She couldn't

Walking down the [...] [...], Katie felt as if she were being pursued by ghosts. Her footsteps rang hollowly on the wooden floor as she bolted into the bedroom. She stared at the walk-in closet for several moments, dragging in lungfuls of air.

She realized she was straining her ears the way she had when she'd first come into the apartment. Did she hear a furtive rustling among the dresses? And she could smell Val's perfume—but also something else. Some*one* else? The scent teased her memory, but she couldn't give it form.

With a shake of her head, she turned to the closet. The door was open, but the interior was dark as midnight. She waved her arm around as she stepped inside, feeling for the cord. Her fingers grazed a row of dresses before hitting something more solid.

Air drained from her lungs as the solid object moved. In the next moment, she felt the cold steel of a knife blade against her throat.

Dear Reader,

We appreciate your warm response to *Life Line,
Shattered Vows* and *Whispers in the Night,* the
first three books in our 43 Light Street series.
We're sure *Only Skin Deep* will provide enough
excitement to warm up a cold winter's eve.
Harlequin Intrigue is keeping us busy writing the
kind of fast-paced, romantic suspense stories that
we love best. The next twelve months promise to
be another banner year for Rebecca York with
two more Light Street books.

Trial by Fire, our August release, is Sabrina
Barkley's story, and we're already knee deep in
witch research. Sabrina is accused of murder, and
the key to her defense is four hundred years and
an ocean away. And in February 1993, *Hopscotch*
lands paralegal Noel Emery into a frightening
game of international intrigue.

We hope you'll watch for our future 43 Light
Street books, because we're having the time of our
lives writing them. Rebecca York and all the
women of 43 Light Street wish you a sparkling
new year full of romance and adventure!

Sincerely,

Rebecca York
(Ruth Glick and Eileen Buckholtz)

Only Skin Deep

Rebecca York

Harlequin Books

TORONTO • NEW YORK • LONDON
AMSTERDAM • PARIS • SYDNEY • HAMBURG
STOCKHOLM • ATHENS • TOKYO • MILAN

Harlequin Intrigue edition published February 1992

ISBN 0-373-22179-7

ONLY SKIN DEEP

Directory

4 3   L I G H T   S T R E E T

	Room
ADVENTURES IN TRAVEL	204
NOEL EMERY Paralegal Services	311
ABIGAIL FRANKLIN, Ph.D. Clinical Psychology	509
KATHRYN MARTIN, M.D.	509
O'MALLEY & O'MALLEY Detective Agency	518
LAURA ROSWELL, LL.B. Attorney at Law	311
SABRINA'S FANCY	Lobby
STRUCTURAL DESIGN GROUP	407
L. ROSSINI Superintendent	Lower Level

CAST OF CHARACTERS

Katie Martin—One terrible night, she lost her sister and reopened an eight-year-old wound she thought had healed.

Mac McQuade—He owed Tom Houston everything. His self-respect. His sanity. Maybe even his life.

Val Caldwell—She found the secret to flawless skin—and it cost her dearly.

Jo O'Malley—She was on the trail of a woman with a blank past. Could she fill in the page before it was too late?

Tom Houston—He made a deadly mistake getting involved with Val.

Jade Nishizaka—The beauty business was only part of her agenda.

Akio Nishizaka—A brilliant scientist. If his work had taken a different direction, he might have won the Nobel Prize.

Cornell Perkins—He knew the junket was a bribe to get him off the case, but how could he turn down Hawaii?

Greg Scoggins—He had muscles in all the right places, but had trouble exercising his mind.

Chapter One

Kathryn Martin stared into the eyes of madness. Once the wide-set orbs had sparkled with mischief. Now, below the blue of the irises, dark currents of lunacy stirred like vipers slithering into the sunlight.

Katie reached across the leather sofa cushion and laid a gentle hand over her sister's. "Val, are you feeling all right?" she asked softly.

"Don't start that doctor stuff with me. I'm fine. Just fine." Beautifully manicured hands snatched up a copy of *Vogue* from the chrome-and-glass coffee table. With jerky movements she began to fan through the pages.

Katie ran her finger down a sofa seam. She'd been so busy with her research grant and the group of friends she'd made down at 43 Light Street that she'd accepted Val's excuses for not getting together more often. Now she wished she'd brought her medical bag up from the car.

With a little snort Val shoved the magazine at Katie. "Look at this model. Her body's okay, but you can see the lines around her eyes. That's not happening to me, sweetie."

"No, your skin is flawless," Katie agreed.

Val raised her head, a brilliant smile on her lips. All at once there was nothing more sinister in her blue eyes than the familiar self-satisfied flush that compliments had always brought.

It's my imagination, Katie thought as she leaned back into the plump cushions and tried to look relaxed. *I've just forgotten what a couple of hours with Val is like—especially when she's worried about something.* Except that this afternoon was worse. One moment Val was like a porcelain doll that had shattered into a million pieces. The next, she'd glued herself back together.

"No one would guess I'm ten years older than you," Val murmured.

Twelve, Katie silently corrected.

"We could almost be twins—if you'd do something about your hair and your makeup."

Twins.

The observation sent Katie's mind off on its own track. They'd both inherited their blue eyes and fresh-faced looks from their mother. But any similarities ended there. Val had always been the life of the party. Katie had been the shy mouse in the corner until her academic achievements had won her the recognition she deserved.

"You're not listening to me. You never listen!"

"Yes, I am. What should I do about my hair?"

"Why don't you let me fit you into my schedule down at Genesis? It's good enough for half the Washington in crowd. It ought to be good enough for you. I know it's expensive, but I could write up the ticket on my employee discount." Val giggled. "My hair used to be as dark as yours. You need some highlights. And a makeup lesson. Fifteen minutes in the morning with the right foundation and accent colors would do wonders."

Katie couldn't imagine spending that much time on makeup—or anything else so self-indulgent. As an intern, she'd learned how to shower, pull on her clothes and get out the door in ten minutes. Since she'd left hospital practice to work on a genetic study, her routine was no longer frantic, but she'd never gotten into the habit of pampering herself. Maybe it was a holdover from all the years their mother had counted pennies just to keep food on the table. On the other hand, being poor appeared to have worked just the opposite with her half sister. Val seemed determined to gather up every luxury she'd missed as a kid.

"It was sweet of you to come take me to lunch on my birthday, but I've got to chase you out. Tom and I have big plans this evening, and I need to get ready." Val got to her feet.

Katie sucked in a deep breath. She could do things the easy way—the safe way—or she could make a stand. Not wanting to be at a disadvantage now, she got up, too. "Val, I know something's bothering you."

"What do you mean?"

"You've been on edge all day. Maybe I can help. Why don't we talk about it?"

For a fraction of a second, Val seemed to waver. Then her face contorted to the old, familiar look of wrath that Katie remembered so well from her childhood. "Sure. Talk. Spill my guts. So you can lord it over me how much better you've done for yourself with your fancy medical degree and how they've got your name in reference books and all. Well, Miss Who's Who and What's What, you may have gotten hotshot grades in school, but you don't know squat about men. Or anything else really important."

"Val, please don't throw up a smoke screen," Katie protested gently. "If you're sick—or in some kind of trouble— I want to be here for you."

"No you don't. Go back to Baltimore where you belong. And don't come back." She gave Katie a shove toward the door that almost made her lose her footing.

Katie steadied herself with a flattened palm against the wall. When she moved her hand away, she could see a sweaty mark on the dove-white paint. No one knew better than she how dangerous Val could be when provoked. She simply couldn't handle this by herself. At least not right now.

"I'll call you later. We'll talk then."

"Don't do me any favors."

Val turned her back, walked to the sliding glass door and stood looking out as if there were no one else in the room.

Katie stared at her sister's rigid neck. "If you need anything, just let me know. I mean that." As she backed toward the door, she felt consumed by a sudden, overwhelming emptiness.

As soon as she got rid of meddling little Katie, Val fixed herself a very dry martini. *The nerve. Trying to pump me for information.*

She took a gulp of the potent drink. It didn't help her head or the clawing fear in her chest. For weeks she'd felt like the guy in that sci-fi movie—what was it? She shook her head. The name wasn't important. It was that guy. The one who looks perfectly normal until he collapses at dinner and starts to scream. Then this horrible little monster digs its way out of his chest.

Val shuddered and clamped her lips together, afraid she was going to start screaming like the man in the movie. And once she started, she was never going to stop. There was a monster inside her, too. Maybe not something with teeth and claws and a body, but something trying to scratch and gnaw its way to the surface where everyone could see it. Not in her chest, in her head. It was in there, buzzing and snarling. Making it hard to think.

When Katie had made that big sob-sister play, she'd almost started babbling to her. But she'd held herself together. The way she always had when things got tough. She couldn't share the fear. Especially not with self-righteous little Katie.

With jerky, automatic motions she pulled off her clothes and lurched into the bathroom. After filling the tub, she sank into the warm, scented water. As she leaned back against her inflated rubber pillow, she tried to make her mind blank. After a while, the pain in her head began to diffuse.

Wondering why she'd been so upset a few minutes ago, she began to hum a pop tune. By the time she pulled the plug and stood up, she felt one hundred percent better. Her only problem was that she'd been staying out too late with Tom. Sixty-three and he wanted to dance all night.

Val executed a little two-step as she rubbed a towel across her shoulders. Not just dance. The old mule thought he was a stallion in bed. But she liked him more for what was in his pants pockets than what was in his pants. If she wanted fireworks between the sheets, she called Greg, the great-looking stud she'd met at the gym a couple of months ago.

Smiling saucily at her high-breasted figure in the mirror, Val reached for a little dab of Flawless Skin Restorer. She'd tried all the Genesis products and treatments, and this almond-scented cream was the best. It went for a hundred dollars an ounce, and only Genesis's most valued customers could purchase the limited supply. But she'd watched Ming open the cabinet enough times to write down the combination. The trouble was, Ming counted everything, so she couldn't snitch a whole jar. She could only take a smidgen out of the top of the new ones. But even a little bit was enough to make a big difference in the way her skin looked, she thought with satisfaction as she examined her face in the magnifying mirror beside the sink.

THE RUSH-HOUR TRAFFIC crawled up Connecticut Avenue toward Chevy Chase Circle with the speed of a disabled caterpillar. Katie had been waiting for a string of motorists to turn left when a horn in back of her blared. With a start she realized that while she'd been worrying about Val, the line of cars had moved.

She wasn't her sister's keeper, she told herself firmly as she stamped on the accelerator and plowed through the intersection just before the light turned red. When Val was on a rampage, the best thing to do was to clear out of the way and wait for the dust to settle.

But as she eased the car into the stream of traffic rounding the circle, she couldn't keep a particular legal phrase from flowing through her mind. *A danger to herself or others... A danger to herself or others.* That was just about the only criterion left for forcing an unwilling patient to have a psychiatric evaluation. But had the situation with her sister really come to that? Reluctantly Katie tried to supply an answer.

She'd seen Val angry. She'd seen Val spiteful. She'd seen Val hostile. But never quite like this.

What would her older sister have done to her if she hadn't left? Was Val a danger to herself? How did the law work in D.C.? And what about that man she had a date with? Did he know what he was walking into this evening?

Purely on automatic pilot, Katie continued toward the Beltway. But as she approached the turnoff, her foot faltered on the accelerator. Pulling onto a side street lined with solid-looking brick houses, she cut the engine and sat for a moment hunched over the steering wheel.

"Stop being a coward, Kathryn Martin," she whispered. Still it was several moments before she eased the gear lever into reverse, backed up, and started retracing her route into Washington. If she didn't find out what was making Val so edgy, she was never going to forgive herself.

AFTER FINISHING her makeup, Val ambled into the bedroom and threw open the door of her walk-in closet. It took forty minutes and three complete changes to settle on a slinky red velvet dress. She was just stepping into snappy slingbacks when the door chimes sounded.

Early again. Damn him.

She didn't dare let her annoyance show as she answered the door. Tom Houston's gray hair was carefully parted on the wrong side, and his square jaw sported a couple of shaving nicks. Tacky. But his first words made up for the deficiencies.

"You look beautiful, honey."

Val accepted the compliment with a glittering smile and a little tingle of anticipation as she thought about the expensive birthday present she'd hinted she wanted. Tom could afford it. That Medizone Lab of his was a gold mine. At least if he'd stop sharing so much of the profits with Mac McQuade. She'd tried to say something about that and had gotten a lecture on the great stuff Mac was doing. You'd think the guy walked on water.

When she and Tom were settled on the couch, he pulled a small box from his pocket. "Happy birthday, honey."

"Oooo. You shouldn't have," she cooed as she tore into the wrapping. However, when she lifted the lid on the suede box, her face fell. Nestled inside was a dinky opal pendant on a silver chain.

Tom watched expectantly. When her lips drew into a pout, he frowned. "Wasn't that what you said you wanted?"

"No." Val leaped off the couch, walked to the sliding glass door, and stepped onto the balcony. The temperature had dropped since she and Katie had come home, and the cold air made her shiver. If she'd been alone, she would have gone back inside. Instead she wrapped her arms around her shoulders to ward off the wind and drew in a deep breath.

It brought the pain back to her head. This time it felt as though a steel needle stabbed her brain. "Don't you know anything?" she snapped, without looking at Tom. "Springs don't wear silver. They wear gold."

"Springs? What do you mean?"

"My season. My colors. Don't you know anything?" she repeated.

Shaking his head, Tom came out to the balcony. After hesitating a moment, he tried to draw her back against his chest. "Sorry. I guess I got mixed up again. I don't know." He shook his head. "It's been happening a lot lately. But it doesn't matter. We can go down to the jewelry store tomorrow, and you can show me what you want."

Val barely heard the words. All at once, the touch of his square hands was revolting. Trying to get away, she leaned forward, her body slanting over the wrought iron railing.

"Val, that's dangerous. Come on back inside, hon."

Wrenching out of his grasp, she whirled. "I'll come in when I damn please. How dare you give me something so cheap!"

"Cheap? That bauble set me back two hundred bucks." His eyes were cold. "I'm starting to think Mac was right all along. You've been using me, baby, and I'm not going to eat dirt anymore."

"Mac. That jerk who works for you. You care more about him than you do about me." Anger exploded in her head like a heat-seeking missile. She lunged forward, her daggerlike nails striking at his eyes.

Tom's hands came up to protect his eyes as he dodged backward and to the side, so that the nails only scraped down one cheek.

With his bulk removed from her path, Val was thrown off balance. Restricted by the tight red dress, she couldn't check her forward momentum.

"Help me!"

Tom dropped his hands from his eyes just as Val grabbed for the railing. She clawed desperately at empty air, but couldn't stop herself from pitching forward. Even though Tom made a frantic grab for her, there was no way he could reach her in time. A scream of mingled surprise and terror tore from her lips as she took flight. It followed her down to the pavement ten stories below.

ON A RAINY DAY in April eight years ago, everything had changed for Mac McQuade. The dark hair and lean body were about the same—except for one small detail. But something in the gray eyes had altered like smoke shifting unexpectedly in a strong wind. Once he'd been an optimist. Now he was a realist. Once he'd chased the American dream—comfort, money, prestige, love. Now he went after less conventional rewards. If his goals took him to the jungles of Borneo or the bottom of the Pacific Ocean—away from other people—so much the better.

Skin like fine leather crinkled at the corners of his eyes. The trouble was, when the trip was over, you had to write a report, and Mac considered report writing in the same league with walking barefoot over hot coals. Which was why he was here at his desk after everyone else had gone home— planning to work straight through until he got the damn thing done.

Hearing a door slam somewhere in the distance, he looked up, annoyed. Then footsteps pounded down the hall of the lab building, and Mac's personal warning system went from irritation to full alert. Pushing his six-foot frame out of the comfortably padded chair, he turned to face the door. Ever since he'd come back from Central America, he'd felt something malevolent hovering just at the edge of his perception like a predator waiting to strike. The worst part was that there'd been no way to head it off.

Remorse billowed up inside his chest when he saw Tom Houston hurtle into the room. Mac knew he should have done something before this. But how? What?

The man's eyes were dazed. Streaks of blood had dried on his face. "Thank God you're here. I need you...I need you to make it come out right."

"Tom, what happened?"

Tom's shoulders hunched as he sank into the desk chair.

"Were you mugged? In an accident?" *Did you kill someone?* Mac's last question went unasked. It was a measure of how bad the situation had gotten that he hadn't been able to censor the thought.

The older man began to tremble.

Struggling for outward calm, Mac grabbed a sterile cloth and distilled water from the supply cabinet. When he reached toward the scratches on his friend's paper-white cheek, Tom jerked away. "Don't!"

"These cuts need attention."

"Just leave them alone."

Mac let the sterile pad and the subject drop. "Does anything else hurt?" The most likely explanation was a mugging, he decided as he gently probed for broken bones. He used his good right hand. With his left hand—the one made out of stainless steel—he loosened the older man's tie, the delicate operations of the metallic fingers almost second nature now.

The metal hand was a very fine precision instrument. But then, he'd had considerable input into the microchip-controlled prototype. And the rehab department had made some refinements since he'd begun field-testing it. Probably when they brought it to market, they'd go for flesh tones. Right now, it was performance he wanted, not looks. If the new batteries just held up under jungle conditions, he'd use the thing when he went back to Honduras for some more snake venom.

"You've got to help me," Tom pleaded.

"I will." *Why didn't you come to me as soon as I got back?* he wanted to shout. Instead he kept his voice steady. "Whatever it takes."

Until a couple of months ago, Tom Houston had been the most intelligent, forceful and stubborn man he'd ever met. About the only thing still intact was the stubbornness— along with a new defensiveness and secretiveness that had made it impossible to reach him.

What did you do when the man who'd been like a second father to you went off the deep end? Hope he'd snap out of it? Drag him bodily to the hospital for a mental and physical exam? For the first time in years Mac McQuade had been paralyzed into inaction.

"She's dead. Her sister."

Mac's head snapped around. "Whose sister? What are you talking about?"

"Damn. I never told you that part. I was gonna. Honest. And now it's all a mess." Tom started to sob. It took a long time to calm him down and get the disjointed story out of him. Even then Mac could hardly believe what he was hearing.

"Val was angry with you. She tried to claw your eyes and went off the balcony," he clarified, his voice measured.

"Yes. I tried to grab her. But I couldn't—I couldn't get to her in time."

It was strange to hope he was simply listening to a sick man's ravings. Still, that was all he could cling to now. "What's her number?"

"Seventy-three—" Tom stopped and shook his head. "Or thirty-seven. Can't remember."

Mac looked away so that he wouldn't have to meet the sudden confusion in Tom's eyes. He'd been calling Val's apartment for months. Now he couldn't remember the number. Picking up the receiver, Mac got it from information.

"May I please speak to Ms. Caldwell?" he asked when a man answered Val's phone.

"Who's calling?"

"Who is this?" Mac countered.

"Fred Richmond, the building manager."

"I'd like to speak to Ms. Caldwell," he repeated.

"I'm afraid there's been a serious accident."

"What happened?"

"Ms. Caldwell is, uh, deceased. Wait a minute. There's a police officer here who wants to speak to you."

Mac's eyes swung toward Tom as he cupped his palm over the mouthpiece. "The police are at her apartment."

The older man's hand whipped out like a spring-loaded dart, snatched the receiver from Mac's grasp and slammed it back onto the cradle.

"Tom!" Mac stopped abruptly and made an effort to curb his own frustration. "Why don't we go down there together, and you can tell them what happened."

"No!" The syllable was as full of fear as anguish.

"It's all right. I'll be with you. We're a good team, aren't we?"

The older man wasn't listening. Scrambling up, he backed away, his eyes focused on some unseen terror. When his shoulders hit the wall, he moaned and looked around as if searching for an escape route.

"Tom, take it easy."

"Not the police. Don't you understand? They want to pin this on me. They'll find out I was paying the rent on her apartment, and my fingerprints are all over the place. They'll want to put me away for murder."

"But if it was an accident, you don't have anything to worry about."

"No! If you tell them I had anything to do with Val's death, I'll kill myself."

"Tom, please." Mac pushed back his own chair and took a cautious step toward his friend.

"Stay away from me. I'll do it. I swear." He snatched up a letter opener from the desk and held it like a dagger.

"I won't come any closer." Mac stopped in midstep and stared at the man who had picked him up when he'd hit rock bottom and convinced him he had a choice about the way he was going to spend the rest of his life. He hadn't figured out how to cope with the way the strong bonds of their relationship were dissolving as if they'd been eaten away by acid. But he did know one thing for sure. He owed Tom Houston everything. His self-respect. His sanity. Maybe even his life.

"You've got to find out if—if—they suspect anything, and take my stuff out of there," Tom pleaded.

"What stuff?"

Tom dropped the letter opener and cradled his head in his hands. "Underwear. Monogrammed shirts, maybe. And, oh God, those pictures we took in the Bahamas."

There was probably more, Mac thought, and it was highly unlikely that he could accomplish the kind of clean sweep that Tom wanted with the police crawling all over the place. The feeling of helplessness that had been building over the past few weeks twisted in Mac's gut again. What did he do now? Risk Tom's life by calling the authorities and laying it all on the line? Risk leaving him alone? Unfortunately he believed what Tom was saying. "Do you trust me?" he asked.

"I trust you."

"I trust you, too," he murmured, hating the way the lie swelled and expanded in his throat. "If I go back to Val's, and see what I can find out, will you promise you'll let me take you to a doctor tomorrow morning?"

Tom twisted his big hands. "I—okay. But you gotta get my stuff. I want it back here."

Mac sighed. Partial victory. And while he was down-town, he could take care of his own agenda. "You've got to promise not to get into any trouble while I'm gone," he admonished Tom, aware now that he was speaking the way he would to a child.

"I promise. I won't get in any trouble. Mac, I won't for-get this."

"You're going to lie down on the couch in your office and wait for me."

"Yes. Anything you say."

"I'll give you something to help you relax while I'm away."

He ushered Tom down the hall to the medical dispen-sary, unlocked the door and found a sedative. Then he handed his friend one of the capsules and a glass of water.

Tom threw his head back with an exaggerated flourish as he swallowed. Then his gaze skittered away from Mac's.

"I assume you've got a key to the apartment."

"Um." Tom felt in his pocket and handed over a leather case.

"Which one?"

It took several moments of fumbling before the older man detached a brass-colored key.

"You'll wait right here for me," Mac reiterated.

Silently Tom lay down on the couch, pressed his arms against his sides and squeezed his eyes closed. As soon as the door shut behind Mac, they snapped open again—glitter-ing and feverish in the dim light. With a grimace he spit out the medication he'd pretended to swallow and sat up.

Chapter Two

She'd been here only a few hours before. Now a strip of yellow tape barred the entrance to apartment 1015. It read: Police Barrier. Do Not Cross.

Katie's heart began to thump against her ribs. "Val? Val?" she called.

The door was thrust open by a tall, broad-shouldered black man in a rumpled sport coat. His hair was military short, and his voice held the note of a drill instructor addressing impossibly incompetent recruits. "I told you people, this isn't a circus. Now clear out." Dismissively he turned away.

"My sister. Val. What's happened to my sister?" Although Katie stood her ground, the question came out high and strangled.

The borderline hysteria apparently caught the man's attention. Pivoting back toward the door, he peered into Katie's bloodless face, and his own expression softened. "There's been an accident. I think you'd better come in and sit down."

She looked up pleadingly into his brown eyes, sensing compassion but also reserve, as if he were withholding judgment about her until he found out more.

"I'm Detective Perkins. D.C. police," he said as he led her into the living room where several other men moved about taking pictures and dusting black powder onto the credenza.

"My sister," Katie repeated. "Valerie Caldwell."

"I'm sorry. There's no easy way to tell you this. She jumped off the balcony."

"Is she..."

Perkins nodded. "I'm sorry, ma'am."

She'd known something terrible was going to happen. Somehow she'd known. Now, as her worst fears were confirmed, Katie's knees buckled, and she dropped to the couch. The same couch where she and Val had been talking only hours before. "But we just had lunch," she protested weakly.

Perkins's expression sharpened. "You were with her this afternoon?"

"A couple of hours ago."

"Then you may be the last person to have seen her alive."

Katie's throat felt raw. The last person. No. Unless Val had canceled her plans. "What about her date? She asked—asked—me to leave," Katie stammered, "because she needed to get ready." It wasn't a complete account of the way they'd parted but it would do for now. "I thought about going home. But I decided I'd better drive back to my office because I had a lot of work to do," she added, unable to keep random facts from tumbling out under the spotlight of Perkins's scrutiny.

The detective had taken out a notebook. "I didn't catch your name."

"Kathryn Martin."

"Your office is downtown?"

"No, I live in Ellicott City and work in Baltimore."

"And your sister had a date with whom?"

Katie racked her brain. It was simpler to try and answer the man's questions than deal with her own shock. Val had mentioned a couple of guys when they'd talked on the phone to set up the luncheon date. Greg. No, he was the one from the health club. The one she was seeing this evening was Ted. No, Tom.

"Tom," she murmured.

"His last name?"

Katie shrugged. "I'm sorry. That was all she told me."

"You said you were on your way back to Baltimore. Why did you return to Ms. Caldwell's apartment just now?"

"I was worried about her."

"In what way?"

"She was nervous—on edge about something. But she didn't want to talk about it." Katie gulped. "I guess that was one of the reasons she asked me to leave."

"Was someone threatening her? Tom? Was she apprehensive about the date?"

"Not the date," Katie said slowly, her numbed brain coming to grips with the direction of Perkins's thoughts. Funny how differently a policeman and a physician approached the same set of facts. It hadn't even occurred to her that someone might have really been threatening Val.

Perkins's dark eyes focused on Katie's face as if he suspected she might be withholding important information.

She bowed her head. Her own theories were hard to talk about, yet what was the point in being evasive now? Drawing in a steadying breath, she met his probing gaze. "I'm a physician. I was worried about my sister's mental health."

Perkins wasn't able to hide his surprise. "You're a doctor?"

"Georgetown Medical School. You want a summary of my vita?"

"No. Sorry, Dr. Martin." He cleared his throat. "Do you think Ms. Caldwell was depressed?"

She tried to answer in the same professional tone with which the question had been asked. "No. Not in the clinical sense. Frightened is a better description. Agitated. Paranoid."

"Did she have a history of mental illness?"

"Well, she was troubled. And unstable. She was married and divorced three times. But she never shared the details of her medical history."

"Umm."

Katie laced her fingers together in her lap and squeezed until the knuckles were bloodless. She could feel Perkins watching her again. If she didn't explain, he wasn't going to appreciate how it had been between her and Val. Suddenly she wanted him to understand why she'd run away this afternoon—and why she'd come back. Still, when she began to speak, her voice was barely above a whisper. "Val is— was—twelve years older than I am. We're half sisters, actually. After Mom divorced Val's father, she married mine. He died when I was only two." She swallowed painfully. "Val was the star of the family. She was pretty and popular. A cheerleader. The homecoming queen. When I was little, she treated me like a kind of pet—styling my hair and painting my nails. Then when I went to school and my teachers started talking about how smart I was, she became resentful." Katie stopped and closed her eyes for a moment as if that could shut out the hurtful memories. "First she teased me. Then she escalated to mean tricks—like getting me to chew on a hot pepper—or spilling nail-polish remover on my homework papers."

Perkins seesawed his pen between large fingers. "Sounds like a serious case of sibling rivalry."

"After I went to college, we didn't even see each other." Katie plowed on, talking quickly now so she could get the telling over with. "But about four years ago, when my mother died, we sort of mended our fences. I—I guess I wanted to keep seeing her, so I let her set the rules for the friendship. It was important for her to feel superior to me.

I think that's why she didn't want me to know there was something wrong with her. I didn't press her this afternoon, and now it's too late," she finished bitterly.

Perkins laid a broad hand on her shoulder. "Don't blame yourself, Dr. Martin. A person who's disturbed and wants to commit suicide, they'll find a way to do it."

"She didn't leave a note, did she?"

"Not that I can find. But before you arrived, a couple of old ladies who live on her floor were eager to tell me that your sister had been acting weird lately. However, I'm still going to keep investigating—follow up some other leads. See if I can locate this Tom person. Find out if he was here this evening. Make sure I can rule out foul play."

Katie and the detective regarded each other for several moments. Then Perkins cleared his throat. "There's one more thing I'm afraid I'm going to have to ask you to do for us."

"I was Val's only relative. I guess you want me to identify the body."

"If you would. I can have one of my men drive you down to the morgue."

IT WAS DARK by the time Mac reached Val Caldwell's apartment building. After finding a parking space in the next block, he sat in the plush front seat of his silver Jaguar looking at the way the light from an overhead street lamp reflected on his high-tech hand. Reaching up, he used the mechanical fingers to adjust the rearview mirror so he could see the sidewalk in back of the car.

In a lot of respects, the precision-made digits were better than the real thing once you got the knack of making them work. They were stronger. Almost as dexterous. Impervious to pain. And designed to carry out a number of specialized operations. However, he wasn't ready to recommend that the rest of humanity line up for a similar set.

Metal fingers had no sensitivity. And wearing an artificial body part was a pretty good test of peoples' values and prejudices. The two responses he hated most were being pitied or being dismissed as less than competent because he didn't have two flesh-and-blood hands. However, it was damn useful to know where you stood with someone right from the first. That was one reason he never dodged the issue by hiding the prosthesis. The other was that he'd made some promises to himself when he'd agreed to work for Tom. He was never going to pretend he was something he wasn't. If you didn't like Mac McQuade the way he was, too bad. What you saw was what you got.

This evening, however, he couldn't keep a hypothetical scenario out of his mind. *Police officer: "Did the man skulking around Ms. Caldwell's apartment have any distinguishing physical characteristics?"*

Witness: "Nothing special. Just a stainless steel fist."

If he was going to do some checking up on Val, it was essential that no one connect him with Tom. So before getting out of the car, he thrust his left hand into the pocket of his trench coat. He also turned up the collar around his face, as if he were seeking protection from the biting wind. The tactic hid not only his features but also his grim expression as he hurried along the sidewalk.

All the way into the city, he'd been wrestling with unpleasant thoughts. Given the time to reflect, he couldn't help being angry with Tom for putting him in the position of having to choose between personal loyalty and the law. He'd been in enough primitive environments to know that society's rules were part of the glue that held a civilization together. And he appreciated being able to return to a world where you didn't have to watch your back every moment.

Realizing he was marching through the gathering gloom with his teeth clenched, he made an effort to look like a more normal part of the city scene.

Deliberately he turned his mind back to Val Caldwell. Tom had bragged about some of his expensive presents to her. Now he'd let it slip that he'd been paying her rent, too. Had the woman been milking him for thousands every month? Had money problems been part of Tom's recent anxiety? And what other mess had Val gotten him into? At first he'd wondered if Tom had Alzheimer's disease or something. But maybe his girlfriend had introduced him to drugs. That would certainly explain his personality changes and erratic behavior.

Mac grimaced. He and Ms. Caldwell had never met, but there wasn't much he'd heard about the sexy little beautician that he'd liked. She'd been demanding, unstable and manipulative. Now she was dead, and before her relatives started dismantling her apartment he was going to have a crack at finding out exactly what kind of trouble she'd gotten Tom into. Then once he had his friend safely under a doctor's care, he'd tell the police what he'd found out.

A patrol car was still sitting at the curb when Mac rounded the corner. Instead of entering the apartment building, he detoured to the little restaurant across the street. After buying a *Washington Post,* he found a booth in the back and ordered a cup of coffee and a hamburger. While he waited for the food and pretended to read the sports section, he listened to the talk around him.

"Did you see her lyin' there on the sidewalk? They picked her up and the whole right side of her face was crushed."

Unbidden, Mac's mind flashed back to the evening when he'd lain on a cold, cracked sidewalk with a crowd of curious spectators gathering. He'd fallen on his left, not his right. And he'd instinctively put up his hand to soften the impact. That had been a mistake.... Underneath the table, he pressed his metal fist against his middle and brought his mind back to the present.

"She was a real hot number..."

"Yeah, she came on to me once like gangbusters..."

"But she had a temper..."

"I'm not surprised she jumped..."

The excited chatter continued. But how much of it could you believe, now that Ms. Caldwell wasn't here to set the record straight? Mac wondered.

After twenty minutes, he noticed the police car had left. Still, he dawdled over the newspaper and a second cup of coffee. He knew he was stalling, but while he'd been sitting here, he'd been having serious second thoughts about what Tom had asked him to do.

WITH EXAGGERATED CARE, Jade Nishizaka set down her cup of tea on the marble-topped table beside her contour recliner.

"I'm not sure I understood. Please repeat that information."

The young manservant she'd hired as much for his looks as his martial-arts skills and a number of other useful talents bowed slightly and flattened his palms against his sides. His name was Koji, and she'd brought him over from Japan on one of her trips to the laboratory complex that developed Genesis's expensive cosmetics for her.

"We have a report from the police that one of your employees is dead," he enunciated carefully.

"Who?"

"Valerie Caldwell."

There was a slight elevation of Jade's classically arched brows. Otherwise the expression on her youthful face didn't change. In fact, nothing much about her ever seemed to change—unless one observed her quite carefully. She was almost sixty, but she was a faithful user of her own products—and the well-equipped gym she'd installed in her luxury condo. With her trim figure and flawless complexion she might have passed for a woman in her mid-thirties. "Do they know what happened?"

"The officer in charge has turned in a preliminary report. The most likely explanation is suicide."

Only a small exhalation of breath betrayed Jade's tension. "How horrible. I must send my condolences to the family. Check our personnel records and get me the address."

"*Hai,* mistress."

"You will have that information on my breakfast tray in the morning. For now, I wish to be alone with my sadness. But I will require your services later—for a massage." Her eyes met his, and a small smile played at the corners of her beautiful lips.

"*Hai,* mistress." Koji's eyes flickered for a moment as he bowed again and backed out of the room.

Yes, he was the perfect servant for her needs. But not until later. Not until she had thought through this crisis.

Alone once more, she sat with her eyes closed for several moments, trying to calm the storm that swept through her spirit. She knew herself well. If there was any fault in her personality, it was the inability to find the peaceful center of her being.

But she had reason to be troubled. So much was at stake. She'd worked for years to achieve her goals. Tomorrow the wife of the deputy secretary of commerce was coming to Genesis for the first time. Talk of Val's death in the salon would hardly make a good impression on a new customer. She would have to remind the staff about the penalties for spreading gossip.

Jade swung her lithe body from the recliner and crossed to the porcelain vase of cherry-blossom boughs decorating a black lacquered table. Her vision blurred as she stared at the fragile pink flowers, inviting their velvet petals to take away her tension. She knew now that she should have done something about Valerie Caldwell long before this. But there was no point in regretting errors in judgment.

Val had been good at her job—one of the few beauticians whose skills met Genesis's exacting standards. Which was why she'd been hired. After she'd begun working on the salon's exclusive clientele, she'd built up a steady base of repeat business. But lately, the woman had started showing symptoms of instability. Jade's first impulse had been to fire her. Then she'd decided it was dangerous to turn her loose. Better to keep her close at hand where she could be watched. Just in case.

Had the judgment been wrong? Jade went to the Louis XIV desk under the window. There was no hesitancy as she looked up a number in her private directory and placed a call. It might be after hours, but she was paying for special services—it was better to be safe than sorry now. She wanted someone to have a look around Val Caldwell's apartment. And she wanted it done tonight. Then she'd have to make some other calls.

IT WAS ALMOST NINE by the time Katie and her police escort got back to Val's apartment building. "Are you sure you're going to be all right?" Officer Bryant asked.

"Yes." Katie's muffled assurance was automatic. For hours she'd felt as if she were walking around at the bottom of the sea. The weight of the water made even the smallest motion almost too much effort. And when she'd stood in front of her sister's pale, lifeless body, the pressure against her chest had been suffocating.

"Where did you leave your car?" Bryant asked.

"Around the corner. But, uh, I'd like to go back inside for a few minutes."

"I guess that would be all right."

Katie opened the door and felt a cold blast of air knife through the light coat that had been fine for the middle of the afternoon. Suddenly the evening chill seemed to penetrate all the way to the bone. She knew she wasn't just reacting to the cold. It was Val, too. The way she'd looked laid out under a white sheet—one side of her face looking perfectly normal, the other ruined.

In the impersonal little viewing room, self-preservation had demanded that Katie keep a tight hold on her emotions. Now tears gathered in her eyes, and she blinked.

"You're sure you're gonna be okay?" the young officer repeated. "Anyone you want to call?"

Katie shook her head and pushed the door wider, determined not to break down in front of this stranger. Quickly she stepped out to the sidewalk.

"Thanks."

His unintelligible reply followed her as she fled into the apartment lobby and tried to warm her icy hands in front of the radiator. Really there was no need to go upstairs now. There was no hurry about sorting through Val's things. Yet she wanted to wipe out the terrible image of her sister lying there broken and vulnerable and so silent. She wanted something else to remember tonight. Some tangible token of Val's life, of the things that had made her happy. Turning away from the radiator, she strode to the elevator and pressed the button.

Was it all right to take a few mementos from the apartment? she wondered as she made her way down the hall. Perhaps she should call Detective Perkins tomorrow and tell him what she'd done, she decided as she entered Val's apartment.

After the earlier bustle of police activity, it was dark and silent as a tomb. She noticed a plastic garbage bag beside the door. Had the police set aside some evidence that they intended to pick up later? Or was one of the officers still on the premises?

"Is anyone here?"

No answer.

"Officer Perkins?"

From somewhere back in the unseen rooms, Katie thought she detected a muffled noise. Standing very still, she waited to find out if it was repeated. She heard nothing, except the beating of her own heart.

Katie shivered, unable to shake the fancy that she wasn't alone in the apartment. Was Val's ghost returning for one last visit? *Oh, come on,* she rebuked herself. *You're just hearing the people in the next unit.*

She was reaching for the light switch when she let her arm drop against her side. Leaning her head back, she stood with her body pressed against the door, needing the support to keep herself on her feet. As if drawn by a flashing red beacon, her eyes swung to the sliding glass doors and the balcony beyond. Only a few hours ago she'd watched Val standing at the floor-to-ceiling window looking out. Had she already been thinking about jumping? Or had she stood there with her back to her sister unable to ask for help?

"Oh, Val, why didn't you trust me?" Katie whispered into the darkness.

An answer reverberated in her mind. *I wanted you to look up to me the way you did when I was little. I wanted you to think I was perfect.*

"Nobody's perfect," Katie choked out. "Not you. Not me. Especially not me. There were times I needed you, too. And I couldn't ask. Oh, Val, why couldn't we help each other?"

The tears she had been struggling to hold back began to flow. Wrapping her arms around her shoulders, she stood in the foyer weeping silently.

She wasn't sure how long the emotional storm lasted. Finally she fumbled in her purse. With a crumpled tissue, she wiped her eyes and blew her nose.

She should go home, get some sleep, and come back in the morning. But she didn't want to do that now. What she wanted—needed—was a token of the time when everything had been all right between her and Val. That had been years ago. She'd been in nursery school, and whenever she'd come into her big sister's room, she'd been drawn to the fuzzy green-and-yellow *W* with the little gold megaphone pinned to the front. The letter had been one of Val's prized possessions, an emblem of her glory days at Woodrow Wilson High School, and she'd never discarded it. In fact, Katie had seen it in a box of memorabilia right after Val had moved in here. Now she felt a compulsive need to find it.

Val had probably put the box in her closet. It would be easy enough to grab it and take the whole thing home.

Yet as she started down the shadowy hall, Katie was unable to shake the eerie feeling that she was being pursued by ghosts. Her footsteps rang hollowly on the wooden floor as she bolted into the bedroom. There was no light switch by the door, so she rushed to the bedside table and turned on the lamp. The puddle of illumination made her feel a little more steady. Still, she stood staring at the walk-in closet for several moments and dragging in lungfuls of air.

She realized she was straining her ears the way she had when she'd first come into the apartment. Did she hear a furtive rustle among the dresses? Not very likely.

Here in the bedroom she could smell Val's perfume. It was almost as if her sister had just stepped out for a moment and was coming right back. But she could also smell something else. Someone else? The scent teased at her memory, but she couldn't give it form. Well, Perkins and Bryant and a bunch of other guys had been here for hours. Maybe she was smelling their after-shave. Or maybe it had nothing to do with the police. Val had been getting ready to see a man named Tom. Had they been in here together?

Katie glanced toward the bed. The spread was smooth and unwrinkled, and she felt suddenly like a voyeur. It wasn't any of her business what Val had been doing with Tom—unless it had some bearing on her death.

With a little shake of her head, she turned again to the closet. The door was open, and the interior was as dark as midnight. But there was probably an overhead light, maybe with a pull chain.

Stepping into the unlighted chamber, she began to wave her arm around, feeling for the cord. Her fingers grazed a row of dresses before hitting something more solid.

Air drained from her lungs as the solid object moved. In the next moment, she felt the cold steel of a knife blade against her throat.

Chapter Three

A scream tried to tear itself from Katie's throat. It was cut off as hard fingers clamped over her mouth. Stark, elemental terror lanced through her, giving her an urgent strength she hadn't known she possessed.

Perkins had been right, and she had been wrong. Someone had been after Val. Now they'd come back to get her.

The unseen attacker grunted as he tried to hold her fast, the hard fingers of one hand digging painfully into her side. They seemed to clutch at her with inhuman strength. Struggling backward, she was thrown off balance as her shoulders sank into the folds of a fur coat.

Regaining her footing, she tried to pound her fist against his broad chest. He didn't go after her with the knife again. Had he dropped it in the struggle? A tiny corner of her mind thanked God for small favors, even as one of her wildly flailing arms hit the pull chain for the light.

As if it were a lifeline, she clutched and yanked at the slender cord.

In the instant the bare bulb flashed on, blinding her with the sudden brightness, she realized she'd made a mistake. Her assailant would know exactly where to aim now. Blinking, she cringed away from the blow she knew was coming.

However, nothing was—nothing could be—what she had expected. Ever again. Awareness was a rocket bursting in her brain. Or perhaps it was more like the world heaving and buckling as if a fault in the earth's crust had suddenly opened up beneath her feet, leaving her dangling helplessly over a gaping pit.

Katie heard a strangled cry that was part shock, part astonishment. She couldn't say whether the sound had come from her own lips or the man who held her in his grasp. There was simply no place left in her mind for rational thought. She was standing in a closet crammed with fur and silk and velvet and other expensive apparel. None of it registered. The universe had shrunk to much more circumscribed dimensions.

Mac McQuade. A ghost from her past. A man she had known she would never see again.

Dizzy, disoriented, her breath frozen in her throat, she stared up helplessly into smoky gray eyes. The only way to save herself from falling into the abyss was to anchor her hands on the broad shoulders in front of her.

Moments ago they'd been antagonists in the dark. Now his arms came up—holding her as a lover might, pressing her against the tensile strength of his lean body. Her face lifted toward him. His head lowered.

"Mac." The name was a shuddering cry. It had been such a long, lonely time since he'd held her like this.

The sound of his name—or perhaps the emotion behind the strangled syllable—broke the spell. She felt his body stiffen. Then his head lifted as if he had finally realized where they were—and when.

"Mac, please."

A stiff arm thrust against her shoulder. "No."

Reality was like a bucket of frigid water sloshing over her. She took a step back and became enmeshed in folds of silk. The fabric had no more relevance to her reality than imaginary cobwebs. Nothing had changed. Eight years ago she'd tossed away her pride and begged him not to shut her out of his life. And he'd dismissed her with a coldness that had frozen her heart.

The memory and the way he had thrust her away again now gave her the strength to look him in the eye and demand some answers. "What in the name of God are you doing skulking in my sister's closet?"

She had the satisfaction of seeing the shock register on his face. "Val Caldwell was *your* sister?"

"Yes. And what are *you* doing here?" she repeated.

He sighed. "It's a long story." The weariness in his voice was reflected in his countenance. She'd been seeing memory as much as present reality. At that moment she became aware of how much he'd changed. The dozens of lines etched into the tanned flesh around his eyes were startling. But it wasn't simply that his skin was weathered. The Mac McQuade she'd known had been equal parts boyish devil, dreamer and serious student. All the boyishness had been scoured away along with the dreams. He'd matured, but the process had not been gentle. My God, what had happened to him?

"Did you go back and finish medical school the way you told me you would?" she asked.

His stony gaze held hers. Instead of answering, he raised his left arm and held it a foot from her face.

Her gasp of surprise as she focused on the metal replacement brought a cynical look to his eyes. "It works pretty well, but it's not the hand of a surgeon."

For several seconds, she couldn't find her voice as she remembered the knife against her throat and the rigid fingers digging into her ribs. Now she understood what she had been feeling.

"You probably know, Dr. Martin—" He stopped abruptly. "It is Dr. Martin, isn't it?"

She nodded.

"You probably know that in the field of medicine, first opinions aren't always correct."

"But you said you were going to be all right," she insisted like a school child who'd memorized a set of facts without really understanding them. "That you didn't need me."

"That's right. I didn't. I don't." He pushed past her out of the closet and left her standing amid Val's fancy clothes trying to cope with her surprise and hurt—and new insights.

He'd lost his hand. Seeing the metal one had been like a rabbit punch. But her reaction had been from shock and surprise, not revulsion—although she suspected he wouldn't believe her if she tried to tell him. When Mac McQuade was sure he was right, he was too stubborn to listen to another opinion. Had he known he was facing amputation when he'd made it clear that he never wanted to see her again? Or had the doctors already done it? That would explain a lot. Or it might explain nothing at all.

She watched his rigid posture as he disappeared down the hall. Eight years ago he'd hurt her so deeply that it had taken every drop of strength she possessed to reclaim her self-respect. Afterward she'd told herself she didn't give a damn about Mr. McQuade. That was before he'd taken her in his arms a few minutes ago. For that brief space of time, the past had been wiped away. She'd thought she had both feet firmly planted in the present. Suddenly she knew that she'd been fooling herself for a long time. She wasn't over Mac McQuade.

However, there was more than an old wound or her own confused feelings to deal with now. Her sister was dead, and Mac was snooping around in her closet. Had he been involved with her? Or was it worse than that? Did he know something about Val's death? Had he come here to remove incriminating evidence?

Her suspicions were confirmed as she saw him pick up the plastic garbage bag beside the front door.

"Wait a minute! You can't just walk away."

"Why not? It'll be better for both of us if you pretend you never saw me."

Sure, she thought. Take the easy way out again. "How did you know Val? Were you dating her?"

He laughed. "I wasn't that crazy."

The words and the harsh tone of his voice sent a stab of pain driving into her chest. "You're talking about my sister. My sister who went over the balcony tonight. My sister who's dead." The protest came out high and fragile.

Mac paused, his good hand resting on the doorknob. His gaze flicked to Katie's face as if he were finally taking in her red eyes and pale skin. His own features softened. "I'm sorry."

She squeezed her eyes shut, wishing he'd look away as she struggled to keep the tears from spilling onto her cheeks again.

After long moments, he stared down at the plastic bag on the floor. When he spoke again, his voice was almost gentle. "This can't be easy for you. I guess you have a right to know why I'm here. Tom Houston is a friend of mine."

The mysterious Tom? "The man Val was supposed to be meeting tonight? What happened?" Katie watched Mac closely. He didn't shift his position. But his Adam's apple bobbed. "Officer Perkins thought Val was being threatened," she prodded. "Was it Tom? Did he kill her and send you to cover up for him?"

"Don't jump to crazy conclusions."

"What am I supposed to think? Stop playing games with me and spell it out."

Mac crossed the room, maneuvered Katie onto the couch and sat down beside her. "Tom was wild about Val. For months she was all he could talk about. He bought her anything she wanted—this apartment included. I can't believe he would hurt her—if he'd been in his right mind."

"In his right mind? What are you talking about?"

He wiped his hand across his forehead. "I wish I knew what the hell happened this evening."

"Then he was here! When she died?"

"Maybe. Or maybe he came over after it happened and saw her. He was too incoherent for me to tell for certain. But I was sure of a couple of things—Val was dead, and he was going to commit suicide if I didn't bring back the personal effects he'd left in the apartment."

It took several moments for Katie to digest the new information. "Who exactly is this Tom Houston?" she finally asked.

"My partner."

"In what?"

"Medizone Labs."

"*You're* a partner in Medizone Labs?"

"Tom's the president and founder of the company. He gave me a job about seven years ago. Since then, I've worked my way up."

Katie suspected that the simple statement wasn't the whole story. Anyone who kept up with the biotech industry knew that in the past half-dozen years or so Medizone had rocketed from a small research lab to one of the country's most innovative developers of pharmaceuticals and treatment modalities. A promising therapy for rheumatoid arthritis. A vaccine for encephalitis. A combination of drugs effective against ovarian cancer.

"How did Tom hook up with Val?"

"Would you believe he picked her up in a bar?"

Perhaps casual contacts weren't Tom's style. But Katie silently acknowledged that even in an age of sexual caution, Val had been reckless about her personal life.

"Is he married?"

"Of course not! His wife died a couple of years ago."

Katie sighed. "Trading veiled accusations isn't going to get us anywhere."

"You haven't lost your piercing insights, Dr. Martin."

"I said—"

"You're right. This isn't getting us anywhere. I'm angry with myself as much as anything else. I shouldn't have agreed to come here. Probably I just should have called the police and forced Tom to face reality. But I owe him one. More than one."

She heard the self-accusation in his voice. Whatever else was true, Mac cared about Tom Houston, and he'd wanted to protect him. "Sometimes it's hard to know what's the right thing to do," Katie said softly.

He nodded almost imperceptibly.

"Has Tom been acting ... out of character lately?"

"Yes." His brows arched. "Why do you ask?"

"You implied he wasn't in his right mind."

"Yeah. Right."

"What are his symptoms?"

"Paranoid. Secretive. Forgetful. Wild mood swings."

The description sent a tremor racing up Katie's spine. "My God. That's exactly what I've been going through with Val. The worst part was that she wouldn't let me help her."

"Tom, too." Mac leaned forward, his eyes intense. "But was there anything physically wrong with her? As far as you could tell, I mean."

"Physically, she seemed better than ever."

They stared at each other, both wondering why two previously healthy adults would exhibit the same set of symptoms.

"Maybe they were hooked on the same drug. What was Val into?" he asked sharply.

"She wasn't into anything that I know of before she met your friend Tom. What wonder drugs has he been cooking up in the lab lately?"

"Nothing illegal. That's not Tom's style."

"Maybe Medizone has a secret operation you don't have a clue about."

"Tom wouldn't do that!"

Katie stood up. "I vote we try to find some evidence one way or the other."

"As a matter of fact, I already started searching the apartment," Mac admitted grudgingly.

"And?"

"Your sister's clothes closet's clean. So is the kitchen. I was just about to tackle the bathroom."

"All right. I'll look in here," Katie volunteered, getting up off the sofa.

They might not want to work together, but for now it was the most efficient way to get the job done.

ARNIE BEALE'S stringy hand froze as he reached for the doorknob.

Blessed Mary! There was someone in the apartment. More than one someone. Ready to spring back if anyone inside made for the door, he pressed his ear against the cold metal. It was a man and a woman. And they weren't exactly having a friendly discussion.

Of all the rotten luck. He'd wanted to make sure the police were gone before he came over. Which was why he'd figured it was okay to stop at Flanigan's for a couple of quick ones.

Bad move, Arnie. Somebody beat you to the goodies. But who?

The man and woman inside had stopped talking, but they were still in there. Because he knew there wasn't another way out of the apartment. Unless they were planning to take a flying leap off the balcony like the previous occupant.

Damn. Now how was he supposed to do the job? Should he risk a quick look-see? No. That was too dangerous. What if one of them was still in the living room? Lifting his hand to his mouth, he began to gnaw on his left thumbnail—which was already bitten almost to the quick.

Whoever was in the apartment couldn't stay all night. He'd just have to wait until they'd left. Looking around, he spotted the stairway, a dozen yards away.

With a sigh, he plopped down on the stairs, inspected his nails for a suitable candidate, and began to chew at the tip of his middle finger. This was supposed to be an easy job. It wasn't his fault someone had gotten there first, and he sure as hell wasn't going to tell anyone about it when he made his report.

The bravado lasted a couple of seconds, until an involuntary shiver danced across his skin. Suppose he made up a story and the people he was working for found out he was lying? They'd hang him out to dry.

MAC DISAPPEARED down the hall. Remembering some of the details she'd read in newspaper articles about the places people hid drugs, Katie began searching under furniture and cushions and lamp bases. Should she unscrew the grilles on the heating ducts? she wondered.

"Got something interesting! Come look at this," Mac called out, a note of accusation in his voice.

Katie's heart began to thump as she hurried down the hall. She found Mac gesturing toward the linen closet. He'd folded back a stack of towels to reveal two small opaque jars. Her hands were trembling as she drew one out and unscrewed the top. Inside was about a tablespoon of a milky-white, faintly glossy cream. It looked like moisturizer. When she lowered her nose to the jar and sniffed, she caught the trademark scent of almonds. A Genesis product. Scooping up a dab, Katie smoothed a little bit between her fingers. It felt lush and silky—almost like a fairy godmother's touch. She could picture her cells soaking up the rich concoction.

"What is it?" Mac leaned over and sniffed the almond scent.

"Moisturizing cream. From Genesis."

"Genesis. Yeah. There was some expensive-looking makeup in the medicine cabinet with that name. What is it, an exclusive brand?"

"That's right. You can only get it at the salon where Val worked. I've never been there, but Val's told me it's kind of an Elizabeth Arden-type place, where they'll do just about anything you want, even collagen injections and body wrapping. Or you can spend a half hour vegging out in their special environmental room."

Mac grabbed the other jar, unscrewed the top, peered in and sniffed. It had the same almond scent and the same glossy appearance. "More moisturizing cream. But if it's from Genesis, why isn't it in one of their fancy jars? And why is it buried in the middle of a stack of towels? You'd think she'd stolen it or something."

"Don't *you* jump to crazy conclusions. Val was doing all kinds of strange things. Probably there's money hidden in the flour canister."

"I didn't find anything." He sighed and slipped the small jar into his pocket before turning abruptly back to the bedroom. Still clutching the other jar, Katie followed him, determined that she was going to be in on any more discoveries. But as he began to open drawers and boxes, she realized that her body felt leaden. She'd been through so much today, and now her energy reserves were zero. After hesitating for a moment, she sank into the boudoir chair by the window. If she'd been alone, her eyelids might have fluttered closed. Instead she found she couldn't take her eyes off Mac as he made a quick but thorough search of the room.

He didn't ask for her help, and it was clear he didn't need it. He was fast and efficient. But she wasn't really surprised. The confident, lithe way he moved was one of the things that had made her notice him in the first place back in medical school.

Against her will, she found the old memories flooding her mind. Back in medical school, even though she'd wanted to get to know the very appealing Mac McQuade, she hadn't made the first approach because she hadn't had a clue about how to interest popular guys. On the other hand, she was one of the best students in their class. That's what had made him notice *her,* she supposed. He was on a scholarship, too, she'd discovered when he'd invited her for coffee in one of the little cafés near the campus. It turned out that talking to him was easy. They'd gone from discussing test results to studying together, from sharing supper to spending the night in each other's apartments when they were studying late. Maybe if she hadn't been so focused on seeing that both of them passed their senior midterm exams, they would have been making love, too. They'd come pretty close. They'd both wanted to. At least that's what she'd told herself later. Although maybe that part had simply been her fantasy.

Resting her chin on her knees, Katie clasped her arms around her legs as if the protective posture could give her some comfort. Over the years, she'd spent a lot of time wondering about how things might have turned out if Mac McQuade hadn't left right after exams to fulfill a previous commitment to work for a couple of weeks in a free clinic in Morgantown, West Virginia.

She'd known he was going to be terribly busy, and she hadn't expected to hear from him right away. But after a week she'd gotten worried and called the clinic. Mac had never gotten there because his motorcycle had been struck by a pickup just inside the Morgantown city limits.

Frantic, her fingers stiff with dread, she'd dialed the hospital where they'd told her he'd been taken. To her enormous relief, Mac had been well enough to talk to her on the phone, although he'd insisted she not come down. Three days later, she disobeyed instructions. When she'd tried to find his room, she'd learned to her shock that he'd flown home to his family's Montana ranch without telling her he was leaving.

They'd only talked once after that, and he'd assured her that he was mending nicely—including his badly injured hand. But he was going to take some time off from school to get his head together. They'd been so close to each other that at first she couldn't believe he was coldly saying goodbye. But he'd made it very clear that any plans for the future didn't include her.

Katie winced with remembered pain. His rejection had been like a deep incision cutting away an important part of herself, and the only way to cope with the hurt was to go back to school and pretend that studying was the biggest thing in her life.

Realizing she had a death grip on the arms of the chair, Katie unlocked her fingers and glanced up quickly. Thank God Mac wasn't paying any attention to her, because she could picture the wounded look that had settled over her features. She wasn't going to make a fool of herself over something that had died and been put to rest years ago. Except that when he'd held her, for just a moment she'd thought that he . . .

As if her disturbing memories had drawn his interest, he stopped and turned. Color flooded her face, and she blurted the first thing that came to mind. ''You can do an awful lot with that hand.''

"Yeah. It's almost as good as the real one."

"I mean—" the heat in her cheeks grew more vivid "—I haven't seen anything that sophisticated before. Did you design it?"

"Not my specialty. But I had some input."

"What is your specialty?"

"Exotic toxins—and antitoxins."

"Oh."

"Look, we're both tired. I don't think we're going to find anything else here tonight."

Katie nodded.

"The best thing for you would be to go home and get some sleep."

She sat up straighter and pressed her heels against the carpet. "The best thing for me would be to talk to Tom Houston."

"No."

"What do you mean, no?"

"Just what I said. Tom was in pretty bad shape when I left him. And he's going to have to face the police in the morning. I don't think talking to you is in his best interests."

She'd been grieving, hurt, shocked and numb by turns this evening. Now she was angry. "Since when do you make my decisions for me? What if I call the police tonight and tell them he was with Val when she died? What if I tell them I met you over here removing evidence?"

She saw the fingers of his right hand clench, but his face remained impassive.

"That's up to you, of course. But I'm not going to make it easy for you."

Before she could continue the argument, he turned abruptly and stalked out of the room. A few moments later she heard the front door open and close.

Katie glanced at the closet. She'd come here to get her sister's school letter. That would have to wait now. Pushing herself to her feet, she headed for the living room and snatched up her purse.

The door to the stairs whooshed shut as she stepped into the hall, and for a moment she thought Mac had gone that way. Then she saw him standing by the elevator at the end of the hall. He must have heard her coming, but he didn't look up, and he didn't hold the car for her.

However, the next one came almost at once. Out on the street, she spotted his familiar stride as he rounded the corner.

Score one for her. Apparently the thought of being pursued by docile little Katie Martin didn't even enter his head. A few minutes later he got into a low-slung sports car and pulled out into traffic. Luckily her car was around the corner. She caught up with Mac at Connecticut Avenue and followed him out of the city. Keeping her quarry in sight wasn't difficult because the traffic had thinned in the late-evening hours. Where was he heading? she wondered. To his apartment? Tom's house? The lab?

Flipping on the radio to keep herself company, Katie tried not to think about the strange twists her life had taken since this afternoon. The confrontation with Val. Her death. The awful trip to the morgue. And then a surprise encounter with the man who had been haunting her dreams for eight years—transformed into flesh-and-blood reality in her sister's closet. Her hands locked around the steering wheel as she followed the sports car onto the Beltway. Maybe Mac was right, and she should let the police take care of things in the morning. Still, she didn't give up the pursuit. Ten minutes later she realized that their route was taking them into the outskirts of Columbia, a planned community just south of Ellicott City where she lived. The thought that Mac had been working, or living, so close without her knowing it brought a lump to her throat.

They had turned off the main highway and onto the curving roads of a quiet industrial park full of research-and-development companies that had been attracted to the high-tech atmosphere of the new town. At this time of night, the park was almost deserted, and Katie dropped back several hundred yards, afraid that Mac would realize he was being followed. Up ahead he swung into a parking lot. She drove past, her headlights illuminating a Medizone company sign. At the next driveway she made a U-turn.

The lot in front of the one-story brick building was empty, but she found Mac's sports car around back beside a rear entrance.

Katie turned off the engine and sat twisting the keys between her suddenly cold fingers as she battled with more second thoughts. Was she doing something stupid—barging in there to confront Val's lover? Mac had been adamant about her not seeing Tom tonight. Yet what if Mac couldn't persuade him to turn himself in? What if Tom Houston was so scared that he went into hiding or fled the country? Then she might never know what had really happened in Val's apartment earlier in the evening. Taking a deep breath, she climbed out of her car and marched toward the building.

The door closest to Mac's vehicle was unlocked. Fate was making things easy for her. But she was still torn by doubts as she pulled the door open.

It shut decisively behind her, and Katie found herself in a dimly lighted back hall without a clue about where to look for Tom Houston. However, in the next moment, a muffled exclamation sent her sprinting toward the left.

As she came abreast of heavy double doors, she heard Mac curse. Pushing the doors open, she stepped into a well-equipped lab—as it might have been set up by a horror-movie director with a weird sense of humor.

Glassware littered lab tables. A printer spewed out paper. Equipment hummed ominously. And an uncaged white rat scurried across the tiled floor.

Mac had just turned back toward the entrance. His face went from dismay to shock as he spotted Katie.

"Get down," he shouted as his body shoved hers back out into the hall. Seconds later an earsplitting explosion rocked the room.

Chapter Four

Flying glass shot past Katie's head like shrapnel from a bomb and pierced the wall behind her. The breath was knocked from her lungs as she landed with a thud on the hard tile floor. Mac had flung himself between her and the source of the danger as he shoved her down.

For several seconds there was eerie silence. Then a second explosion shattered the air. Mac's large body covered Katie's, and his arms came up to shield her head. More glass rained down, striking the floor around them like hail hitting a tin roof.

Katie pressed her face tightly to Mac's chest, feeling the staccato beating of her own heart. She knew it would be perilous to look up or open her eyes with the glass showering around them. Just above her ear, a shard pinged against metal, and she guessed that Mac was using his steel hand as a deflector. Then she heard him wince sharply and knew the flying glass had connected with his flesh as well.

"Mac, what happened? Are you hurt?" she whispered urgently, struggling to see the damage.

He pulled her face closer to his chest and tunneled his fingers through her hair, the pressure against her scalp holding her still. "Don't move yet."

"You've been hit."

"I'm okay. My coat's taking the worst of it."

For endless seconds she clung to him. Shifting, he cradled her slender form against his sturdier one, enfolding her protectively. If she hadn't known better, she might have said the gesture was fiercely possessive. Except that he was just giving her the aid and comfort he'd give any other woman in similar circumstances.

Her mind worked out the logic. Her body knew that she was in Mac's arms again for the second time in as many hours. She could feel her breasts pressed against his chest, her thighs glued to his, all her soft contours molded to his harder ones. Despite the peril, she couldn't stop herself from reacting in the old familiar way. Fear had made her pulse race. It raced faster now. The reality of Mac McQuade was too much for her to handle. Or did the fantasies she'd spun over the years give him this power over her?

Katie breathed in and out with shallow regularity and tried not to move again, tried not to do anything that would make her more aware of him. But her nerves felt raw as she strained her ears for a change in the barrage. A second before she realized she was listening to silence once more, Mac was shifting his weight off her. Apparently he was as anxious to break the intimate contact as she. Shrugging out of his overcoat, he spread it on the floor over the glass and eased into a sitting position. Yet his eyes searched hers, and his fingers slid over her face. "Did I hurt you when I threw you down?" he asked, his voice concerned as he dropped his arm.

"You saved me from a face full of glass, I think." Katie smoothed her fingers over her cheeks, aware that he was following the motion with his smoky gaze. Her hand fell to her side. Then she flexed her arms and legs. "I'm okay."

Standing up, he pulled her to her feet and watched her take a couple of tentative steps, her shoes crunching on the broken glass.

When he saw she was all right, his voice took on a different tone. "You followed me back here."

"Yes."

"You shouldn't have."

"It was my decision."

"Well, it's too dangerous in here for you to stay." He turned her around in the direction of the door to the parking lot.

Katie had started for the exit when she realized Mac wasn't behind her. She whirled and saw him reentering the lab, grinding glass under his heels with every footfall.

"Mac! No!" As he disappeared through the doors, fear leaped in her throat, blocking her windpipe. If it wasn't safe for her, it wasn't safe for him, either.

Acrid smoke was billowing into the hall now. Something in there was burning. But surely the building had an automatic sprinkler system. Why wasn't it pouring water onto the flames?

Casting around for the fire alarm, Katie located the panel several feet down the hall. As she pulled the handle, she braced for the loud clanging of the warning bell. It didn't sound. *My God, none of the safety systems is working.*

But at least there was a good old-fashioned fire extinguisher near the alarm panel. Without stopping to think about her own welfare, Katie wrested it from its bracket. Unhooking the nozzle, she bolted into the lab after Mac.

Immediately her eyes began to burn from the smoke as she looked frantically around for him.

"Mac!"

He was bent over a computer terminal cursing under his breath as he worked the keyboard with a right-handed typing system and thumped down on the shift with his metal fist.

His head jerked up when he spotted her. "Get out of here before something else happens."

"Not without you."

"The damn automated system's got to be shut down before it does any more damage. Get out before the whole place goes up in smoke," he repeated.

As if to punctuate his words, a pile of steel-wool pads in back of Katie began to flame and spark. Turning, she coated them with foam. When the papers from the printer blazed up, too, she doused them as well.

Tears streamed down her face, and she began to cough. Across the room, Mac was choking, too. How long would either one of them be able to stay here? The speculation was cut off as her attention swung to a third small fire, which had taken hold on the seat of a lab stool, sending choking fumes into the air. As she saturated the fabric, she watched Mac out of the corner of her eye. He had moved away from the computer and was yanking open windows. Then he grabbed the fire extinguisher he'd been using earlier and began to soak a trash can that had turned into a bonfire. There were no more flames in the room, but thick smoke still hung around them like poison mist.

Between gasps for breath, Mac turned back toward her. "The air's too bad. Get back in the hall."

"You?"

"One more thing I've got to take care of. I'll be out in a minute."

She was about to protest, until another spasm doubled her over. If she didn't get out of here soon, she was going to faint—and then she'd be more hindrance than help. Chest aching and eyes watering, she staggered into the hall and sucked in several grateful drafts. She wanted to go back into the lab, but her lungs vetoed the plan, and she was forced to wait in white-knuckled silence. Finally Mac reappeared, and she threw her arms around him and clung.

He held her just as fiercely, his heart thumping against her breasts and his hand stroking over her back and shoulders. "You don't take orders very well," he growled.

"I didn't like the ones you were giving."

He reached up and began silently picking glass out of her hair. As she watched the unguarded look of tenderness in his eyes, her chest tightened.

"Mac." Spontaneously, her face lifted to his just as it had a few hours ago. His head lowered. This time their lips met. She'd thought she'd figured everything out. But nothing was as simple as it seemed. Not when he was holding her in his arms again. Not when his mouth moved over hers. Urgent. Claiming. Making demands he had no right to make. She yielded freely. For long moments they were both lost. Then he broke the contact. As though nothing earthshaking had happened, he took a step back and inspected her hair.

"That's the worst of it." He looked over his shoulder toward the disaster area. "I'm sorry. I'm not thinking very clearly."

What exactly was he apologizing for? she wondered.

"I finally remembered that every lab has an emergency exhaust system. I turned it on manually. The smoke'll be gone in a while."

She could be just as cool about the kiss as he. "Shouldn't we call the fire department—just in case?"

He nodded. "But I've got to check on Tom first. I left him sleeping in my office. Thank God it's at the other end of the building. We can call from there."

Before she could ask what had triggered the explosion and why none of the safety systems had kicked in, Mac was striding down the hall.

Katie ran to catch up. "Tom slept through *this?*"

"I gave him a pretty strong sedative before I went back into the city."

Despite the explanation, Mac's voice betrayed his concern. Katie couldn't match his rapid gait as he hurried into the executive wing of the building. She got a quick impression of walls and furnishings in a pleasing combination of mauve and gray, and thick carpet muffled their footsteps. They passed an L-shaped seating area, a secretary's desk and an oak door with Mac's name and the words Vice President on a polished brass plate. An identical door led to Tom's office. Except that his title was President.

Inside, the furnishings were rosewood and leather. But Katie's eyes honed in on the shelves behind the desk where a picture of Mac and a forceful-looking older man was prominently displayed. Mac was dressed in a safari outfit. His smiling companion, who wore a conservative business suit, was clasping him on the back. The vice president and president of Medizone.

Mac made a rapid check of the office, his manner more frantic than she'd ever seen it. "Where the hell is he? I watched him take the medication. It should have put him out," he muttered.

"Is this it?" Katie held out her hand. A small red capsule like a poison berry lay in the middle of her palm.

He snatched the medication out of her hand. "Where did you get that?"

"It was on the rug beside the sofa."

"Oh, Lord. He only pretended to take it." Cursing under his breath, Mac thumped the metal fist against the desk in a gesture of defeat and frustration. "I didn't want to believe it. But I guess he's the one who set up that Rube Goldberg experiment down the hall. Whatever it was supposed to be."

"We didn't see him in the lab," Katie soothed.

"But I've got to go back there and check. He could be under a table. Or behind a storage cabinet." The last words were tossed over his shoulder as he sprinted back down the hall once more.

Katie trotted after him.

The smoke had cleared, and the small fires that might have enveloped the room were cold and dead. Katie and Mac both glanced around for signs of structural damage. Although the place looked like a war zone, there didn't seem to be any twisted posts or blasted-out walls. Encouraged on that point, Katie helped Mac search behind the tables and under the desks. They found no one.

"Thank God for small favors. At least he's not in the lab." Mac led the way into the hall again. "Maybe he left. No. His car was still in the parking lot when I arrived."

"He could have walked out of the building. Or called a cab."

"I didn't think about that." Mac brushed back his hair with his fingers. "What the hell did he think he was doing? And why was he sterilizing all that equipment?"

Katie shook her head slowly. As she'd helped search, she'd realized what had caused the explosions. Two autoclaves—the machines that sterilized glassware and instruments with steam pressure—had exploded, shattering their contents and spraying deadly missiles all over the room. Superheated glass had started the fires.

She gestured back toward the mess. "I can't believe you didn't have automatic cutoffs. Or did someone disable every safety device in the building?"

Mac sighed. "We've been trying to go on-line with a computer-controlled total operating system for each lab. It runs the machinery, the ventilators, the sprinkler systems. Everything. It's going to be wonderful when it's working right. But all the bugs aren't out of it yet, and it's only supposed to be activated for carefully monitored tests. Anyone who wants to access the program has to know the password. And any time it's turned on, a whole series of warnings flash across the screen. You'd have to be suicidal or crazy to ignore them.''

Katie saw the impact of the last sentence hit Mac like an avalanche hurtling down a mountain. Yet all he said was, ''Tom has a hell of a lot of explaining to do.''

''But where is he?''

''I guess he's hiding, since he knows I'm going to be damn angry with him.''

Katie had a hard time imagining the forceful-looking man in the photograph cowering in a broom closet or some other dark corner. But most of the things that had happened this evening had been hard to imagine.

''We can cover more territory if we split up. Do you mind?'' Mac asked.

For the first time this evening, he was actually asking for her help, and she felt her heart squeeze. But there was no time to let herself examine that emotion. ''Of course I don't mind,'' she said softly.

It was Katie who found Tom—in the anteroom to the hematology lab. Wearing a grease-streaked white shirt and gray slacks, he was sprawled on the floor. His sightless eyes were focused on the open refrigerator door, and his fingers were curved as if they had been clutching something. But his hand was empty. Beside him were instruments and glassware that looked as if they'd been swept off the lab table when he'd fallen.

Another death. Although she'd never met this man, his lifeless body brought a stab of pain. Yet she forced herself to do the things that were necessary. Kneeling, she checked for a pulse in his neck. As she touched his flesh, she felt as if a river of sadness were flowing through her. This man had cared for Val. Now they were both gone. The only thing she could still do for him was try to catalog details that might be important later. His skin was still warm, and his limbs were still flexible—which meant that he'd only been deceased for a few hours.

Mac came in as she was gently closing Tom's eyes. She heard the breath whoosh out of his lungs as he focused on his friend's face. Like Katie, he had no trouble recognizing death. Yet he knelt beside Tom and grasped his shoulders urgently, raising him up slightly as both the good hand and the metal one dug into the fabric of his dress shirt.

"Oh, Lord. What was I thinking about? I never should have left him alone."

"Mac, you did what you thought you had to."

"No, I had a pretty good idea of the kind of shape he was in. He was distraught. He told me what he was going to do. I should have stayed with him!" Anguish seeped out of him with every word.

Katie felt tears gather in her own eyes as he laid Tom carefully back on the floor.

"He asked you to go down to Val's apartment. He said he'd feel better once you brought his belongings back."

Mac didn't seem to hear her. When she reached for his hand, he stood up before she could make contact and exited into the hematology lab where he stood with his back to her. He was a man who knew how to control his reactions. At least on the surface. Now he looked as if he were staring intently out the window into the night. As far as Katie could tell, there was nothing to see but the parking lot.

Her own emotions in turmoil, she got up and closed the refrigerator just to give herself something to do. Then she tiptoed to the doorway. The tension gathering in Mac's broad shoulders was like a physical force. His back was rigid as a stockade fence—with a No Trespassing sign slapped in the middle.

Katie gripped the door frame with stiff fingers, knowing he wanted her to turn around and leave so she wouldn't see any more of his pain. But she'd already stopped taking orders from him—both spoken and unspoken—once and for all tonight. Before she lost her nerve she crossed the room, slipped in front of Mac and slid her arms around his middle to hug him close.

His arms hung at his sides.

"Please. We've each lost someone tonight. Someone we cared a lot about. Please, hold me."

She knew some iron band inside of him had snapped when he whispered her name. His voice came close to breaking as he folded her into his embrace. For long moments they simply held each other, each drawing strength from the human contact—from each other.

"I was a fool tonight, charging off to your sister's apartment to play cops and robbers when I should have been taking care of my friend. Now Tom's dead because of me," he finally said.

"You weren't playing cops and robbers. You were trying to reassure Tom. If he was acting like Val, I'll bet he made it pretty hard for you to say no."

Mac didn't answer, but she felt the truth of her guess in the way a little of the tension eased from his shoulders. "You were looking for evidence," she continued. "Well, it didn't come out the way you expected. Now you feel the same way I do about Val. Guilty." She gulped. "I shouldn't have left her alone this afternoon, either. But I did."

His hand soothed over her back. "Maybe we both did the best we could."

"God, I hope so."

He held her for a few minutes longer. Then she felt him begin to ease away and knew that they couldn't stand there forever. They were going to have to call the police. Mac would have to face the same ordeal she'd been through. But he wouldn't be alone. Whether he wanted her support or not, she was going to give it to him.

She looked around the room, her eyes following the trail of broken glass and scattered instruments on the floor back to the lab table. The polished surface was a disordered mess, although not quite as bad as the scene down the hall after the explosion. Maybe Tom had forgotten he was sterilizing equipment. Or maybe he'd abandoned his lab experiment and come back here to take care of something more important. But what?

Katie's scalp tightened when she spotted something she hadn't noticed in the middle of the debris on the table. An empty hypodermic. No, not empty, she noted as she glided closer. There was a bit of pink liquid in the bottom.

Had Tom given himself an injection? Medication? Had he taken an accidental overdose? Or was this some designer drug? Was that the cause of his death?

Her gaze swept the cluttered countertop. A few yards away from the syringe was a small bottle with what looked like the dregs of the same stuff. Snatching it up, Katie read the label. It consisted of a series of meaningless letters and numbers and told her nothing.

HI 320 DQ

"Was Tom taking any medication that had to be injected?"

"Not that I know of."

"Then what's this stuff?" Katie held out the bottle and the hypodermic on her flattened palm.

Mac turned, focused on the syringe, and closed the distance between them in a few giant steps. Lifting the bottle from her hand with cold metal fingers, he inspected the contents and the label.

"It looks like it's from one of our experimental batches."

"Batches of what?" She couldn't keep the accusation out of her voice.

"I told you before, we don't make illegal drugs at Medizone."

The sharp denial meant that his mind had at least been skirmishing with the same thoughts as hers.

He sighed. "I do most of my work in the field. Tom is in charge of development. But he's a stickler for careful documentation. Everything we produce is logged in and updated on a regular basis."

"Then let's see what your records say about HI 320 DQ."

The challenge in her voice made his eyes narrow, but his voice was deadly calm. "If you insist, Dr. Martin."

Folding the bottle into the prison of his steel fingers, Mac ushered Katie out of the room by a different door so that they avoided the body in the anteroom. Earlier his strides had been decisive, now he walked more slowly.

Second thoughts? Katie wondered.

She had her answer after he sat down at a computer terminal and typed in a hidden password. "These files contain proprietary information."

"I'm not going to reveal your company secrets."

Mac nodded and entered the code number from the bottle. A moment later, the screen brought up a lab status report for HI 320 DQ.

Katie leaned over Mac's shoulder, scanning the test. According to the background summary, Mac had brought back the basic compound being used from an expedition to Nepal. It was a plant resin that was native to the central highlands of that country, but Medizone had succeeded in establishing several specimens at their Beltsville greenhouses. Next was documentation on concentration and purification.

"Yeah, now I remember this stuff," Mac muttered. "Tom was talking about it a couple of months ago. He was excited about the preliminary results. Let's see what came of it."

"This is all very interesting, but what are you using it for?" Katie asked.

Mac scrolled down to the next page of the text and moved the cursor to one of the paragraphs.

Katie read rapidly through the information and then read it again. Puzzled, she turned back to Mac. "Do I have this right? You're using this compound against HIV?"

"Correct. In early laboratory trials, it was shown to slow down the growth of the AIDS virus."

He brought the next several paragraphs into view on the screen. "The problem is, it turned out to have highly toxic side effects."

"But the bottle. The hypodermic. Why would he inject himself with that?" Katie asked.

"I don't know." Mac scanned the figures on the screen. "But if HI 320 DQ was really in the bottle, it was enough to kill a grizzly bear."

Chapter Five

Mac looked up from the computer screen, rubbing the side of his hand down his jaw. It scraped against the evening stubble of his beard, and for a moment Katie found herself focusing on the barely audible rasp. It was a very male sound and a very familiar one that reminded her of long nights studying together in her tiny student apartment. Now they were together again in the middle of the night. With another problem to solve, she reminded herself. One that was a whole lot more immediate than the study of diseases in textbooks.

"This isn't getting us anywhere. And the longer I wait to call the police, the worse it's going to be." Mac paused and gave Katie a direct look. "Maybe you don't want to be here when they arrive."

Katie met his level gaze. "I'll stay."

"And tell them what? That you followed me here because your sister killed herself this evening and you thought Tom Houston might be able to tell you something about it?"

She sucked in a sharp breath. "I didn't know Tom's name. But Perkins, the detective who interviewed me, wanted to talk to him."

"He can't do that now."

She was so tired, it was hard to think. "It's not right for me to leave. I was here. I found him. Couldn't we just tell the police what happened after we arrived at Medizone?"

His gaze swept her disheveled appearance and focused on her face, making her vividly aware of how she must look.

"It's three in the morning, and you've had a hell of a day. Do you really think you're up to sorting through questions and deciding which ones to answer honestly?"

"I—"

"Do you want to go through the story of Val's suicide again?"

Katie shook her head wearily. He was right; she didn't know if she could face that again.

"It's better if we keep things separate—Tom and Val. Until we know what's going on."

Katie still didn't like the idea. But as she considered the evening's events, she realized that if she stayed, she might have to explain how she'd met Mac down at her sister's apartment—where he'd gone to remove evidence. That wasn't going to look very good for Mac now that Tom was dead. "Will you call me when it's over?" she asked.

"No. It's already late."

"Then we'll talk tomorrow."

He nodded tightly. "Go on. Get out of here so I can make the call."

WHEN CORNELL PERKINS came in at eight-thirty Wednesday morning, there was a blue memo sheet in the middle of his blotter. It read: "See me ASAP." There was no signature, but he knew the handwriting. The message had come from Captain Gantry.

Now what? Perkins checked to see that he wasn't wearing scrambled egg on his tie.

He'd never seen himself as Eddie Murphy in *Beverly Hills Cop*, he reflected as he started down the hall. He was just a homeboy who had made it in the big city by doing his job. But after forty years in the department, the strain was starting to wear him down. And all he was going to get for his efforts was a D.C. pension if the city government didn't run out of money.

Gantry's secretary ushered him through to the inner sanctum after barely a five-minute wait. Something was definitely up.

"Close the door and have a seat."

Perkins complied. As he dropped into one of the imitation leather chairs across from the chief's desk, he felt his mouth go dry.

"I've got some good news," Gantry murmured but didn't immediately elaborate.

"Oh?"

"The task force on drug abuse has gotten funding for a departmental liaison to check out how the problem is being handled in various other locations around the country. Honolulu. New Orleans. San Juan. It's a four-week tour. And there's per diem on top of the base salary."

"Yeah? Which lucky son of a bitch has the job?"

"You do."

Perkins's jaw dropped open. "You've got to be kidding."

"No joke."

The detective stared across the desk. "How long do I get to make up my mind?"

"They want to know right away." Gantry hesitated, then continued in a lower voice. "Somebody's either rewarding you for a whopping big favor I don't know about—or they want you out of the way for a while. If it's the latter, you'd better accept. Otherwise, they might come up with some other bright idea that isn't quite as pleasant."

Perkins sat back in his chair. In a few moments, he looked up at Gantry. "When do I pack?"

"After you report to the District Building this morning."

"What about the cases I'm working on?"

"I've had your folders pulled. Everything's being reassigned."

Perkins had always gone with his hunches. Now his spider senses told him someone was pulling him off the Caldwell case. And it looked like he'd better go along with it.

Gantry waited until Perkins had closed the office door behind him. Then he reached for the phone and dialed a Chevy Chase exchange.

"Hello."

"Blackbird has flown west," he said in a stiff voice and hung up. If the police commissioner got wind of this, his thirty-year career was down the tubes. But like he'd told Perkins, when the right people called in a favor, you either played ball or applied for disability retirement.

THE MOMENT Katie opened her eyes, everything came back. Val. Mac. Tom. For silent moments she stared at the clock. Ten a.m. Mac hadn't called. Did that mean everything had gone all right with the police last night? Or had it gone badly? When she sat up and reached to find a phone book in the stand beside the bed, she winced. Her body felt as if she'd gone fifteen rounds with Mike Tyson.

More cautiously, she stood up and tentatively flexed her arms and legs. Being slammed against the floor during the explosion hadn't done her body any permanent harm, nothing a hot shower wouldn't relieve. But how much was it going to do for the ache in her heart? The ache had a cable link to the emotional elevator she'd been riding since the previous afternoon. Most of the trip had been straight to the subbasement. But when Mac had kissed her, she'd gone all the way through the roof. That had made the subsequent plunge all the more sickening.

The best thing for her would be if she never saw Mac
McQuade again. Last night he'd made it very clear that he
didn't want anything from her. Not her help. Not her support. Not her comfort. And certainly not a resumption of
their relationship after all these years. But that didn't stop
her from worrying about him and wondering how he'd gotten through the police interview.

After finding Medizone in the phone book, she dialed the
number. When she asked to speak to Mac, she was put
through to his secretary.

"Who's calling, please?" a motherly-sounding voice
asked.

"Dr. Martin. A friend of Mr. McQuade. Is he available?"

"I'm afraid not. Our company president died suddenly
last night, and Mr. McQuade has a lot of things to deal
with."

Katie caught the protective note in the secretary's voice.
The woman obviously cared about Mac.

"Is Mr. McQuade all right?" she asked.

"Yes. If you want to leave a message, I'm sure he'll get
back to you when things calm down around here."

Katie left her name and number. She could imagine Mac
had an awful lot to cope with today. Maybe even the police. At least he could call his family if he needed someone.
No, he wouldn't do that. She remembered he'd never asked
them for help when he'd been in school. Probably he'd
hated having to go back to the ranch after he'd lost his hand.
How long had he stayed? What had he done before he'd
joined up with Tom? Katie brought herself up short. She
had her own problems to worry about today. Like her sister's funeral.

After turning the shower taps to full blast, she adjusted
the temperature and stepped under a hot spray. While she

washed her hair, she made mental notes about what she needed to do.

As she was drying herself off, she spotted the little jar of face cream she'd taken from Val's last night—and remembered the lecture her sister had delivered on morning beauty care. Well, she certainly wasn't in the mood for makeup, but maybe the expensive moisturizer would help soothe her skin. Scooping up a dab, she smoothed the cream over her cheeks and around her eyes. It felt marvelous. She rubbed a little on the sore spots over her ribs where Mac's metal fingers had bruised her flesh. Probably it wouldn't help. But it wouldn't hurt, either.

Although her body was feeling less creaky by the time she'd gotten dressed, she wished she didn't have to go down to the office. But since she didn't have a secretary to rearrange her appointments, that was the only way she was going to clear her calendar.

When she'd begun her genetic study on Huntington's disease, she'd planned on working at home—partly because she'd been through a rather bad experience in her last job. She'd been on the staff at a private hospital called the Sterling Clinic, which had been rocked by a series of unsavory revelations. Katie hadn't been involved, but the clinic had finally been forced to close, and the negative publicity had made it difficult for her to get another hospital job.

So she'd designed a research study and applied for a grant. Then her friend Abby Franklin had mentioned she was looking for someone to sublet her office at 43 Light Street in downtown Baltimore while she and her husband Steve were on an extended trip to India. The timing and the location were perfect, since Katie had found her home wasn't really a very good setting for the interview phase of the project. Now she was hoping to lease her own office at 43 Light Street.

She'd come to love the charming old building. And Abby had introduced her to a whole group of supportive women who worked there. They shared not only their good times but also their problems. The feeling of having someone to turn to when you needed her was one of the best things she'd gotten from the experience.

However, this morning when Katie walked into the black-and-white marble lobby, she felt more withdrawn than she had in months. Which was probably what set off Sabrina Barkley's radar. Before Katie could press the elevator button, the vivacious redhead waved from the engagingly cluttered shop—called Sabrina's Fancy—where she sold herbs and other merchandise.

Stepping through the door, she gave Katie a critical inspection. "You look like you need a cup of mulled cider."

"Sabrina, I—I have some stuff to take care of."

"Come on in and tell me about it."

It was hard to refuse her friend's warmth and encouraging smile. Over a mug of spiced cider, Katie found herself talking about the evening before—leaving out the intimate details of her encounter with Mac.

"I'm so sorry about your sister," Sabrina murmured. "What can I do to help?"

"Thanks for asking. But there's nothing I need right now. I think I'm just going to have a simple graveside service. No open casket, not when Val cared so much about how she looked."

"Oh, honey. It must have been terrible for you having to go down to the morgue all alone. Why didn't you call one of us?"

"It's a long drive to D.C." Katie's voice choked up, and she stopped abruptly.

They were both quiet for several moments while Sabrina straightened up a shelf of herb-vinegar bottles and Katie collected her scattered control.

"I'd better go make those calls," she murmured. "Before my interviewees start showing up."

"Yes."

As she stood up, Sabrina patted her arm. "By the way, do you want me to put a hex on that guy who popped out of the closet? Warts on his face. A rash on his bottom. A flat tire on his fancy car."

The images coaxed a little smile to Katie's lips. "Don't tell me you've added a new service."

"No. But it's fun to read about the old superstitions. When you're up to it, you can come over to dinner and I'll show you some of my books."

"Maybe after I get through the next couple of weeks."

Sabrina walked Katie to the elevator. "Remember, call me if you need anything."

"Yes. Thanks."

Katie unlocked the door to her fifth-floor office and flipped on the lights. Sinking down in the leather desk chair, she spared a quick glance at the answering machine. No calls, she observed with a little sigh of relief. At least she wouldn't have to spend time returning them.

It took longer than she expected to cancel her appointments because word quickly spread around the building about Val's death. During the morning there was a steady stream of people in and out of the office all wanting to offer comfort and support.

By lunchtime she'd rescheduled all her interviews for later in the month and turned to the task she dreaded: Val's burial arrangements. First she dialed Craigstone's, the funeral home she'd used four years ago when her mother had died. They'd helped her and Val through a number of difficult decisions at a time when she'd felt least capable of making them. Now as she went through a similar set of questions, a wave of unreality swept over her. No viewing. A graveside service. Hillside Cemetery. Yellow roses. Val had always loved roses. Even to Katie's own ears, her responses sounded like tinny echoes through a cheap microphone.

"I think we can take care of everything from here. All we need to know is when the body will be released," the funeral director said.

"I'm not sure," Katie replied. "But I'll call the morgue and let you know as soon as I find out."

Noel Emery, Laura Roswell's paralegal assistant, stopped by with a crab-cake platter for lunch. Ordinarily Katie would have considered the seafood a treat. Today she could hardly force herself to take a few bites. Finally she stuffed the plate into the office refrigerator and called information for the number of the D.C. medical examiner.

What should have been a simple task turned into another ordeal that ate up much of the afternoon.

"I'm sorry, Ms. Martin, an autopsy is required whenever the deceased was not under the care of a physician," a clerk explained. "According to my files, the police department hasn't signed off on the procedure."

"Dr. Martin," she corrected.

"I'm sorry, *Dr.* Martin. We can't release your sister's body yet."

"Does that mean the autopsy showed something abnormal?" Katie asked.

"We only received the remains last night, so it may not have even been done yet. Besides, I'm not allowed to give out pathology information without specific authorization."

Katie silently fought her exasperation. As next of kin, surely she was entitled to the results. But that really wasn't the important issue, anyway.

She took a calming breath. "All right. I understand you have your rules. But I need to make funeral arrangements."

"You might try talking to someone at district police headquarters."

Katie hung up and went in search of her purse, where she'd put Detective Perkins's number. As she removed the business card, she also took out two aspirins. Her ear ached from the pressure of the receiver, and the knot of tension at the base of her neck was growing tighter by the moment.

Perkins had seemed curt with her at first, but after he'd heard her story, he'd been more sympathetic. Maybe he could tell her what was going on. Picking up the phone again, she tried his number. It rang five times before the call was transferred to another extension.

"Sergeant Nathans speaking. Detective Perkins is out of town on police business, could someone else help you?"

Out of town on police business? He hadn't mentioned that when he'd given her his card and told her to call him if she had any more questions. "Is someone else working on the Val Caldwell case? I'm her sister."

"I'll check." She was put on hold for a few minutes.

"Sorry to keep you waiting," Nathans said when he returned. "I don't seem to have any record of a Caldwell case. Are you sure it was assigned to this office?"

Katie stared at the phone. All she wanted was to schedule her sister's funeral. "I'm sure about which detective interviewed me for hours last night," she said, enunciating every word carefully. "Don't you people have logs? Can't you get in touch with Detective Perkins and find out what he did with the file?"

"Calm down, ma'am. I'm sure the report is here somewhere. Leave me a number and I'll get back to you."

Katie left her number with Nathans, wondering if she'd hear from him again. Lacing her hands together, she massaged her white knuckles with the fingers of the opposite hands. But it was impossible not to keep imagining Val's body lying in some storage freezer while the police hunted for a misplaced file and made up their minds about the autopsy report.

Maybe that was S.O.P. in an overworked big-city police department. Maybe she was so stressed out that her expectations were unreasonable, Katie told herself. Or maybe there was another explanation, she thought with a sudden chill.

Last night she'd gone from thinking Val was paranoid to wondering whether her sister and Tom were on the same drug, to coming up against the brick wall of Tom's suicide. But what if this wasn't just some personal tragedy that had destroyed two lives? What if she'd walked into the middle of some sort of cover-up? What if Val and Tom had been into something illegal that the D.C. police department wasn't prepared to talk about yet?

Once the idea surfaced, Katie found it was hard to keep her imagination from going wild. Had Tom really died from an injection of HI 320 DQ? Or had someone wanted it to look that way? And what if the experimental drug was in his bloodstream? Had he injected himself? Or had someone else done it for him?

Maybe she and Mac should put the Howard County Police into the picture. Except that Mac had wanted her out of the way when he talked to them, and she still had no idea what kind of story he'd come up with.

Her chest began to tighten as she thought about the way he'd rushed her out of the Medizone building last night. And, as she considered a number of other incidents from their evening together, it became hard to breathe. My God, look at the way they'd met! In her sister's clothes closet.

He'd given her a plausible explanation for what he was doing there—and his insistence that she leave Medizone before the law arrived. But what if she'd been too off balance to see the real truth? Her feelings about him were colored by the warm glow of good memories. But it was obvious that he'd changed. How much? What was he really like now?

Blood pounded in her ears, and it was several moments before she could get her mind to function effectively again. Yet there was a very disturbing possibility she had to consider. What if Tom and Mac were involved in something illegal, and he was trying to cover it up? She closed her eyes, as if that would shut out the terrible thought. But it hung there behind closed lids. Scrabbling for a replacement, she came up with something that wasn't quite as damning. What if he'd uncovered something very damaging about his friend Tom—something that he was determined nobody else was going to dig up? What lengths would he go to in order to cover it up? All at once, she knew she had to find out.

BY NOON, Mac had accomplished a day full of essential tasks. He'd gotten a confirmation from the fire marshal that the Medizone building was safe for occupancy. He'd brought in a cleaning crew. He'd called a meeting of all his employees to break the news of Tom's death and to assure them that the tragedy would not have an adverse effect on their jobs. And he'd also talked to several reporters who'd been camping on the front walk when he'd returned to the office at seven-thirty. Then he'd canceled his return trip to Latin America. He'd have to be stateside for the next few weeks.

Thank God that over the past few months he'd assigned a number of Tom's administrative duties to Marlin Stoner. The man was up to speed on company projects and policy and would be able to run the day-to-day operations while he took care of funeral arrangements and other unexpected details.

After talking to Tom's lawyer, he put down the phone and tried to roll the tension out of his shoulders. Walking to the window, he stood and stared at the traffic going by on Green Branch Road.

Marcia, his and Tom's secretary, stuck her head in the door to find out if she could get him some lunch. She'd come to work for Medizone six years ago after her kids had graduated from college, and would have mothered the management team if they'd wanted that kind of relationship. But he'd never acquired the habit of letting women smother him with concern. Today she looked shocked and weary, and he suspected she was having almost as bad a day as he was.

"What did *you* have?" he asked.

"Just coffee."

"I'll take some, too."

Marcia didn't bother arguing that he needed to eat. Eventually his body would force him to do that. Right now, the idea made his throat clog.

"Mac, I can call Phil and tell him I'll be staying late."

"Thanks for the offer, but not tonight. The next few weeks are going to be tough on all of us. I don't want you burning out on the first day."

"If you need me, all you have to do is ask."

"I know."

After Marcia went back to her desk, his fingers tightened on the white crockery mug she'd brought. It had his name on the side in gold lettering. Tom's was sitting on the shelf over the coffee machine. Could you give away a monogrammed mug to Goodwill or some other charitable organization? Or should he keep it?

Taking a too-quick gulp of the hot brew, he grimaced as it burned his throat. He was doing everything at a frantic pace, which was a deliberate ploy to keep him from thinking too deeply. Now that he had a moment alone with his thoughts, there was nowhere else to hide.

Eight years ago he'd given up on himself. You couldn't sink much lower than sleeping under the Whitehurst Freeway and scratching out a living by volunteering to be a guinea pig in experimental drug-testing programs. Tom had turned him down flat for a Medizone protocol. But he must have seen some spark of talent in the grubby, one-handed former medical student sitting on the other side of the desk—because he'd gotten him to talk about his lab skills and then he'd offered him a job. Not something easy. A research project the company had already given up on. At first he'd been angry. Then he'd been curious. Finally he'd been challenged. And by the time he was halfway through, he knew that Tom Houston had suckered him into caring again.

Oh, Tom, what am I going to do now, he wondered silently. *I'm a good researcher. You proved that. But can I really take on this whole company?*

He didn't want to think about that now, and that left his mind open for another topic he'd rather skip. Katie.

He sighed. She ought to be the least of his worries, the one factor he could control; yet every time her image stole into his mind, he had to struggle to banish it.

Suddenly there was nowhere else to hide from old pain and fresh new wounds. He'd told himself he'd gotten over Katie Martin. Except that seeing her again had been like tumbling into a jungle pit full of sharpened stakes. The physical impact of realizing how much he wanted her had been both astonishing and agonizing.

Part of the shock had been the way he'd reacted to the new Katie Martin. The last time he'd seen her she'd been a girl, dewy with promise. Now she was a mature woman. But maturity had only made her more beautiful and more desirable. And another dimension had been added. Eight years ago, when he'd coldly explained that he wanted her out of his life, she had meekly acquiesced. Last night when he'd warned her to keep her nose out of Tom's business, she'd followed him back to Medizone. The pointed questions she'd asked had made him angry. He suspected that the only reason she'd agreed to go home before the police arrived last night was because she thought that saying too much would get *him* in trouble. He didn't want to think about that. Besides, all the reasons why he'd severed the relationship still stood.

He pressed metal fingers against the side of his leg, focusing for a moment on the small stabs of pain as if that could drive away the memories. It didn't work. Eight years ago when he'd lain in that hospital bed contemplating his altered future, he'd known that when Katie saw his hand, shock would come first—and then pity. He hadn't wanted her pity then. And he didn't want it now. Not hers or anyone else's. Back then, he'd told himself he didn't want her to spend her life picking up the pieces of his broken dreams. He hadn't been able to admit how much his own pain and pride had influenced his decision. He and Katie had both been at the top of their class, and friendly competition had added a spark to their relationship. More than that, they'd been convinced that life was going to be a succession of happy choices and easy triumphs. Then, suddenly he'd been forced to drop out of the race—and out of the winner's circle. But Katie had still been there—and on the brink of the career that had been denied him. It was hard enough adjusting to a new physical image of himself. Having her around as a daily reminder of his deeper loss would have been unbearable. It still was.

Standing up, he set the half-full mug of coffee down with a thunk and strode across his office. Maybe Tom's computer files would take his mind off Katie.

Tom had an encrypted directory that Mac had never accessed, but he knew the password. With the touch of a few keys he was staring at Tom's most private files. Several were obviously intended to be read by him. One labeled MAC1 was date-stamped three years in the past—when Tom had made him vice president. It contained a very detailed message reiterating their partnership agreement and giving instructions for the continuation of Medizone if anything should happen to the senior partner.

Mac had to stop reading for a moment when he realized he was trying to see through a film of blurry moisture. Here it was—proof if he'd ever needed it of how much faith Tom had in him. It was a hell of a lot to live up to. Frightening. Or a challenge—depending on the way you looked at it.

"Sorry pal," the message concluded. "I know you're good at field work. And I know why getting off by yourself has been important to you. But I've watched you grow and mature over the past couple of years. The company's going to need you at headquarters, and I hope you'll accept my judgment that you're going to have to stay put for a while."

Mac felt his eyes smart again as he read words written by the old, logical, prepared-for-any-contingency Tom. The man knew him pretty well. He knew his vice president would do what needed to be done.

Another file was labeled MAC2 and was date-stamped several months ago. Right before Tom had gotten sick. Mac's fingers tingled as he keyed in the password. His whole body started to tingle when he saw the first words.

"I'm just making a couple of notes here in case I don't get to finish this project. Buddy, if you're reading this, you're probably going to be angry with me for messing in your affairs. But I've decided that it's time for a little fatherly counseling. Since Brenda died, I've been doing a lot of thinking about what I've had and you've missed. Every man needs a personal life—a chance at happiness. And if you didn't want me to try and do something about the way you're killing part of yourself, you should never have told me about that woman in medical school—Katie Martin."

It was a while before Mac could keep reading. The note went on to talk about some private research Tom had been doing. Research that had started with Val Caldwell. Tom had met her at a singles bar she frequented. But it hadn't been an accidental encounter. Tom had gone looking for Val because he'd tracked down Katie Martin's sister. His original plan had been to ask for her help in staging a reunion between Mac and Katie.

But things hadn't turned out the way he'd anticipated. Val didn't seem close to her sister, and he'd decided it might take time to get around to the subject. Meanwhile, he'd soon realized how thrilled he was to be dating someone as pretty and sexy as Val. Probably when he'd gotten sick, he'd almost forgotten about the original scheme.

"Oh, Lord," Mac muttered. "That's how he got hooked up with her. Some crazy plan to save me from myself." For the past twelve hours he'd been cursing fate that the woman who had walked into that closet was Katie Martin. It wasn't fate. It was poor old fatherly Tom's plan. And the irony was that he'd accomplished his purpose at the cost of his life.

Mac was cursing as he signed off the computer. He wasn't emotionally prepared to deal with any more of Tom's private files right now. Instead he stalked down the hall to the ruined lab, hoping he could find out what his friend had considered so important last night.

Inside, he began poking through the equipment and papers littering the tables. Even with his heavy load of administrative duties, Tom had usually kept his hand in a few experiments. He'd always taken careful notes, but as far as Mac could see, the documentation on this project was about as decipherable as hoofprints on a rocky trail. Still, he kept pawing through the paper, hoping to find some clue.

Outside, he could hear people walking around, and realized with a start that it must be near quitting time. It was almost twenty-four hours since this whole nightmare had begun. When he'd gotten home last night, he'd hardly closed his eyes. But there was no point in leaving again now. Better to stay here and keep busy.

A slight movement to his right brought his eyes up from the notebook he was thumbing. The woman he'd been trying not to think about stood in the doorway.

KATIE'S EYES swept over Mac, noting the pallor below his tan, the circles under his eyes, the lines of strain across his forehead. His day had probably been as bad as hers. Worse, since a prominent biomedical company had suddenly become his sole responsibility. And even worse yet if he was in the middle of some kind of cover-up.

It looked as if she was the last person on earth he wanted to see. His greeting did nothing to dispel the impression. "What are you doing here?" he demanded.

"You said we'd talk. I want to know what you said to the police," she came back at him in the same tone of voice.

"I've been busy. And I wasn't planning on your coming out here."

Katie's chin lifted. "As far as you and I are concerned personally—I agree. But there are other issues involved."

He didn't bother to dispute the assertion, but he didn't jump in to advance the conversation, either.

"Did you do a chemical analysis of the liquid in the bottle?" she asked.

"That isn't any of your concern."

"Let's pretend it is."

He sighed. "I had one of my technicians take care of that. It was what it said it was. HI 320 DQ. I guess the medical examiner will let me know if a lethal dose was in his bloodstream."

"You told the police about his taking the injection?"

"Of course!"

Well, that would be a matter of record, if she wanted to question the police report later.

"What else happened after I left last night?"

"I talked to an Officer Butterfield. I told him about the explosion. And about finding Tom—leaving you out of the story."

"Why did you say you came back here?" As she asked the question, she watched his face carefully.

"I was worried about Tom. He'd shown some signs of instability over the past few weeks, and I knew he was here late."

She could see the tension around his mouth and eyes. Maybe he was telling the truth, but not the whole truth. "You didn't mention anything about Val?"

"No. Did you give Perkins Tom's last name?" he shot back.

"No. Actually, I couldn't. He's made a sudden trip out of town. The records on the case are missing from his precinct. And the medical examiner's office won't tell me if they've done an autopsy on Val. What do you think about all that?"

He looked surprised. "That sounds like a couple of interesting coincidences."

"You have any hypotheses?"

"Like what?"

"You're keeping something from me," she challenged.

"Nothing relevant," he snapped back. "Just the messages Tom left me about how to run the company if he was out of the picture. Forgive me if I'm a bit brusque, but reading your best friend's last instructions to you is a little hard on the emotional equilibrium."

Katie pressed her hands against her sides, holding back the impulse to open her arms to him. Obviously he didn't want her help dealing with any of this. And she couldn't let her feelings distract her from her purpose. There were ways to find out if he intended to be honest with her. "Let's try another approach," she suggested in a businesslike voice. "Does HI 320 DQ require refrigeration?"

Mac seemed relieved at the abrupt change of subject. "No. Why?"

"The refrigerator door was open when I came into the hematology lab."

"I didn't notice."

"At the time, it just seemed like part of the general disarray in the room so I closed it. But, I've been thinking about the way Tom was lying on the floor. He was staring at the refrigerator. I don't suppose you checked to see what was in there."

"No."

"Why don't we?" Without waiting for his permission, she turned and started down the hall. Mac caught up with her after a few steps. From the corner of her eye, she saw he was about to say something. Then he abruptly closed his mouth. When they arrived in the hematology lab, she noted that the room had been cleaned and tidied.

Before she could cross the room, Mac yanked open the refrigerator and began shuffling through the contents. As expected, there were several racks with vials of blood. But she heard Mac suck in his breath as he pulled one of the tubes out and held it up.

The label was barely legible. But she could make out an initial and a last name. T. Houston.

"Tom's blood," Mac muttered.

"Was he planning to test it for something?"

"The whole time I worked at Medizone I knew exactly what he was thinking. But the past few months, I gave up trying to figure out what was in his mind."

"What did you do before you came to Medizone?" The question was out of Katie's mouth before she had time to censor it.

"Nothing constructive."

"What?"

His gaze turned inward as he remembered his earlier thoughts. It was almost as if she'd gone in and plucked them from his brain. "I was hanging around D.C. picking up a few bucks here and there volunteering for medical protocols. I was one of the first group that tested an experimental malaria vaccine. I did a new cold-remedy trial, a test of saturated fat on cholesterol levels in healthy males in their 20s."

"Oh, Mac, you didn't. That stuff can be dangerous."

"Somebody has to do it."

"Not somebody like you, somebody with a future."

"That's what Tom said. I met him when Medizone advertised for volunteers to try an antidepressant drug."

"Mac!"

"Tom read my questionnaire and told me I wasn't suitable for the study. I was getting up to leave when he surprised the hell out of me and offered me a job with the company." Mac's voice clogged and he stopped speaking.

"He saw the potential in you when you'd given up on yourself," Katie whispered.

"Yes. Now do you understand what I owe him?"

She nodded. Mac had just revealed an awful lot—about himself and why he felt so strongly about Tom Houston. But he didn't give her a chance to dwell on the information.

"So let's find out what the hell he was trying to accomplish last night." Mac grabbed a glass slide, spread it with a drop of the blood, and set it under one of the microscopes on the counter against the wall. Adjusting the focus, he stared into the eyepiece.

"I don't see anything unusual." He sighed. "I guess we could try some standard drug tests."

"We could. Or we could have a look at a blood sample using an electron microscope."

Mac was silent for several seconds. Then he gave her a direct look. "Okay, last night we were talking about AIDS. You think that's what Tom really had? You think he infected your sister? You think that's what made them both flaky? That quickly? Without any of the more obvious symptoms?" The questions came out low and gritty.

"I don't know. But AIDS is a sexually transmitted disease." She swallowed and looked away from Mac. "And I assume they were lovers."

"Yes, I think that's a pretty valid assumption."

"Whether Tom had AIDS or not, that appears to be what he was thinking about."

"Okay. We'll look at the blood under the electron microscope and see if we can find any virions," Mac clipped out.

"Yes. Good." She felt something unfurl inside her chest. He wasn't happy about agreeing. But he wasn't trying to block their mutual investigation, either.

It had been eight years since Katie and Mac had worked together on any kind of project. Now they fell back into their old rhythm as if there had never been an interruption in the partnership. That at least hadn't changed. For a moment Katie felt a surge of pleasure—until she reminded herself what they were doing and why.

Once the specimen was ready, Mac sat down at the keyboard of the scanning electron microscope and began to adjust the resolution and the magnification. As Katie stared at the CRT screen she realized that Medizone had one of the most sophisticated instruments available. The resolution was the best she'd ever seen.

She drew in a sharp breath as she realized what she was seeing.

Beside her, Mac muttered a low exclamation. "It's loaded with virus particles. But what the hell are they?"

Katie stared at the screen, her mind trying and failing to fit the images into a familiar pattern. "I don't know. But it's nothing we studied in school, and nothing I've ever seen before."

Chapter Six

"Not very pretty, are they?" Mac muttered, stealing the words from her.

"No." Katie slid a sidewise glance at him. Obviously he was as perplexed as she.

Viruses were tiny. A thousandth of a thousandth of a millimeter. Even with an electron microscope, their image was apt to be indistinct—perhaps a fuzzy-looking sphere or a blurry filament. But with Medizone's state-of-the-art equipment, Katie had a better view of this one than she'd ever had before. It reminded her of an octopus, and she shuddered as she watched the limp, dead arms. She could imagine them when they'd been moving—scrabbling at Tom's tissues, getting a grip, choking off his life.

Mac pressed a button that activated the camera in the microscope's lens. Thirty seconds later they had a Polaroid of the picture on the CRT screen.

Katie stared at the photograph, the researcher in her challenged by the medical mystery. Hundreds or perhaps thousands of viruses could cause illness in humans—ranging from acute respiratory infections to chronic hepatitis and AIDS. But the form of a virus could change as it mutated or recombined with DNA borrowed from its host. Take the flu, for example. One form could make you achy and congested for a couple of days. The next mutation might be deadly—like the flu virus that had killed twenty million people in 1918-19. Often these seemingly new variations of an old virus came from tropical areas where they had already infected local populations—or been transmitted from animal reservoirs. And sometimes medical science was called on to do battle with something that seemed to be entirely new—like the HIV virus.

"Has Tom been in any exotic locations?"

"No."

"What about animal imports?"

"The only animals we have here are homegrown white lab rats."

"The first place they found Seoul virus was in Baltimore alley rats."

Mac pointed to the screen. "But that isn't Seoul virus." He got up from the console and walked over to the table against the wall where he stood shifting a pen back and forth between his good hand and the metal one. "Tom hasn't been on any trips out of the country in the past six months, but I have," he said, enunciating the words carefully. "Honduras. Borneo."

As she took in the deadly implications of Mac's words, Katie felt an arctic wind sweep over her body. It penetrated her flesh, all the way to the marrow of her bones. "Mac, no! You don't have any of the symptoms." She wouldn't allow it to be true.

"Not yet."

"Let's be logical. If *you* brought it back from the jungle then you should have run into trouble before Tom."

"Okay. You're right. Maybe I'm not at risk. Maybe I'm just a carrier."

"No." She wouldn't accept that conclusion, either.

"I hope to hell it isn't true. But we've got to find out." He went dead still. "When Tom came back to the lab last night he wouldn't let me clean up the scratches on his face. He must have suspected his blood was contaminated."

Struggling for an outward calm that masked her internal trembling, Katie nodded.

"I guess we can start by looking at some of my blood," Mac said.

How could he be so cool about this? Katie wondered as she followed him back to the hematology lab. Her own heart was thumping like the bass line in a rock number as she assembled a tray with a syringe, glass tubes and the other supplies she'd need.

Mac sat down in one of the lab chairs and began to fumble with his right shirtsleeve. As she watched a metal finger stab through the fabric, she knew he wasn't as cool as he wanted her to believe. She longed to roll back the sleeve for him. She knew he wouldn't accept the help. Turning away again, she pretended she wasn't quite finished with the tray.

"Put on rubber gloves," he growled as she prepared to take the seat opposite him.

"It's a little late for that."

"We don't know exactly how this virus is transmitted."

Their gazes caught and held. Last night he'd kissed her very thoroughly. Now a flush blossomed on her skin as she recalled every nuance, every subtle pressure of his lips moving over hers. His smoky eyes shifted to her mouth, and she knew he was remembering the same things she was.

For a long moment, neither one of them seemed capable of moving. Then Mac stretched out his arm along the chair armrest, and the spell was broken.

"Let's get this over with."

She nodded and sat down opposite him, pulling her stool closer to make it easier to work. She'd taken blood enough times so that the procedure should be easy. Yet this was different. As she tied the rubber tourniquet around Mac's upper arm, her nerve endings noted every touch of her fingers against his warm flesh. The disquieting sensation was even more acute as she investigated the inside of his elbow looking for a good vein.

"I never like having blood taken." His voice was gruff.

"Me neither. I'll try to be quick—and accurate."

He didn't wince when she inserted the needle. He didn't move while she drew two tubes of blood. But when she turned back to him with a small adhesive bandage for the needle mark, he took it out of her hand, and she knew he was worried about her coming into contact with his blood.

Her fists clenched as she kept her face averted. *Talk to me, Mac. Tell me how you're feeling. Let me share it.* The plea remained locked in her throat as he silently picked up the tubes of blood.

They looked at the sample with the electron microscope. Katie felt a surge of elation when they didn't find the nasty-looking virus particles.

"Not conclusive," Mac muttered.

Katie wished she could protest the summary judgment. Instead she nodded tightly. Mac could be in a different stage of the infection. The only way to be sure he didn't have the virus would be to grow more of the organisms from Tom's blood, inject them into an animal to obtain antibodies, and check for those antibodies in Mac's blood. Their absence would be the definitive proof.

"I wish it didn't take twenty-four hours to get enough of the virus," Katie murmured.

"It may not. Medizone's been experimenting with accelerated techniques."

"I'll help you set up."

She'd half expected him to insist that he didn't need her help to continue the work. Except that they'd be using "hot lab" procedures where hazardous material was handled in an isolated environment to prevent the spread of dangerous microorganisms. You had to reach inside the sealed hood with rubber gloves permanently affixed to access ports. If metal fingers could tear through shirt fabric, they could just as easily tear through the glove while he was working. That was one of the realities he lived with, and his accommodations had become automatic.

IT HAD BEEN a long, tense day, and the raw edges of Jade Nishizaka's nerves were frayed as if she'd been lashed repeatedly with a bullwhip. Still, a warm smile was fixed on her face as she glided across the Italian tile floor to one of the hairstyling stations. Like the rest of the Genesis salon, it was decorated with white wicker furniture, beveled mirrors and dozens of hanging plants.

"Mrs. Castleton, stardust blonde looks wonderful on you," she murmured.

"I just love it." Donna Castleton patted her elaborately coiffed hair. "The other wives at the country club will be green with envy."

"Be sure to tell them where you had your hair done. And before you go, you might want to stop by the cosmetic counter. Ming will be glad to show you our line of cosmetics including our exclusive cell-building moisturizer. It can take years off your skin with nightly applications. I've been using it myself since our exclusive lab began experimental trials."

"But you're so young!"

Jade gave her a mysterious smile. "No, I'm fifty-nine."

The blonde's eyes widened incredulously. "No one would ever guess. And you're right, I definitely must have that moisturizer."

The patronizing expression fell away from Jade's lips as she closed the door to her office. Sinking into her cushioned leather chair, she sat with her head bowed and her eyes closed, trying to steady herself.

With trembling fingers she unlocked the traveling campaign chest beside her chair and took out the ivory inlaid box. Inside was a worn picture album.

Slowly she began to turn the pages, studying the old black-and-white photos with their agonized faces and twisted bodies. She'd longed to bring them beauty. But it had been too late. Now the beauty belonged to her. And the women with the money to pay for Genesis's expensive treatment.

As always, the pictures tempered the iron of her resolve. Closing the book reverently, she slipped it back in its special place. Then she opened the personnel file on her desk. Val Caldwell. Age: forty-five. Marital status: divorced. Parents: deceased.

Was the information true? Or was it all a pack of lies? There'd been no evidence in her apartment to mark her as a spy. But perhaps she'd had a cover tight enough to breach the Genesis security check.

Jade's eyes scanned down the form. There was no one to notify in case of emergency. Had the omission been careless or was there really no one who'd be interested in Val's death? During the day, Jade had talked to her staff individually, telling them of Val's demise, reminding them not to discuss the tragedy with customers and tactfully pumping them for information about the dead woman's personal life. But her efforts had yielded very little. Val seemed to be a shallow woman interested in little else but herself, her sexual conquests and impressing her customers with her skill. Had that all been some kind of act to throw them off guard? Several of the other staff members had been told she was seeing an exercise instructor at a health club and a man who bought her expensive jewelry. Were they the same person? And what about the half sister she met for lunch occasionally? Truth or lies?

Jade was about to phone the detective agency she'd often employed, when she was interrupted by a knock on the door. "Who is it?"

"Ming."

"Come in."

A diminutive brunette carrying a cardboard box that had once contained bottles of Genesis setting lotion pushed open the door. "Here are the things from Val's station and her locker."

"You can put them on the table."

Ming followed her employer's instruction and waited to be dismissed.

"Before you go, I have a few questions. Is it possible that Val might have helped herself to our exclusive treatments?"

"No, madam. I inventoried the supplies just this morning, and everything seems to be accounted for. Besides, only the two of us know the combination." Ming's voice hesitated on the last word.

"What?" Jade snapped.

"I remember now. She was hovering in the background several times when I was opening the cabinet."

Jade's agile mind followed the train of her assistant's thought. "Go check again. And this time weigh each container on the milligram scale."

MAC HAD LEFT the lab while Katie prepared the tissue culture. When she finished, she found him waiting in the lounge next door. On a square table was a makeshift dinner. He'd brought her coffee, a sandwich and a chocolate bar. For himself there was only a cup of the dark brew.

After stuffing her lab coat into the hamper, Katie sank into the chair opposite Mac and took a long swallow of the coffee. It was just the way she liked it, with sugar and extra cream. Her sandwich was tuna, what she probably would

have asked for if given a choice. For dessert she had a
Mounds candy bar. As she looked at the meal laid out on a
paper-napkin place mat, she was swept with a warm rush of
feeling. After all these years, Mac had remembered her fa-
vorites.

"Not exactly up to your gourmet standards." It seemed
he also remembered that she liked to work off her tension
after a trying day by preparing elaborate dishes.

"This is great. Thanks." Hunger had finally caught up
with her, and she tore into the food with enthusiasm.

When she realized he was watching her eat, she set down
her sandwich. "Sorry, I must look like a pig at the trough."

"You look like you're starving. When was the last time
you had a meal?"

"Lunch with Val yesterday, I guess." She gestured toward the other half of her sandwich. "I'll bet it's been about
that long for you, too."

"I'll have something later." Once more he rubbed the side
of his hand against his jaw, and she heard the scratching
sound of his beard. This time it seemed to rasp against her
nerve endings.

Katie busied herself blotting her lips, but her eyes
searched Mac's face. He looked tired—and tense. But ba-
sically healthy. Of course, appearance could be deceptive.
"I wouldn't like having to wait for the antibody tests, either," she murmured, hoping she could get him to open up
with her.

"Maybe this will be an incentive for Medizone to de-
velop some superacceleration techniques."

"Uh-huh."

She finished her sandwich and unwrapped the candy bar.
"How did you remember I like Mounds bars?" she asked.

"Are you kidding? I used to call them your K rations.
There was always one in your purse and a couple in your
locker."

"So you're trying to see if I still have the addiction."

"You couldn't or you'd weigh three hundred pounds by now."

"Thanks."

He laughed, and all at once she knew that since he'd come back into her life, some deeply buried part of her had been waiting to hear that glad sound. The transformation was startling. The harsh lines in his face softened. The flatness went out of his gray eyes, and they took on depth, as though she were standing on a high mountain and looking down through layers of cloud to the ground far below. For just a moment, he was once again the engaging companion she remembered.

"I've missed you." As soon as the words had tumbled out, she wished she hadn't revealed so much.

"You miss that time in your life when everything was spread out in front of you like a Sunday brunch waiting for you to dig in."

"Yes, I miss that. I missed you, too."

"I'm not the same man you remember."

She'd thought that, too. Yet the old Mac McQuade had peeked out from behind his granite facade long enough for her to know that he was still there. She knew he'd only dispute her if she commented. Instead she shredded the bread crusts on the table in front of her. There was a question she was afraid to ask him. Yet what else did she have to lose? "When you said goodbye eight years ago, did you already know you were going to lose your hand?"

He crushed the coffee cup between a metal thumb and finger.

"So what if I did?"

He hadn't exactly answered the question. Except that he had.

"It's late, we're both tired," he continued. "And it won't do any good to sit in the lab staring at the petri dishes."

Pushing back his chair, he stood up and began to clear the table. Watching him, Katie was struck with a sudden piercing insight. Eight years ago, when Mac had known he was facing amputation, he'd sent her away because he hadn't wanted to rely on anyone else for strength and comfort. Now he was waiting to find out if he had the same virus that had killed his friend. But he wasn't going to let her help him cope with the terrible uncertainty. She was just here as a lab assistant.

His back was to her, so she could watch him carefully as she tested the theory. "Yes. I think I'll go home and get some sleep."

Tension seemed to ooze out of his shoulders like water seeping from a broken main.

As quietly as possible, she pushed back her chair and stood up. When he turned from getting rid of the trash, she was standing a foot behind him. "But I'm not quite ready to leave yet," she murmured, her voice husky with both determination and trepidation.

For a breathless moment, she preserved the slight distance between them. Then she stepped forward and circled his body with her arms.

He tried to move out of her grasp but wasn't quick enough to prevent her from locking her hands together behind his back. She heard him suck in a sharp breath as she rested her cheek against his chest and closed her eyes, absorbing the warmth of his body, giving him back as much of her own warmth as he would let himself take.

"Katie, you don't know what you're doing."

"You're wrong, I know exactly what I'm doing."

"The virus. You're taking a stupid chance getting this close to me." She could feel him swallow. "Tom gave it to your sister."

"You don't know that."

"Come on. They had the same symptoms. Those nasty little things we saw under the microscope turned Tom's brain to mashed potatoes. From what you said about Val, she was the same way."

"And you're not."

"Katie—"

"You don't have it!" she insisted fiercely.

"Until we know for sure, we have to assume I do."

She could feel him try to ease away. She didn't loosen her grip. "You know, really dangerous viruses aren't highly contagious."

"Oh yeah? What makes you think so?"

"The fact that the human race has survived all this time."

"Humph."

"Besides, that's a direct paraphrase of Joshua Lederberg," she added, referring to the Nobel Prize-winning geneticist who had recently turned his professional attention to emerging viruses.

"You always were a smartass." Grudging admiration mingled with a chuckle in his voice.

"Only some of the time."

"What about the rest of the time?"

She didn't answer. Instead she tipped her head up and stared at him. Neither one of them stirred, except that his eyes shifted so that he focused on her lips, the way they had earlier in the evening in the hematology lab.

"Would you mind telling me what kind of a game you're playing?" he grated.

"It's not a game, Mac."

He stared into her upturned face. It had always been pretty and intelligent. Maturity had added depth and beauty. The old Katie had haunted him through so many sleepless nights. This new woman he didn't understand—who wouldn't defer to him anymore—had taken her place. She certainly wasn't a match for his superior physical

strength. It should have been easy to slip out of her grasp.
Yet tonight he'd stopped trying to break free of her embrace. He couldn't.

Once before, he'd told her he didn't need her. He'd delivered the message over the phone, because he'd known what
would happen if she took him into her arms and offered him
the things he'd been afraid to ask for. Now he was caught in
precisely the trap he'd feared.

Only it didn't feel exactly like a trap. It felt like warmth
and sharing and all the other tender emotions he'd denied
himself all these years because he hadn't been willing to let
down his guard.

He'd never thought of Katie as provocative. Now as she
reached out to stroke the stubble on his cheek, her fingers
brushed erotically against the bristly hairs, sending little
tremors deep into his body. She saw he was looking at her
mouth, and her tongue flicked out to delicately touch her
top lip. The back of his throat burned as he remembered the
taste and texture of her. At that moment, he would have sold
his soul for the chance to drink in those pleasures again. His
soul. Not her life.

He wasn't going to take the chance. He couldn't. Yet he
was powerless to break away, powerless to stop his arms
from coming up to cradle her back.

A tiny shudder racked her body. It fired an answering
charge in every one of his nerve endings. Life force seemed
to surge through him. Life. The denial of death.

"Katie, this is crazy." The words were little more than a
hoarse whisper.

As if in a trance, she shook her head in denial.

He had to stop. Now. Before things got completely out of
control. But he couldn't stop. Not yet.

Her lips were parted. Her skin was flushed. Never taking
his eyes from her face, he brushed his body against hers,

watching the blue of her eyes darken and the red of her cheeks deepen.

The hard little buttons of her nipples against his chest made his own body tighten to a level that approached pain. The knowledge that she was as aroused as he almost sent him over the edge.

With the back of his left hand, he pressed her hips more tightly to his. But there was no need to hold her captive. Her body moved against his now of its own accord. His left arm moved, tipping her upper body back. Still watching her face, he cupped one soft, rounded breast in his palm.

For just a moment her eyes fluttered closed. Then they snapped open again—and locked with his.

He ordered himself to stop touching her. His fingers didn't follow the instructions. She was too alluring, too perfect, too responsive. And he needed her too much. Her little gasp was transformed into a moan of pleasure as his fingers played across her knit top and teased her nipple. The bulky fabric was a frustrating barrier. Slipping his hand underneath, he claimed her through the silky fabric of her bra, his hand moving greedily from one breast to the other.

Her breath came in a series of little gasps now.

His own breath was no more than a ragged counterpoint to the frantic pounding in his blood. She was in his arms again—offering him all the sweet passion he'd craved through all the lonely years.

His head lowered. Her lips parted, trembled.

They were a whisper away from contact when he realized what he was doing.

"No. God, no."

He took a step back, saw her sway and put a hand out to steady her. Her expression was dazed as she stared up at him.

"Katie, we both know how Tom gave the virus to Val. Through intimate contact."

"You don't know that for sure. We don't even know Tom was the source of the infection. And you don't have it."

"I hope to hell you're right. But if you're not, you may have to finish the investigation by yourself."

"Mac." Her face went white as driftwood in the moonlight, and he thought she might go to pieces. Then she seemed to visibly pull herself together.

"You need to go home and get some sleep." He resisted the impulse to tell her she wasn't thinking very clearly.

"All right. But I'll be back in the morning."

The look on her face told him there was no point in arguing.

Chapter Seven

Katie lay rigid in bed, her mind refusing to shut off and let her succumb to fatigue. Mac was right. There was a chance he could be infected. But she wouldn't allow him to be right. And like an earthquake victim clinging by her fingernails to an ever-widening chasm, she clung to the desperate belief that he had escaped the virus.

Sometime during the darkest hours of the night she finally fell into a restless sleep. And sometime in the expectant time just after the sun had crested the eastern horizon, she awoke with a fine sheen of perspiration on her skin and her heart pounding with fear.

"Mac." His name was a breathy sigh on her lips. "You're going to be all right," she whispered. "You have to be."

She might have sat up and turned on the light, or gotten up and drawn herself a drink of water. Instead she burrowed deeper under the covers, away from the pale light seeping around the curtains, and tried to stop her mind from churning. But the effort was wasted. Mac was in her life again—and the worst part was that there was no control over this time, either.

Her mind fled from the present and found the past just as painful. During the first three and a half years of medical school, she'd decided exactly what she wanted in a mate. The man she married would have to be her intellectual match. He had to be curious. He had to love solving problems. He had to be willing to take risks, to stand up for his convictions, to buck the system if that's what it took to accomplish his goals. He had to be able to make her laugh. He had to make her feel wild, singing passion when he took her in his arms.

Later, after she'd graduated, she'd admitted to herself that she was describing Mac McQuade. Perhaps, even though she'd gone on with her life, she'd never given anyone else a chance to show her he could step into the matrimonial profile. Years ago she'd decided if she couldn't have what she really wanted in a husband, there wasn't any point in settling for second best. So the only course for her had been to make the most of other things.

She'd been very successful, except for one stunning disaster in her professional career—the episode at the Sterling Clinic. Now that she'd put it behind her, her work was challenging and satisfying. She had a great group of friends. She loved her house and her garden. She loved to cook. She'd taken some memorable vacations.

She'd convinced herself that was enough. After a while it had been. Until Mac McQuade had come barreling back into her life, and she'd suddenly realized that all her rational thinking was as substantial as dandelion fuzz floating in the wind.

"Mac." She whispered his name, and this time she wasn't sure whether it was a curse or a benediction.

It hadn't been a one-sided exchange last night. She might be inexperienced with men, but she'd known he wanted her. Not just wanted. Needed. Enough to almost shatter his iron control.

However, *almost* was the operative word. At the last moment, he'd wrenched himself back from lowering his mouth to hers, from taking what she was so obviously offering.

Which didn't make things any easier now. Because she knew that he'd been thinking of her safety, not his own desires.

Pushing things that far had been her fault. No, she was being too hard on herself. She and Mac had both been caught up in the terrible uncertainty of the moment.

There wasn't any point in trying to go back to sleep. Swinging her legs out of bed, she headed across the carpet to the bathroom.

Under a mild pounding from the shower massage, she struggled to bring her fragmented thoughts to some sort of resolution. Mac couldn't be harboring the virus. And once they were perfectly sure that he was all right, it would be better for her emotional stability if she simply went about her own business. However, she couldn't leave this investigation to him. He needed her help to track down the infection to its source. Which meant she was going to have to walk into the lab this morning and act as if nothing out of the ordinary had happened between them. Logic told her he'd act that way, too, because the situation couldn't be much easier for him than it was for her. Yet she was going to be the one who got hurt if they couldn't pull it off.

MAYBE MAC hadn't expected her to come back, after all. When Katie arrived at the entrance to the hot lab at eight the next morning, he was giving directions to one of the technicians. Before she could stop herself, Katie searched his eyes again for signs of the illness that had ravaged Tom and Val. His countenance was haggard—but essentially unchanged. He didn't have it, she told herself again.

She was willing to bet that he hadn't gotten to bed at all. However, either he'd gone home to shower and change into the fresh blue shirt and dark slacks he was wearing under his lab coat, or he kept a change of clothing in the building.

She saw him go very still when he glanced up and found her standing in the doorway. He didn't look her directly in the face, but he didn't need to, to make her heart start pounding as if it might batter its way through the wall of her chest.

The attack of nerves diffused as he introduced her to the woman who was taking in their silent exchange with apparent interest.

"Dr. Martin, Ms. Prager."

"Hello," they both said in unison.

"Ms. Prager was in early today to check on some cultures in the research department. I asked if she'd mind giving me a hand." Mac pointed to the isolation hood where they'd been growing the cultures. "There was enough of the virus to go on to the next step this morning."

Katie favored the technician with a smile she hoped was warm and reassuring as she took a clean lab coat from the drawer. "Thanks for filling in, but I think I can take over now."

The woman looked from Katie to Mac, seeking clarification of contradictory instructions.

Mac slipped his hand into his coat pocket. "I wasn't sure Dr. Martin would be back so early. Thank you, Ms. Prager. I'll call you if we need any further assistance."

There was another awkward moment after the technician had left, and Katie wondered if she should have been so quick to dismiss her. In a way, it made things easier to have a buffer between them.

"What did you tell her you were doing?"

"She can see what we're doing. An antibody test." He paused for several seconds. "I was getting ready to bring the serum from the refrigerator."

Katie tried to swallow past the sandpaper coating her throat. She hadn't realized he was almost ready for the crucial step.

It was hard to control the telltale shaking of her hands as she slipped them into the rubber gloves fixed to the side of the isolation chamber. The trembling was only slightly less apparent as she selected the necessary equipment inside the chamber and lighted the Bunsen burner. At least while she was setting things up, she had her back turned to Mac. It gave her the time to compose her face when she turned to take the serum from him. He was holding it in his metal hand—to make the contact as impersonal as possible, she supposed.

Neither one of them spoke as she operated the air lock. Nor could they think of any conversational gambits as she heated the serum.

Mac watched as she added the antibodies that had been produced overnight. If he had the same virus, they'd see antibodies clumping under an ordinary light microscope.

After preparing a slide using negative staining techniques, Katie turned to the microscope built into the wall of the chamber. When she'd set the slide on the platform, she felt Mac's hand on her shoulder, his touch a light caress that delayed the moment of truth. Then his fingers squeezed more tightly.

"Let me look."

Not trusting her voice, she nodded and stepped aside so he could stand in front of the microscope.

Her gaze was glued to his face as he bent to the eyepiece. His expression was absolutely neutral while he adjusted the focus.

For heart-stopping moments, Mac studied the slide. Finally she couldn't hold back the anxious question blocking her windpipe.

"Mac, what do you see?"

"Nothing."

"You mean I didn't prepare it correctly?"

"Your technique was faultless. I don't see any reaction."

"Thank God. Oh, Mac, thank God." The release of tension was like a tidal wave sweeping across a coastal plain, uprooting trees, tumbling boulders in its wake.

"You'd better take a look, too. Just in case I'm fooling myself."

He stepped aside and stood stiffly a few feet away. Pulse pounding, Katie lowered her face to the eyepiece and repeated the visual inspection. "You don't have any antibodies," she whispered.

Behind her he let out a deep, thankful breath. "I was afraid I was seeing what I wanted to see."

"You're clear," she repeated. "You don't have the virus."

The look of relief on his face made her ache to take him in her arms and hug him fiercely to her breast. For one unguarded moment he stood staring at her as if he wanted the same thing. Then he turned away and started stripping off his lab coat. After stuffing it into the hamper, he rolled his shoulders.

"Tired?" she asked softly.

"Yeah. But at least the waiting's over."

"How long have you been here?" she asked.

"It seems like forever." He pressed his hand against his forehead. "Since yesterday morning."

"Then you need a change of scene." She made her voice light. "Do you ever have breakfast at Vie de France in the Columbia Mall?"

"You mean the place with the chocolate croissants?"

"The very same."

There was a wistful note in his voice. "That sounds good. But there's so much to do here."

"Mac, you've just been through a pretty tough twenty-four hours. You're entitled to a break."

He sighed. "I guess you're right. I'd better make sure Marcia doesn't need me for anything urgent."

There was a look of relief on his secretary's face as she practically shooed Mac out of the office.

"Nice day," he observed as he sucked in a hearty draft of air before heading toward his car.

"Uh-huh." Katie followed, a little smile flickering around her lips. The weather wasn't really all that wonderful. In fact, it looked as if it might be going to rain. However rain and clouds probably had little to do with Mac's perspective on life.

Katie smiled again as she settled back into the plush upholstery of Mac's sports car. The comfortable seats weren't the only luxury. The windows were the same kind of dark glass that you saw in limousines—which gave the car a feeling of privacy. Mac fiddled with the radio until he found a rock number with a strong beat. Yesterday he'd been as uptight as a man getting ready to face a firing squad. This was much better.

THE PHONE RANG as Helen Austin-Wright was sitting at the inlaid marble kitchen table of her Georgetown home going over her weekend social calendar.

When she picked up the receiver, a familiar voice began, "Hello, Helen, it's Donna. Is it too early to call?"

"No. It's fine. George and I always get an early start on the day."

"I tried to call last night, but you must have been out. I just *had* to thank you for recommending that I try Genesis. What a wonderful place. My first appointment was yesterday afternoon, and you won't believe how well my hair turned out."

"I can't wait to see it," Helen murmured.

"You will tonight at the Commerce Club."

"Tonight?"

"At the Ides of March party."

Helen glanced across the table at her husband, George, buried behind a copy of the *Wall Street Journal*. She knew Wright Chemicals was fighting off a takeover bid. George had been worried about that for months, but lately he'd stopped talking about it. And now he was staying home from the office in the mornings. Had he given up the fight to save the company? Were things worse than he was letting on?

In the past he'd always put a good face on problems—especially with his colleagues. Surely, as a board member of the prestigious Commerce Club, he ought to be attending the party. But he hadn't mentioned it, had he? A worried look wrinkled her brow as she thought about just how many other things he'd forgotten lately.

"Helen, are you still there?" her friend on the other end of the phone line broke into her thoughts.

"Yes, sorry, Donna. I just need to talk to George before he leaves for work. I'll call you back later."

After replacing the receiver, Helen cleared her throat. "Darling, do you know anything about a do at the Commerce Club tonight?"

"What?"

"The Commerce Club. Did you forget about the Ides of March Party tonight?"

"No!" George flung the paper down on the table, his face contorted with anger. "Stop bugging me. Why are you always bugging me?"

"Darling, I just—"

Slinging the paper down on the table, he glared at her. Then he picked up his cup of coffee and slammed it back down into the saucer, sending brown liquid splashing all over the creamy-white surface of the table.

Helen shrank back, the violent look in his eyes sending a tremble of fear down her spine.

In the next moment, the fury was wiped away, replaced by confusion. George stared at the mess on the table. "Did I do that? I—I'm sorry."

Helen began to mop at the coffee with her napkin. "It's all right. You're just under a lot of stress, that's all."

He reached across the table and squeezed her hand. "Stress. That's right. I have to leave. I've got a meeting. You call the Commerce Club. I'm sure we have a reservation. I'm sorry I forgot to tell you about it."

IT WAS ONLY a fifteen-minute drive to the mall, and Katie directed Mac to the parking lot closest to the *patisserie*. As they drove up and down the lanes of parked cars looking for a space, she noticed a dark blue Ford doing the same thing. Apparently the situation brought out the old competitive streak in Mac that Katie remembered from medical school. As he and the other driver approached an empty spot from different directions, Mac stepped on the gas and zipped into the space.

"Tough luck, buddy," he murmured as the other car pulled away and began to circle again.

"Men," Katie muttered under her breath.

"Just testing my reflexes."

And feeling frisky, Katie added silently. She was smiling as they strolled down the lane to the mall door. But she tensed for a moment at the entrance to the restaurant when she spotted the driver of the blue car heading in their direction, one hand lifted to his mouth. He looked as if he were biting his thumbnail. Somehow the nervous gesture didn't seem to go with the broad shoulders and football player physique. Was he nervous? Was he coming to start a fight? However, he loped on past, and she soon forgot all about him.

Because it was late for breakfast and still early for lunch, there was no one ahead of them in the cafeteria-style line.

Once they'd gotten their food, they had their pick of tables in the eating area. Instead of pastry, Katie opted for crab soup and Swiss cheese on French bread. She bit back any comment as she watched Mac pick up his chocolate croissant and a cherry Danish. The man had eaten hardly anything in twenty-four hours, but there was no point in lecturing him on nutrition. In fact, under the circumstances, he was entitled to anything he wanted.

Leaning back in his chair, Mac stretched out his long legs beside the table. "Thanks for suggesting that we get away for a little while like this. Sometimes I wonder if I've forgotten how to relax."

"I know what you mean. That's why I force myself to do something wicked every once in a while—like take the afternoon off for some marathon shopping."

Mac laughed. "Sure. Really wicked." He regarded her fondly. "It's strange to realize you're living right in the same area."

"I grew up in D.C."

"Right. I remember."

Katie found herself wanting to catch up on all the old news she'd missed. "How's your mother doing? I remember you were worried about her being able to keep the ranch," she asked.

There was an oddly strained look on his face, and Katie prepared herself for bad news. But his answer was positive.

"She's fine now."

"I'm glad."

"I've been able to funnel some of my Medizone profits into building up the herd and repairing the buildings. Chip, my younger brother, is running the spread."

"You never did want to be in charge of a ranch."

"No."

The conversation petered out, and they munched their respective meals in silence for several moments. From under lowered lashes, Katie watched Mac. He didn't look as relaxed anymore. Was there something he was holding back about his family? She remembered some of the things he'd told her about the independent, demanding McQuades who had been disappointed when Mac had announced his choice of career. As the oldest son, he'd been expected to carry on the family tradition. They'd had a hard time adjusting to his leaving the ranch. Probably they'd had trouble adjusting to his handicap as well. Had she made him think about that now? Or was he worrying about something else? As more patrons came into the little restaurant, he kept glancing around, as if he was feeling crowded. Maybe he was.

"I can't stop thinking about that crazy experiment of Tom's," he finally said. "I think he was looking for a cure or a treatment for the virus."

Katie jumped on the new line of conversation. "Then when things didn't work out, he went back to Medizone's AIDS research."

"But he wasn't thinking things through very clearly."

"I want to know if this virus has shown up anywhere else in the country. We should have packed up a sample and sent it right to the CDC," Mac muttered.

"We can do it when we get back."

He set down his coffee cup and cleared his throat. "You probably have your own work to catch up on. You don't have to come back there to the lab with me."

Katie chewed the bite of bread in her mouth, wondering how she was going to swallow it. Mac's offhand remark was an easy way of telling her goodbye. Probably there wasn't any point in protesting. Maybe it was better this way, after all. Hadn't she been warning herself something like this was going to happen?

"I'm afraid I need a ride back—to pick up my car."

"Yeah. Your car." He had the good grace to look embarrassed as he put down the cherry Danish and folded his napkin. "I, uh, haven't really thanked you for your help. And for putting up with me."

"I was glad to help. Besides, you were certainly entitled to be edgy. I was, too. I was worried about you."

"You don't need to be concerned about me."

There was nothing left to lose, no need to censor her reactions now. "Of course not, Mac. You're perfectly capable of taking care of yourself."

The sharp note in her voice made him raise his head.

"By the way," she continued. "What was your mother's reaction to your losing your hand?"

His eyes shifted away from hers, and he appeared to be staring at a spot somewhere over her left shoulder. "My mother is a good woman. Salt of the earth, as they say. When I came home after the accident she told me it wouldn't have happened if I'd stayed where I belong. I think she never did come to terms with my defection. Anyway, being in the same room with me makes her uncomfortable." He held up the stainless steel fist. "She couldn't deal with this. I send her money, but I haven't been out to Montana since right after the accident when I needed a place to recuperate. If she doesn't see me, she doesn't have to think about my disability."

"Oh, Mac, I'm so sorry."

"The last thing I want from anyone is pity."

"I wasn't offering pity. I'm just sorry you and your family don't know how to deal with each other. That's the way it was with me and Val. So I know how sad it is."

He made a noncommittal sound.

"And I don't think of you as disabled."

"Then you should go back to the dictionary and check the definition."

"If it makes you uncomfortable to be with me, that's your fault, not mine."

She saw his Adam's apple bob. "Katie, I'm sorry. It isn't going to work. Not with someone I was close to before."

"Not if you don't give it a chance."

"There's too much old stuff in the way."

"A lot of old stuff. Yes. Or is that just an excuse?"

He fished some change out of his pocket and slapped a tip down on the table. Without waiting to see if she was following, he stalked toward the door.

It flashed through Katie's mind that she could call a cab to take her back to Medizone, and then Mac McQuade wouldn't have to suffer her company for another fifteen minutes. But why should she go to the trouble and expense? she asked herself as she trailed after him toward the exit. And why should she make things easy for him?

While they'd been in the restaurant, the sun had come out from behind a bank of clouds. As she stepped through the door, Katie squinted against the sudden brightness and fumbled in her purse for her sunglasses.

When she glanced up again, Mac was over toward her right, head down as he made for the space where they'd parked the car. Apparently he wasn't paying much attention to his surroundings, because he didn't seem to notice the blue car heading along the circular drive toward the mall entrance. It was the Ford that had passed them several times in the parking lot.

Now that it was closer to lunchtime, half a dozen people were heading for the mall entrance. The driver should be slowing down as he approached the pedestrian walkway, Katie thought. Instead the vehicle was speeding up.

"Mac! Watch out!" Katie shouted as he stepped off the curb. Before the words were out of her mouth, she was already sprinting across the sidewalk.

Everything seemed to happen in slow motion after that. Hearing the warning, Mac stopped and looked up. He saw the car because he took a quick step back. But that wasn't going to keep him from being hit. While Katie watched in horror, the wheels on the right side of the Ford came up on the sidewalk as the vehicle bore down on Mac.

Chapter Eight

Katie crashed into Mac at a forty-five-degree angle, knocking him back and to the side. Her sunglasses went flying as they both lost their balance, hit the sidewalk and skidded against the cement.

The car's engine roared in her ears. When she glanced up, she gasped. She'd tried to knock Mac out of harm's way. But the effort hadn't been good enough.

From her position on the ground, the car bearing down on them looked like a tank trying to crush wounded enemy soldiers. The grinding sound of crumpling metal broke around her. Katie squeezed her eyes shut and braced herself, expecting to feel the wheels crush her body. The impact never came.

Instead of plowing into her and Mac, the speeding car had collided with one of the two-foot-high concrete posts that flanked the entrance to the mall and served as seats for shoppers waiting near the curb.

Dazed, Katie reached desperately for Mac. He was already pushing himself off the sidewalk—lurching toward the blue car. The vehicle gunned its engine, made a hard left and careered away.

She could hear Mac cursing. When he knelt beside her again, she saw worry gnawing at his features. "Are you hurt?" His voice was low and intense.

She tried to talk and found her jaw was trembling too badly. The trembling spread to her limbs. Somewhere in her peripheral vision she noted that a crowd was forming around them, but the entire focus of her attention was on Mac.

"My God, what did that maniac do to you?" he asked.

Katie struggled to choke out a response. "I'm—I'm all right."

Wrapping an arm around her shoulder, Mac angled her gently toward him. "You're sure?"

She nodded. "What about you?"

"I'll survive."

He helped her to her feet and watched as she flexed her arms and legs. She wanted to make sure of his condition, too, but it had become impossible to block out the commotion around them.

Someone handed Katie her sunglasses, and she jammed them back on her face. She was astonished to realize that her purse was still slung over her shoulder. Probably it had helped cushion her fall.

"That guy was insane," a loud voice from the crowd observed.

There was a chorus of agreement.

"He looked like he was trying to mow you down."

"Did anyone get the license number?" Katie asked, swaying slightly on rubbery legs. Mac steadied her by pulling her tightly against his side.

No one answered her question.

"You sure you're okay, fella?" The man who'd asked the question was staring at Mac's prosthetic hand.

"I'm fine."

"Want me to call the cops or an ambulance?" a denim-clad young man asked excitedly.

"I'll take care of it," Mac told him. He turned to Katie, his face carefully neutral. "Let's get out of here."

"Hey, you can't just leave the scene of an accident," someone objected.

"Why not? The driver didn't stay to exchange insurance information." Mac's arm was still around Katie's shoulder as he led her to the car.

At least none of the crowd followed them. As soon as Mac opened the door, Katie sank into the seat, grateful for the special tinted glass that meant no one could look in on them. They were in the middle of the mall parking lot, but at least they had some privacy. She felt the back of Mac's hand press her cheek and reached up to cover his fingers with hers.

"Pretty stupid of you, dashing into the path of a speeding car." His voice was low and husky.

"I—I saw him bearing down on you, and all I could think about was pushing you out of the way."

"You shouldn't have."

"I wasn't very effective. It was the concrete post that stopped him."

"You were effective, all right. If you hadn't hit me like a linebacker, I would have been on the other side of the post."

She felt his lips brush her forehead, his hand smooth back her hair. Before she could react to the tender gestures, she was wondering if she'd imagined them, because Mac was reaching across her and opening the glove compartment. A moment later, she smelled antiseptic, followed by a wet stinging sensation against her knee. Very carefully so as not to hurt her more than necessary, he began to dab at the raw skin.

"You don't have to do that."

"I want to make sure it's clean." After he finished with the antiseptic, he covered the abrasion with an adhesive bandage.

His next question was asked in a barely audible voice. "How do you think I'd feel if you'd gotten hit?"

"I don't know. How would you feel?"

"Katie—"

She drew in a shaky breath. "Mac, you may want to keep pretending that we don't care a lot about each other. I gave up on that a couple of days ago. If you thought I was just going to let you take me back to my car and then disappear from my life again, you were wrong."

He sighed heavily. "Katie, you don't want to get mixed up with someone like me."

"Why not?"

He thumped his stainless steel fist against the steering wheel. "I'm not the same guy you knew back in medical school. I'm bitter. I'm resentful about your having the career I wanted. I've turned into a loner."

"At least you're being honest."

"I'm no good for you."

"Why don't you let me be the judge of that?"

He bowed his head, and she pressed her forehead against his. There was an ironic quality in his voice when he started to speak again. "You know, this may sound strange, but there are women who are turned on by a guy with a hand like mine. It makes him an interesting novelty."

"I was turned on by you long before you showed up with the trick part."

He kept on talking, as if he hadn't heard her response. "I've never put a relationship to the test. I guess I never wanted to find out whether it was real or not."

"Our relationship was real."

"Maybe once. I don't know how to communicate on a sincere level anymore."

Sadness shuddered through her soul. For all these years he must have been so lonely. So lonely.

Yet somehow at the same time, hope swelled deep inside her. She was sure he'd never confided those feelings to anyone else. If he could trust her enough to confess his failings, maybe he could trust her enough to accept the love she'd buried deep inside her for so many years.

A little shock skittered across her nerve endings as she realized what word she'd silently used.

Love.

There was no use hiding the truth from herself any longer. Not when she'd jumped into the path of a speeding car to push him out of the way. Perhaps later the intensity of her feelings would be scary. At the moment, they gave her a feeling of joy. Mac was here again with her. Maybe she hadn't gotten what she wanted with him the first time because she'd never had the courage to reach out and grab it. Yet what if she tried and failed? Well, at least she'd know she'd done her best.

When she felt Mac shift away from her, she stroked her finger down his cheek. "I'm taking a rain check on the rest of this conversation," she murmured.

"I already said more than I intended."

"Maybe that's a good sign."

"If you say so. But I see mall security heading over this way." He pointed toward a small white truck with a flashing yellow light. "And I don't feel like answering a bunch of questions at the moment."

The bubble of intimacy surrounding them burst. Katie carefully flexed her scraped knee as she watched Mac reach for the ignition key.

"I want to check that license number," he muttered as he pulled out of the parking space.

"I thought you didn't know what it was."

"I didn't say that. It's GXS 734. As a matter of fact, I got it *before* we went into the mall."

"Convenient. I guess Mr. Ford didn't like you beating him out of a parking space."

"Mr. Ford! That's good, Button."

"Thanks." Button. His old nickname for her. For the first time since they'd been together again, it had slipped out of his mouth. It had started when he'd teased her about her buttoned-down image. Then he'd told her she was as cute as a button. Her heart squeezed painfully as all the associations came back to her, but she wasn't allowed to dwell on the moment.

Mac plowed ahead with the business at hand. "Do you really believe that was the reason he came after us? The parking space, I mean."

"I—I don't know."

"I think your Mr. Ford may have had another motive."

"What?"

"I'll tell you after we get back to the office. The first thing to do is pack up that virus sample for the CDC. I want to get them working on the identification as soon as possible."

Looking impatient to set the process in motion, Mac pushed past the speed limit as he headed back to Medizone. His expression changed abruptly when he stepped into the hot lab and peered through the glass wall of the isolation chamber.

"What the hell?"

"Mac, what is it?"

He gestured toward the interior. "It's all gone."

Katie stared through the glass in disbelief. The petri dish with the virus and the rest of the equipment they'd been using had been cleared away.

Turning on his heels, Mac stormed down the hall to the head of lab services. Behind him, Katie trotted to keep up. "Who authorized the removal of my materials from Hot Lab Three?" he demanded.

"Why, *you* did, sir."

"What?"

"Yes, the messenger company arrived while you were out. They took everything away with them, just the way you specified." The woman began thumbing through pages on a clipboard and then tapped a sheet of paper. "Here's the order right here."

Mac snatched the stack of papers away from her and scanned the form. "It's our regular delivery company. But I didn't initiate the request."

"Let me see." Katie reached for the clipboard. When he handed her the form, she looked for the destination. The material was supposed to be going to a hospital lab in downtown Baltimore. "That place doesn't do anything more than standard blood work for doctors' offices," she pointed out.

She and Mac exchanged worried glances, and she could see he was about to voice a comment. Before he could, she shook her head almost imperceptibly. The less they said about this in front of anyone else, the better. Yet they did need some information.

Apparently Mac had gotten the message. When he turned back to the lab supervisor, his voice was more controlled.

"Was it the regular driver?" he asked.

The woman was beginning to look upset. "Why, no, Mr. McQuade. It was an oriental fellow. He said you wanted the materials to go out immediately. I'm terribly sorry if I did something wrong."

"No. It's probably just a mix up. Dr. Martin and I will take care of it."

They went back to Mac's office and closed the door. A quick call to the delivery company confirmed their suspicion that the driver hadn't been from their organization.

"You're right, we shouldn't be talking about this in front of anyone else," Mac acknowledged. "It looks as if somebody went to a rather big risk to get the virus sample. What if we'd been here?"

"But we weren't." Katie struggled to keep the timbre of her voice even. "While they were cleaning this place out, Mr. Ford was trying to run us down at the Columbia Mall."

"Yeah."

"What did you mean when you said he might have another motive besides revenge for taking his parking space?" she demanded.

"It wasn't anything I could prove. But I was wondering if we'd been followed to the mall from here. While we were having breakfast, I kept feeling as if someone were watching us."

"Is that why you were looking around?"

"Uh-huh."

"Well, they didn't get *us*. But all the material is gone."

"No, they didn't get us. And we're going to duplicate the material."

"We can't. We don't have any of Tom's blood."

"Yes we do. I froze the other tube that was in the refrigerator. If it hasn't vanished, too, we're in business." He paused. "However, we're not going to do the work at Medizone. In fact, we're not going to stay in the building any longer than we have to."

Katie felt tiny goose bumps pepper her arms as the implications of the morning's activities sunk in. Someone wanted to eliminate them and all traces of their virus research. And whoever it was, was probably going to come back when they found out the accident in the mall parking lot had failed.

Mac reached for her cold hand. "Come on. The way I figure it, we've got a little window of time to get out of here before Mr. Ford reports back to headquarters. We're splitting as soon as we pack that frozen blood in dry ice and I tell Marcia she's going to have to handle things here—because she's not going to be able to get in touch with me."

Ten minutes later they climbed into Tom's car.

"Your Marcia's worried," Katie murmured as they pulled out of the parking lot and headed north. "Maybe she even thinks you've cracked under the pressure."

"I know. But the less information she's got the better it is for us—and her."

"Who are we up against?" Katie wondered aloud.

"We're going to find out. Too bad I'm not into covert operations," Mac muttered as he checked the rearview mirror to make sure they weren't being followed again.

"I am."

His eyes swung toward her momentarily. "What are you talking about?"

"At least I have the right connections. I've got a friend named Jo O'Malley who's a private detective. Last fall, she helped another friend of mine go underground for a few days."

"Is needing to hide out a regular occurrence in your circle of friends?"

Katie's laugh helped dissipate a little of the tension. "I hope not. But Jo's a good woman to have in your corner when you're in trouble."

"So are you."

"Thanks." She shot Mac a surprised glance, but his eyes were firmly on the road ahead of him.

Katie called Jo from the car phone and briefly explained what had happened to her and Mac in the past hour.

"You'd better not come down to 43 Light Street or go home, either," the detective advised. "If they came looking for Mac at Medizone, they may very well have your office staked out, too." Jo was silent for a moment. Then her voice came back across the speaker. "There's a Marriott Courtyard out near the airport. Why don't I meet you there? Register as Mr. and Mrs. Lam."

"As in 'on the lam'?" Katie asked.

"You got it. Your first names are Lisa and John."

As they drove toward Baltimore-Washington International Airport, Katie risked a glance at the man beside her. His expression was tightly controlled. This time she was glad he kept his eyes on the road, because she was positive her own face mirrored her inner turmoil. Someone had tried to kill them and had stolen incriminating material from the lab. Hiding out made sense, and it was stupid to be worrying about their personal relationship. Yet just the thought of her and Mac spending the night together in a small motel room flooded her system like a brook after a torrential downpour. Yesterday she might have tried to hide her feelings. Now she cleared her throat.

"I'm nervous about sharing a motel room with you, too."

"I'm not nervous!"

"But I think we can handle the situation."

"Of course."

Nevertheless, when they arrived at the motel, Katie was glad it was safest for her to check in alone while Mac waited in the car. That way she didn't have to confer with him when she told the clerk Mr. and Mrs. Lam wanted two double beds instead of one queen.

As she started to pull out a credit card, she realized that wasn't a good idea—for several reasons. She could explain that they'd just gotten married and she hadn't changed her name. Yet that left them open to being traced through the transaction. Paying for one night took most of her cash, and she wasn't sure how they were going to get more.

Just as they stepped into Room 105, Jo phoned from the desk.

"In a jam, are you?" she asked as she breezed through the door a few minutes later.

Seeing her friend, who had dropped everything and come running to their assistance, brought a lump to Katie's throat. Because she couldn't trust herself to speak, she nodded tightly.

Jo gave her a quick, reassuring hug, then inclined her head toward Mac. "Is it this guy's fault?"

"Now wait a minute!" he objected, his posture immediately defensive.

"No," Katie assured her quickly. "Our being in trouble has just as much to do with my sister as his friend Tom." She wasn't absolutely sure the assessment was true, but she was sure that she and Mac were in this together.

Jo continued to stare appraisingly at her friend's companion. "You've got a reputation for causing trouble, you know, McQuade."

"Is that so? With whom? Or are you going to make me play twenty questions?"

"I'm not going to play games with you. Not when Katie is in danger. Remember that cooperative artificial-limb project a couple of years ago? The one where various scientific outfits around the country were donating their services and shared technologies. *You're* the one who held up approval of the design for six months and added thousands of dollars to the cost."

Mac raised the left hand that had been angled away from Jo. "I did a personal evaluation of the upper extremity model. It needed work. And how do you know anything about it?"

Jo's eyes focused on Mac's stainless steel hand, but she didn't miss a beat. "My husband, Cameron Randolph, had a lot to do with the miniaturized electronics."

"*You're* married to Cameron Randolph?"

"Uh-huh. I've been sharing his house full of inventions for the past year."

Mac shook his head and grinned at her. "Well, I'll be damned. I've been wanting to meet the son of a gun since we exchanged that flurry of E-mail. After he reworked the design, that hand was the best I'd ever tried. In fact, I was using it until a few weeks ago, until Medizone came up with this one." He snapped the fingers, and they responded with a satisfying metallic click.

Jo grinned back at him. "Wait till I tell Cam about this. Better yet, I'll arrange an introduction after we figure out what to do about the mess you're in now."

Katie let out the breath she'd been holding. Both Jo and Mac had strong personalities, and for a while there, she'd been afraid that the two of them were going to grate on each other. Now it looked like things were going to work out rather well.

"I want to hear the whole story of how you got yourselves in this fix," Jo prompted. "Every detail. Then we'll try to sort out what's important."

The two women sat down on one of the double beds. Mac took the chair. For the next hour, he and Katie filled Jo in on exactly what had happened since she had visited her sister, leaving out the personal details they'd both decided weren't relevant.

"So you suspect both Val and Tom were infected with a virus that's transmitted by intimate contact," Jo mused. "And you think someone is desperate to keep that information from getting out. Why?"

"At first we thought it might have been imported accidentally from abroad—by insect larva or animal hosts." Katie turned to Mac. "Did Tom meet with personnel from other area labs?"

"Yes."

"Well, the government farms out all kinds of secret research. What if some laboratory in the area is involved in a covert germ-warfare experiment that's gotten out of control?" Katie asked. "That would certainly be worth suppressing."

"By robbery and murder?" Mac countered.

"If the stakes are high enough. What if they've blown a multimillion-dollar contract?"

"Maybe it's not the government. Maybe it's some sort of terrorist group," Jo suggested. "How long did you say Tom was exhibiting symptoms—while he was still partially functional?"

"A couple of months at least," Mac told her. "Which doesn't sound like the virus would have a military or terrorist application. They'd want something that struck down victims quickly."

"What if it was going to be used for covert assassinations? And you didn't want anyone to know the person was a target?" Katie suggested.

"Then you sure wouldn't want his wife to get it," Jo offered.

"I suppose we could be dealing with terrorists. But as far as I know, assassination isn't a policy of the U.S. government," Katie murmured.

"Okay, forget that," Jo agreed. "Let's go back to the germ-warfare theory. Maybe the virus isn't stable. Maybe it's just in the early experimental stages."

"We can speculate until doomsday and not get anywhere," Mac interrupted. "But there might be another way to find out who wants the information suppressed." He wrote down a series of letters and numbers on the notepad beside the phone and handed it to Jo. "This is the license of the car that tried to run us down. Do you think you could find out our Mr. Ford's real name?"

"Was it a Maryland or D.C. license?"

"D.C."

"I have better contacts in Maryland, but I'll see what I can do."

"Meanwhile, we need to grow another sample of the virus," Mac went on. "It's important to send it to the Centers for Disease Control in Atlanta—to see if they've got data on any outbreaks."

"I thought all your materials disappeared," Jo pointed out.

"I still have a frozen blood sample from Tom." Mac gestured toward the thermos container on the floor beside his chair. "Which should be taken to a lab in the next few hours. Then we can duplicate the work."

"I've been thinking about that," Katie interjected. "We don't have to do that part ourselves. I mean, as long as adequate precautions are taken, we can contract out the labor. There are a couple of labs in the area that could handle it—and keep the information confidential."

"How are we going to know they're not the one with a secret government contract?" Mac asked in a level voice.

Katie looked chagrined. "I wasn't even thinking about that."

"Harvey Cohen can tell us," Jo suggested. "I've worked with him before."

"You've worked with Harvey Cohen, too?" Mac asked. "Who don't you know?"

"Who is he?" Katie asked.

"The author of *The Electronic Warfare Game*. Now he's got a watchdog think tank a couple of miles from here, as it happens. He may not know every outfit that has a secret contract—but he'll know which labs wouldn't touch government work with a ten-foot pole."

After a short conversation with Jo, Harvey Cohen recommended R & E Labs in Elkridge.

"Now we just need to find out how this is tied up with the D.C. police's noninvestigation of Val's death." Katie's voice was gritty as she got ready to leave with Mac.

Jo reached out and gently squeezed her arm. "Why don't I make some calls—starting with the D.C. morgue. We can meet back here later in the afternoon. Wait, before you go—" The detective pulled a couple of credit cards out of her knapsack. They were in the names of Lisa and John

Lam. "I've used this account when I needed to establish another identity," she explained. "You can pay me back when you have access to your own accounts."

"Jo, you think of everything," Katie marveled.

"I try. And speaking of that, rent yourselves a car—in case someone gets the bright idea of looking for Tom's."

THE TRIP TO R & E LABS went well. Although the facility wasn't as well equipped as Medizone, the staff was cooperative, and Mac was satisfied that they'd be able to duplicate his and Katie's procedures.

The building wasn't more than fifteen minutes from Katie's house in Ellicott City, and she wished she could go home and pack a suitcase. But she knew that wasn't safe. As they left the lab and headed back toward the highway, she could see Mac checking the rearview mirror. And she kept looking behind them, too, making sure they weren't being followed by a blue Ford or any other vehicles.

"Mac, I'm going to need some stuff. You know, toilet articles, underwear."

"Yeah."

"We could stop at the K mart at Dobbin Center."

Instead of heading for the motel, Mac went back to Columbia. They split up to do their shopping, but met back at the checkout counter. Katie glanced at him as the cashier picked up the long-sleeved flannel nightshirt she'd bought. He was staring at it but quickly reached into the basket to put some more things on the counter.

If they'd gotten married after medical school, they would have been making shopping trips like this for years, Katie thought. Really, it was all so ordinary. A suburban couple stopping at the store on their way home from work. Yet she knew there was nothing ordinary about the circumstances. Even if they were in danger, she was hoarding every mo-

ment of the experience—every moment they spent together—like a pirate filling a treasure chest.

They were both quiet on the drive back to the motel.
When they stepped in the door, it was obvious from Jo's
expression that she hadn't had a very successful afternoon.

"What is it?" Mac asked.

"For starters, my contact at motor vehicles is on leave. So
I can't tell you a thing about that license number, or your
Mr. Ford."

"But that's not the only thing wrong," Katie prodded.

Jo pressed her lips together, and Katie wished she hadn't
put her friend on the spot. "Right. Honey, I'm really sorry.
The best thing to do is give you the scoop straight out.
You're not going to have a chance to check out that virus in
your sister. The D.C. medical examiner's office is very
apologetic. But they say there was a mixup at the morgue.
Valerie Caldwell's body was accidentally switched with another woman—a hit-and-run victim named Hannah Cabel.
She was sent to Flowers Funeral Home and cremated."

Chapter Nine

Sudden tears gathered in Katie's eyes, and she felt Mac's arm come up around her shoulder. She leaned into his embrace. "Val always felt like she was so alone. After Mom's funeral, she told me she was glad she was going to be buried there, too."

"You can still bury her ashes next to your mother," Jo murmured.

"It's not the same!" Katie heard the edge of hysteria in her own voice and knew her irrational reaction was as much to the whole situation as to this latest macabre twist.

Mac eased her to the edge of the bed and sat beside her, stroking her shoulder. Jo brought her a glass of water.

Katie took a few sips and set the plastic tumbler down with a thunk on the bedside table, spilling some of the contents. "It wasn't an accident!" she grated. "They don't care who gets hurt. They did it on purpose to keep us from tracking the virus."

"That fits with the rest of it," Mac agreed, getting up and walking toward the window where he pushed the curtains aside and stood looking out. After several moments he turned back to Jo. "You've done an awful lot for us, and I hate to press you for anything."

"Don't be ridiculous! I'm here to help."

"Yeah, well, now that we don't have anything else to work with, we've got to track that license number."

"I know." She thought for a moment. "Listen, why don't I approach it from a different angle. I've got a lot of contacts in the Maryland office. One of them may be willing to query the D.C. system for me."

"I appreciate that. And while you're gone, Katie will have a chance to get some rest."

Katie, who had been tensely watching the conversation, didn't protest the suggestion.

When her friend had left, she turned to Mac, her expression quizzical. "Okay, I've already caught on to the way your mind works. You weren't exactly being straight with Jo."

"We need to trace that car."

"Stop playing games with me, too! What is it you didn't want to say in front of her?" Katie demanded.

He sighed. "I'm trying to keep your friend out of danger. The less she hangs around with us, the better off she'll be." Mac took a step toward her. "I keep trying to think of some way to get us out of this mess, too. The trouble is, every time we turn around, the plot looks bigger."

"You mean like the way the cop who did the initial investigation of Val's death was pulled off the case?"

"Like that," he agreed.

"Either someone in the D.C. police is being paid off to bury the case, or the department is a shambles."

"Or we're back to the government conspiracy theory."

"No matter what, we'd be taking a big chance if we went to the authorities for help. I can believe someone down there is praying we'll come forward—so he can turn us over to the bad guys."

For a moment Katie felt as if she were standing in quicksand. It was pulling at her feet, trying to suck her under. Were she and Mac going to have to spend the rest of their lives on the run? She sat up straighter. "What if they did an autopsy before they destroyed the body?"

"If they did, *someone* is going to get the information."

"Exactly what I was thinking. Or maybe they're going to get the actual tissue samples."

"Except that those could have disappeared just as easily as the lab samples we had at Medizone. But I won't know until I check."

"What do you mean? What exactly do you have in mind?" Katie demanded.

"Going down to the morgue tonight and doing some private investigating."

"Mac, that could be dangerous."

"I've been in a lot of dangerous situations."

"But you don't know anything about the layout of the morgue. You're going to have to take me along, because I'm the one who had a little tour of the place a few days ago. I have a heck of a lot better chance of figuring out where to look than you do."

Mac considered her reasoning. "I wish you were wrong," he finally admitted. "But you do realize we could be walking right into the clutches of whoever wants us out of the way?" Although the question was spoken quietly, his gaze burned into Katie's.

All at once, it was difficult to swallow around the lump clogging her throat. "Yes" was all she could manage.

"Then we'd both better get some rest." Mac crossed to the window and yanked the drapes closed. Then he pulled back the spread on the other bed and slipped off his shoes. Katie watched him, wishing she could say what she longed to say: *Oh, Mac, put your arms around me. Hold me.* Instead she silently slipped her shoes off, too. Mac gave her a long look before plumping up the pillows. Neither one of them got undressed or climbed under the covers. For the next several hours they lay in the darkened room on their separate beds listening to each other breathe.

THE LAST TIME Katie had been inside the two-story brown brick building that housed the D.C. morgue, she'd been desperate to hold herself together in the face of Val's death. Then she'd been focused on her sister's personal tragedy and her own guilty reaction. Now as Mac drove into the parking lot, she couldn't stop herself from glancing nervously behind them where the walls of the city jail loomed.

Death.

Crime.

It was no accident that the two buildings were so near each other—and both tucked out of the way where ordinary, law-abiding citizens didn't have to see them.

Yet here she and Mac were, coming to the morgue on a moonless night to commit a crime of their own in order to prevent a bigger one. However, the rationale wasn't going to make any difference if they were caught. Now that they had arrived, the plot they'd hatched seemed crazy, their plans flimsy. Still they had to give it a try.

Mac pulled into a parking space and cut the engine. On the way down they'd stopped at R & E for some lab coats. Then Mac had pumped Katie for information about the layout of the building. Now neither one of the them spoke, and she could feel the darkness pressing in around her. It was like a heavy blanket, smothering her, but it concealed her, too.

Katie wasn't sure how long they sat in the deep shadows like two thieves waiting to make their move. Twenty? Thirty agonizing minutes?

Finally the silence was shattered by the wail of an ambulance siren. It was what they had been counting on.

Mac reached for the door handle. "You don't have to come with me, you know. You could stay here."

She reached for his hand and squeezed it. "I was pretty sure you were going to say that. Don't even think about trying this alone."

He didn't stop to argue. Jamming his metal hand into the pocket of his white coat, he strode off toward the red-and-white emergency vehicle. Katie quietly closed the car door and hurried after him. They arrived at the entrance to the building as attendants brought in two gunshot victims.

While the bodies were being checked in, Mac and Katie came in as if they belonged there, too. They faded away down one of the white tiled corridors and slipped into an autopsy room.

Disinfectant, formaldehyde, death. The characteristic reek of the place—and Katie's recent memories—made her throat close. Mac must have felt her shudder. Quietly he laid a steadying hand on her arm.

"Let's do it fast," he whispered.

"I—I've been thinking. We have to make sure the whole thing isn't a lie. About Val's being shipped out of here and cremated, I mean."

"Yes. I was wondering about that, too. She could still be here."

"The room where they keep the bodies is down the hall." Now that they were sneaking around the building, it was impossible for Katie not to imagine eyes drilling into the back of her neck as they tiptoed down the hall. Realizing that her hesitant gait would give them away, she tried to walk more briskly as if they had every right to be in the facility.

She might look collected, but she couldn't control her physiological reactions. Under her borrowed lab coat, her skin had chilled to ice. When she pulled open the door to the refrigerated chamber, the freezing sensation sank into her bones.

Mac was behind her. Paralyzed, she stared at the rows of body-size drawers with neatly typed labels. She'd thought she could handle this, but the other terrible trip down here a few days ago was too fresh in her mind. It was all too personal.

"Katie, if you can't function, you might as well clear out of here."

Mac's matter-of-fact words were exactly what she needed. Her backbone stiffened, and she took several steps into the storage room. "I'm all right."

Silently she began opening the drawers on her left. Mac took the ones on the right. She opened them all, those with labels and those without. She was a physician, but it had been years since she'd confronted so many rigid bodies and lifeless faces. They seemed to accuse her of being warm and alive while they were cold and dead.

It was a humbling experience. Besides, it served no positive purpose. None of the mortal remains was Val's.

"She's not here," Katie whispered as she pushed the final drawer shut.

"Or here, either. Let's check the tissue storage."

They were just closing the heavy refrigerator door when a sound in the hall made them both come to an abrupt halt.

Discovery. She'd been unconsciously waiting to be unmasked for a sneak thief since the moment she'd walked into the building. A uniformed police officer strode into the room, stopped short and looked them up and down, taking their measure. For a heart-stopping moment, Katie forgot to breathe. Out of the corner of her eye, she could see Mac edging around in back of the man.

"Haven't seen you around here before," the newcomer observed. The silver bar on his shirt identified him as Officer Valenza.

As he paused beside a cluttered desk, Mac moved in a little closer and drew the metal hand out of his pocket.

"We're working on a report for the mayor's office," Katie said quickly, snatching up a clipboard from the table beside her. She was surprised that her voice didn't crack in the middle of the lie.

"Homicides?" Valenza pulled out the desk chair and sat down.

"Yeah," Mac confirmed, his tension visibly easing a notch or two.

The officer snorted. "How many is it this month so far? Twenty-five? You can tell Her Honor we need more officers patrolling the streets and fewer statistics for the newspapers to throw back in our faces."

"Isn't it the truth." Mac had quietly slipped his hand back in his coat, and Katie let the breath she'd been holding trickle from her lungs.

"Come on, Dr. Carter, let's finish up."

Katie followed Mac into the hall, closing the door behind them. As she stood there trying to gather the tattered shreds of her resolve, Mac was already striding down the hall. Running to catch up with him, she grabbed his arm. "What were you planning to do back there? Add assault to attempted robbery?"

He shook off her grasp. "I warned you about coming in here. We can't risk getting caught and turned over to whoever's in charge of the cover-up."

Nodding tightly, she stepped ahead of him and opened another door on their right. It led to an office. Katie had to open several more doors before she found the tissue storage facility. A stainless steel refrigerator was filled with neatly labeled samples. None had Val's name.

"I guess this was all for nothing. We've struck out," Mac muttered.

"Unless it's not with the regular material."

"This is a big place. Do you have any suggestions?"

"Another lab, maybe. One of the autopsy rooms."

She could see Mac weighing the options. Either they left empty-handed, or they took a few more risks. He nodded, and they began moving down the hall again, checking labs and offices. One factor was in their favor. At this hour in the morning, only a minimal staff was in the building. No one else questioned their presence.

Security wasn't exactly tight. But then who in their right mind would break into the morgue? Still, Katie felt her tension growing. Every time she opened a door, she expected to see someone sitting inside in the dark, waiting for them.

It didn't happen that way.

Mac was behind Katie in one of the labs when she started to open a door. In the hall, a man was just passing, and she had a quick glimpse of the side of his face. As she stopped short, Mac slammed into her.

"What?"

For a moment, Katie couldn't speak. The man. His face was ordinary, yet the sight of him had sent a scurry of prickly fingers over her scalp. As he receded down the hall, she focused on his broad shoulders, his loping strides. Suddenly the context snapped into place. It was the man who had followed them into the Columbia Mall, the man who had tried to run them down in the parking lot. Now he was *here.*

"The driver. Mr. Ford. The one who almost killed us," she whispered.

"Where?"

"He just disappeared around the corner."

"Stay here." Mac started down the hall. Katie was right behind him.

When they rounded the corner, the corridor was empty.

Mac swore.

Katie wondered if she was so strung out that she'd started seeing things.

The question was answered in the next second when a door to one of the autopsy rooms swung open, and the man they'd been following stepped back into the corridor.

They'd jokingly called him Mr. Ford. This was no joke.

For a split second he stared at them, obviously unnerved as they. Then with lightning-fast reflexes, he reached into his pocket.

Mac, however, was quicker. His arm shot out, catching the assailant's wrist between metal fingers and giving it a whiplike shake.

Mr. Ford screamed; a gun clattered to the floor. Mac kicked it toward Katie, and she picked it up. It was heavy and alien in her grasp.

What in the name of God were they going to do now? she wondered. In the next moment, the issue took on much greater urgency. Someone else must have heard the scream, because feet were pounding down the hall toward the corner they'd just rounded.

Mac threw Katie an urgent look. Grabbing Mr. Ford by the collar, he yanked him back inside the room from which they'd just stepped.

Katie had only a few seconds to decide what to do. Automatically she stuffed the gun into the waistband of her skirt. At least the white jacket concealed it. Now all she had to do was explain the scream.

As a blue-clad leg rounded the corner, she dropped to the floor and tore one of her shoes from her foot.

"Dr. Carter?"

The policeman who'd startled her and Mac earlier in the evening came to a halt inches from her knees. In the next moment, he was squatting down beside her on the tile floor, his service revolver in his hand.

Looking up at him with dazed confusion that was only partly faked, she pressed a palm against her forehead.

"Dr. Carter," he repeated. "What happened? Are you all right?"

Katie continued to stare at him in consternation, until she remembered that Dr. Carter was the name Mac had given her earlier in the evening. "Sorry to bring you running," she gasped. "Yes. I'm okay. Thanks. The lighting's so bad in here, and there must have been something slippery on the floor," she babbled.

He reholstered his weapon, reached for her wayward shoe, and held it out toward her.

"Thank you," she murmured again as she slipped the pump back on her foot. All the while, her ears strained for some clue about what was going on in the autopsy room where Mac had dragged their assailant.

In the next moment, her rescuer reached down to wedge a hand under her elbow, and she knew his fingers were only inches from the gun under her jacket. For a moment, she couldn't draw air into her lungs.

As he pulled her to her feet, he studied her pinched features. "You must have had quite a fall. Want me to take you over to D.C. General?"

"No. I'm fine. Really."

To her horror, now that she was standing, the heavy gun was starting to slip from its makeshift perch in her waistband. Trying not to draw attention to it, she pressed her arm against her side. "Thanks so much for coming to my assistance."

Valenza nodded and looked around. "Your partner leave without you?"

"He had to go back to the office. I'd better get over there before they send out a search party for me."

"Well, take care of yourself."

Valenza wasn't going to move from the spot on the floor until Katie did. Dutifully she started hobbling off down the hall. After half a minute, she risked a quick glance over her shoulder. The officer had disappeared around the corner.

Cautiously, ears straining for any telltale sound, Katie edged back toward the autopsy room where Mac had pulled Mr. Ford out of sight. What was going on there now? She had the gun. How was Mac controlling his prisoner?

As she quietly opened the door, she slipped the weapon out of her waistband and thrust in through the opening, hoping she was ready for whatever she was going to find. However, there was no way to be prepared for the scene that met her eyes. Under the bright glow of a surgical lamp, Mr. Ford was stretched out on the autopsy table like a turkey on a Thanksgiving platter. Several pairs of surgical gloves gagged his mouth. Adhesive tape bound his wrists and ankles and held him firmly to the polished stainless steel surface. Still, she saw his muscles bulge as he strained against his bonds.

No wonder. Mac stood over him, a scalpel clutched in his alloyed hand. It was poised to sweep across his captive's exposed throat.

Chapter Ten

"Lock the door." The menace in Mac's voice sent a shudder rattling down Katie's spine. How did it affect the man on the table? Her eyes flicked toward their captive. Sweat was trickling off his face like water in a thundershower.

Katie stood rooted to the spot, unsure exactly what Mac had in mind.

"Lock the door," he repeated. Fumbling behind herself, she found the knob and pushed the button.

Satisfied that they wouldn't be disturbed, Mac shifted the scalpel away from his captive's throat. The man twitched. "The driver's license in his wallet says his name is Arnie Beale, and he lives in Hyattsville," Mac said in a conversational tone. He reached down and spread the man's fingers for Katie's inspection. "He's a nervous type. He bites his nails." Mac let go of the man's hand and stood staring down at his prisoner.

Katie's breath came sharp and fast as she approached the table. She'd seen the dead laid out like this, never the living. Behind the two men was a diabolical assortment of equipment. Saws. Probes. Clamps. At the moment, none was more menacing than the simple scalpel Mac held.

"What is he doing here?" Katie whispered, as much to distract herself as for information.

"He's been a very busy man. This time he's not trying to run down pedestrians. He's making a pickup." Mac reached behind him and lifted a knapsack off the table. Inside was an insulated specimen carrier. "It's got Val Caldwell's name on it."

Katie stared at the dull gray box with the hinged lid. Tissue samples from Val. The only mortal remains of her sister. Closing her eyes, she fought back tears. It took several moments before she was sure she had enough control to go on with this.

When she opened her eyes, she saw that Mac was watching her. She knew she had to play the scene out—for him as well as herself.

Stiffening her backbone, she took several more steps toward the table and realized she was still holding the gun. She didn't even know if the safety was off, but she pointed it at Beale.

Their prisoner's terrified gaze flicked between the pistol and the scalpel.

"I believe we're going to find out where our delivery boy was heading," Mac predicted, the hard lines of his face a counterpoint to the matter-of-fact words. "Unless I make some kind of fatal slip with this artificial hand of mine." His carefully calculated actions belied the words. With delicate precision, he began to slice the buttons off the captive's shirt.

He had Arnie's full attention. The man's eyes bulged as he followed the progress of the scalpel. Through his gag, he was desperately trying to say something.

Ignoring his grunts, Mac pulled the ruined shirt open and pressed the razor-sharp blade against a broad chest. "Dr. Carter is going to remove your gag, and if you make any sound that isn't an answer to one of our questions, you're going to find you've made a surprise donation to the D.C. organ bank."

With fingers that had turned clammy, Katie struggled to untie the knots in the gloves. They were tight and hard to undo. Finally, the gag came free with a little pop.

Mac's eyes burned into Arnie's, and he raised a warning eyebrow.

"Who are you working for?"

"I don't know." The words were barely more than a hoarse croak.

"Who?" Mac pressed the blade against the man's perspiration-slick flesh and drew a tiny drop of blood. Holding the scalpel up, he rotated the knife in front of Arnie's eyes. "Not so much fun when you're on the receiving end, is it?" he grated.

The hit man began to blubber. "Please. Please. I don't know nothin'. I don't talk to no one face-to-face. I get my orders over the phone."

"You expect me to believe you accept snuff jobs from a voice over the phone?"

"I—yeah. For security."

Mac snorted. A subtle movement of the artificial hand shifted the scalpel so that it was out of the way. With the point of one metal finger, he drew a delicate line down the man's flesh.

As Katie zeroed in on Mac's rigid features, she shivered. The Mac McQuade she'd known had never been this ruthless, this calculating, this diabolical. Yet he wasn't really hurting their captive, she told herself. He wouldn't really hurt him. Would he?

Arnie, who obviously thought he was feeling the knife, rolled his eyes and began to whimper. "Don't. For cripe sakes, don't cut no deeper."

Out in the hall, Katie heard several pairs of footsteps and the squeak of a rolling cart, and her whole body went rigid with dread. God no. Not now. Should she point the gun at the door? Or should she simply pray?

Mac heard the disturbance, too. With a low, dangerous curse, he pressed the blade against their captive's throat again and leaned over the table. "Don't try anything stupid," he hissed.

For a wild moment Katie thought Arnie might be too crazed by terror to cooperate. But the man didn't move a muscle. Like actors in a tableau, the three of them waited in tense silence for the intruder to pass by—or burst in upon them.

When the footsteps and the squeaking cart finally faded, Katie remembered to breathe again.

Mac eased the knife away from the gray, quivering throat. His voice was steady, but a trickle of perspiration at his hairline betrayed his own frayed nerves. "Listen up, Arnie. We don't have much time, and I'm getting impatient." As he'd done with the man's chest, he jabbed with a metal finger against his windpipe.

Arnie gagged. "No! Don't kill me."

"You're not badly hurt. Just a scratch. You'll recover. If you tell us what we want to know."

"Please. I'm supposed to leave the box at a beauty shop."

"Don't give me that!" Mac grated.

"It's the truth. I'm supposed to wrap it like a present and leave it at the front desk. Someone else is gonna take it from there."

"What beauty shop?"

"Genesis."

Over the head of the man strapped to the table, Katie and Mac stared at each other. On the face of it, Arnie's story was crazy. Who would deliver tissue samples to a beauty parlor? Except that they knew that name. Genesis. The shop where Val had worked.

"What other assignments have you gotten over the phone lately?" Mac growled. "Besides orders to kill us."

"Just to search her apartment."

"Whose apartment?"

"The same lady whose name is on that box. Val Caldwell."

Katie felt the breath in her lungs solidify.

"When?" Mac demanded.

"Wednesday night."

The night they'd been in the apartment. Had he been there before them or after? "What were you looking for?"

"Stuff. Face cream."

She wanted to ask him more about it. But several more sets of footsteps sounded in the hall. The building was waking up.

"We've got to get out of here," Mac mouthed over Arnie's head as he replaced the gag.

They withdrew to a corner for a hasty conference.

"I'm not sure how much more we'd get out of him if we had a couple more hours," he said.

"What do we do with him?"

"Leave him."

"But, Mac, what's it going to look like?"

"Damn peculiar. It'll give whoever's behind this something to think about."

Katie wasn't sure she liked it. When she turned back toward Arnie, she gasped. His eyes were rolled back up in his head, and his jaw was as slack as the gag would allow. Had they killed him? Had he died from fright?

Swiftly she crossed to his side and felt for a pulse in the clammy skin of his neck. It was strong but shallow.

The hit man had fainted.

IT WAS A COUPLE OF DAYS into his temporary assignment in Hawaii, and Cornell Perkins was supposed to be observing police-department procedures. But they'd let him off duty at two in the afternoon again. He'd killed the rest of the day with a nap, a swim and dinner. Now he sat in the outdoor lounge at the Honolulu Mainliner Hotel sipping a piña colada and listening to a Don Ho lookalike croon an Island favorite. The casually dressed crowd was enjoying the balmy eighty-five-degree evening. But Perkins was edgy. And not just because he started to realize this assignment was one of those boondoggles that the *Washington Post* would expose in a flash across the front page of the Metro Section if they got a tip. City Faces Layoffs While Police Detective Has All-Expense-Paid Vacation to Hawaii.

Despite the idyllic weather, the gourmet food and the cordiality of the Honolulu police, he felt rotten.

This morning he'd called one of the guys he trusted back at the precinct and fished for information about who had been assigned the Val Caldwell case and how the follow-up was going. All he'd found out was that the death had been ruled suicide and the file closed. So what was the problem? After his conversation with Dr. Martin, he'd been leaning toward that conclusion himself. Until he'd been yanked off the case and sent out here. In the afternoon as he'd lounged by the pool, he'd been brooding about a neat and nasty little cover-up back in D.C. Somebody was getting something out of hushing up the Caldwell investigation, and maybe he was a fool to be sitting here in the sun letting the action pass him by. What the hell was he supposed to do in three weeks anyway? Come back to work as if nothing had happened?

Perkins finished his drink, went back to his eleventh-floor hotel room, and started to pack.

KATIE REACHED for the door handle. She wanted to suck in a steadying draft of air. At the last moment, the mixture of odors in the room stopped her. The taint of Arnie's fear was mixed with all the other evil vapors now.

Out of the corner of her eye, she saw Mac's teeth clench as he jammed his hand in his pocket. She touched his arm lightly but didn't say anything. Silently they stepped out into the hall again.

The building was beginning to fill up with the day staff. There might even be an autopsy scheduled for early in the morning, Katie realized. Which meant they didn't have much time before Arnie was discovered. What then?

As they retraced their steps, people began to pass them at regular intervals. Katie cast her eyes somewhere between the floor and the middle distance. If anyone looked her directly in the eye, she was sure they'd wonder what was wrong. So she concentrated on remaining anonymous, on blending into the institutional green walls.

Finally the door through which they'd entered was only a few yards away, and Katie was about to let out the breath she'd been holding when she came to an abrupt halt.

Another familiar face. The young policeman who had escorted her down here to identify Val's body was talking to the clerk at the desk. Officer Bryant. She even remembered his name.

Mac, who hadn't recognized the danger, was already a few paces ahead of her, but he stopped when he heard her muffled exclamation. Her eyes flicked to his, trying to telegraph a warning as she began to back away. Mac started to follow. But it was already too late. Bryant looked up and saw her.

In her present state, she expected him to pull out his service revolver and point it at her while issuing a stern warning to raise her hands in the air. Instead he gave her a boyish smile.

"Hi, how you doing?" he asked. As he spoke, a look of uncertainty flashed across his features.

"Fine." It was difficult to make the word come out smoothly around the telltale quiver of her mouth.

Beside her, Mac's body went taut—ready to flee, ready to fight. Either reaction was natural. Either one would spell disaster. As much to reassure him as herself, she reached for his elbow.

Bryant looked mildly embarrassed, and Katie suddenly realized what was probably going on. The police officer recognized her, but he wasn't sure of the circumstances under which they'd met. Most likely, he assumed she worked for the D.C. government, and all they had to do was get out of there before he remembered driving her down here to identify a body.

She gave a little sigh. "It's been a long night. I'm dead on my feet."

"Yeah. I know what it's like to pull the graveyard shift."

"Well, see you around."

"Sure."

Mac started to move again. To her mild surprise, Katie found her legs would also function. Moments later they were standing in the watery morning sunshine. Katie sucked in a draft of the chilly air.

Mac tapped her arm. "Come on."

She followed him back to the rented car. They didn't speak again until they'd climbed inside and Katie had reached to lock the doors.

"Who was that guy back there?"

"The officer who escorted me down here after Val died. I guess he doesn't remember where he met me. Let's go before he figures it out."

"Right."

Mac started the engine and swung out of the parking lot onto Massachusetts Avenue.

Katie turned and looked over her shoulder, seeing the grim bulk of the D.C. jail receding in the distance. She felt as if she'd just done ten years at hard labor and finally escaped.

"It's good to be out of there," Mac said.

"Yes. I guess it was worth it. I—I didn't like doing that to Arnie."

"He tried to flatten us in the mall parking lot."

"If we sink to his level, what does that make us?"

Mac was silent for several moments. Out of the corner of her eye, she saw his hands tighten on the wheel. His next words took her completely by surprise.

"What did you think I was going to do, kill him?"

"No."

"Or maybe just cut him up a little? Torture him with the scalpel?"

"You wouldn't have gone that far."

"Did you think I was enjoying myself?"

"Mac, mostly I was frightened. Seeing him strapped down on that table. Seeing you standing over him like— like—I don't know—with your eyes blazing."

"It was a calculated effect. I was trying to scare the living daylights out of him."

"You did."

"You were afraid I'd lose control," he persisted. "Don't you know me better than that?"

She couldn't meet his eyes. Two days ago she'd told herself she was in love with him. Now—"I thought I did. A long time ago."

He sighed. "You're right. I went farther than I had to. I guess I was taking out my anger on him. For days I've felt as if I was up against a faceless enemy, and then I finally had someone to attack." She saw him swallow. "Maybe I don't know myself anymore."

Katie wasn't sure what to say. When she reached out and covered his hand, it stiffened on the wheel. He was doing it again, withdrawing when she tried to make contact. This time she didn't have the emotional energy to push it. After a moment she took her hand away and folded it in her lap.

They were several miles from the morgue before Mac spoke again. On a completely different topic.

"Genesis. That's the place where your sister worked, isn't it?"

"Yes."

"It can't just be a coincidence."

Katie murmured her agreement. "All of a sudden it looks like we've been going at this from the wrong angle."

"Do you think an upscale beauty emporium could be a front for some kind of criminal organization?"

She shrugged. "It sounds crazy. However, if you were trying to hide something illegal, it would be a great cover. Maybe Val stumbled onto something she wasn't supposed to know about. That could be a reason why they'd sent Arnie to look for evidence at her apartment." She stopped abruptly and glanced back in the direction from which they'd come, the hair on the back of her neck bristling. "My God, Mac, maybe he went down there right after I left the first time. Maybe he pushed her off the balcony, and Tom saw what happened."

"I'd like to go back and shake the truth out of him."

"We can't." Katie ground her teeth in aggravation.

"I believe what he said, that he's just a little part of something bigger. The trouble is, we don't know a damn thing about Genesis. As soon as we drop off the tissue sample, we're going to see what we can find out about the place." Katie nodded, suddenly feeling overwhelmed with fatigue and frustration.

HELEN AUSTIN-WRIGHT opened one eye and peered at the green illuminated numbers of the digital clock. 6:32 a.m.

Early.

What had awakened her? she wondered, her mind drifting in a warm, sleepy sea. Sometimes things were so complicated, and it was hard to cope. But not right now. There was nothing that needed her attention for a couple of hours. The decorator was coming at eleven to talk about redoing the family room, and her Genesis appointment wasn't until two. It was going to be a very pleasant day.

She might have drifted back to sleep, except that something was wrong. The room was silent. Too silent. She couldn't even hear George's ragged snoring. Helen patted the far side of the king-size bed and found it empty.

Sitting up, she snapped on the bedside lamp. "George? *George!* Where are you?"

The only answer was a low moan from the bathroom. Helen's throat constricted as she leapt out of bed and rushed toward the closed door. But when her feet crossed over from carpet to tile, she stopped dead and grabbed the wall for support, hardly able to believe what she was seeing.

Naked, George was bending over the sink, a knife clutched in his hand. Blood streamed down his left arm. As she watched, he dipped the knife toward the other wrist.

"No! George, no!" Lunging forward, she grabbed for the weapon. He slapped her away, and she landed with a thud on the hard floor. Staring up at him, she saw the wild, desperate look in his eyes. Somehow she'd known all along that something terrible was going to happen.

It took a moment to catch her breath. "Please, give me the knife, sweetheart. You don't really want to do this. Things aren't as bad as you think. We'll get you some help. Please listen to me."

The words came out high-pitched and trembly, bouncing around the tiled room like an echo in a cheap stereo system. They drove George to a new level of frenzy.

Picking up a three-hundred-dollar china soap dish, he smashed it against the mirror. As his arm swung, blood flew in an arc toward the glass. The dish shattered and the mirror splintered into a tangle of spiderweb cracks and drops of blood.

The look in his eyes when he turned back to Helen froze the breath in her lungs. Before she could back away, George was slamming her into the wall and bringing the bloody knife to her throat.

FOR THE MOMENT, there wasn't much point in continuing to speculate. Katie closed her eyes, giving in to the weariness that had begun to make her limbs feel dragged down by hundred-pound weights. Yet much as she longed to shut everything out, she couldn't turn off the questions swirling in her brain.

Genesis. Maybe this all went back to Genesis. What had Val told her about the place?

The owner was a lady from Japan. A very beautiful woman. Elegant and refined. Who only hired beauticians of the very finest caliber. Val had made sure Katie had known that.

What was the woman's name? Katie drew a blank. But the information would be easy enough to get.

Val had bragged that their line of cosmetics was completely exclusive—available nowhere else in the U.S.—and very expensive. The first salon was in D.C. Soon they were going to expand to other major U.S. cities.

Were their products manufactured here? Or were they imported from Japan? Slowly, reluctantly, her mind began to spiral down a frightening path. What were the sanitation standards in the plant where the cosmetics were manufactured? What were the inspection procedures for nonfood imports into the U.S.? What if the moisturizer Val was using had somehow gotten contaminated with a lethal virus? Arnie had been sent to look for something in Val's apartment. "Face cream," he'd said. What if the owner knew the products were contaminated and was trying to pull in the supply before the authorities found out?

Katie's breath rasped in fast and painfully. "Oh my God!"

"Button, what?"

"Oh God," she repeated as she started to shiver. Suddenly she had to clamp her teeth together to keep them from chattering. Too much had happened too quickly. Panic, the ordeal of the autopsy room, exhaustion had all combined to send her over the edge.

"Honey, what is it?"

She shook her head, unable to tell him. They were on Connecticut Avenue within a few blocks of Chevy Chase Circle. Mac pulled off onto a side street lined with solid old houses and found a parking place under a wide-spreading oak. After cutting the engine, he reached for Katie, but she shrank back, her shoulders wedged against the door.

"Katie! I can't help you unless you tell me what's wrong. Are you hurt? Sick?"

She started to laugh, then had to stifle a sob. "You thought you had the virus. That somehow it came from Medizone. That you'd brought it back from a trip. But that's all wrong. You weren't in danger—except from me."

"Stop it! You're not making sense. Tell me what you're talking about."

He reached for her again. Katie batted his hand away. "Don't!" She didn't know that tears were brimming in her eyes. "Stupid. I was so stupid. I used it."

"What?"

"The face cream. I used the face cream Val had hidden in her closet. I even put some on my sore ribs." Tearing at the tail of her shirt, she pulled it up, exposing the skin over her right ribs. "I don't understand what happened to the bruises," she muttered as she stared at her skin.

"What the hell are you talking about?"

"You were right, Mac. She stole it. That's why she hid it. She wasn't supposed to have it, because it was contaminated, Mac. But she didn't know. She thought it was going to make her younger-looking.''

''Katie—''

''Don't you get it? The face cream. That's where the virus came from.''

Chapter Eleven

Mac tried to pull Katie into his arms.

"No. Don't. Get—away—from—me."

Tears streamed down her cheeks. Her voice was edged with hysteria. Desperately she flailed at Mac. "No. Leave me alone." Her voice rose in a despairing wail.

Ignoring the blows, the words and her confusion, Mac folded her close, stopping her thrashing with his arms and the weight of his body against the door. Pinned, she continued to struggle, sobs racking her body. But Mac's strength and the force of his resolve were simply too much for her. When she had no more will to resist, she slumped against him.

The tears continued for a few more minutes. Finally the husky, low sound of his voice helped to bring her back some measure of calm. Yet they couldn't entirely drive away the fear waiting to swallow her whole.

When he sensed the change in her, he let go his tight grasp on her shoulder.

She winced, and he swore.

"The damn hand—I'm sorry."

"It's okay. You didn't hurt me. I must have gone a little crazy."

He shifted a few inches away, found a handkerchief in his pocket and passed it to her.

Katie blew her nose, her face averted.

Crazy. Like Val and Tom. Was it already starting?

When she shuddered, he tangled his fingers in her hair and gently tipped her face up to his. "You used the face cream you found in Val's closet."

Katie gulped. "Yes."

"And you think it's contaminated?" he clarified in tones that she knew were under tight control.

"Yes." Somehow his manufactured calm helped her get a grip on herself.

"How much did you use? How many times?"

"Just a little bit. But what does that matter, if it's got the virus?"

"You're not thinking the whole thing through. Suppose some of the cream was contaminated? Suppose there were batches that were okay? Your sister was probably using it for months. You only did it once, from one jar. And you're not sick."

She didn't break the eye contact. "Just acting nuts."

"Stop it! You've been up for the past twenty-four hours. You've been through a couple of hellish ordeals. You're entitled to act a little flaky. And if it comes to that, your theory about the face cream is probably a crock of half-baked speculation. It's highly unlikely that it would be harboring a virus."

She ignored the last observation. "You've been up for twenty-four hours, too. You're not wigged out."

"Maybe not now. But I was back in the autopsy room. Or isn't that what you thought?"

"Let's stick to the point. We're talking about my crazy behavior, not yours."

Neither one of them moved. The atmosphere in the car was charged with tension.

"Mac. I'm sorry," she finally murmured, wondering exactly what she was apologizing for. Being afraid she had the virus? Arguing with him? Or pointing out his deficiencies? It was hard to think clearly. Which brought another surge of fear.

Through the panic, she realized that they'd been in this spot before. Only then everything had been reversed. Mac had been the one afraid that he'd been contaminated. And she had been desperate to deny that it was true. He hadn't been a model of rationality. In fact, none of her contentions had made any real difference. Now she knew exactly how he'd felt. And he was in a damn good position to understand *her* feelings.

"I know you're not in any shape to listen to my arguments," he muttered.

"Are you reading my mind?"

"I wish I could."

He pulled her back into his embrace, his lips skimming her hair, her forehead, her cheeks.

"Don't. You shouldn't." The protest was weak.

"I think I need this as much as you do."

The admission made her throat constrict. Wordlessly she let her head drop to his shoulder. After a moment of hesitation, her face turned to press against his neck. He held her, stroked her, murmured soft reassurances.

Oh God, she thought. *If I'm going to lose my mind, if I'm doing to die, I want one last wish before it happens. I want to finally know what it's like to make love to you, Mac.* Yet even as her mind silently formed the request, she knew it was impossible to grant. Putting him at risk like that was something she'd never do. She'd have herself locked in the psychiatric ward of a hospital before she took that kind of chance.

Katie allowed herself to cling to Mac for a few moments longer. Then she lifted her head. "I want to go back to R & E," she said. "I want that blood test."

"Yeah. We'll both feel a hell of a lot better when we know you don't have it."

"Sure." Then another thought struck her. "Mac, what if there's a window when you can't tell someone is infected?"

"That won't be a problem. We'll be using new procedures developed at Medizone."

There wasn't much to talk about on the ride to Elkridge. Katie sat with her hands clenched in her lap, trying not to think, trying not to focus on the knot tightening in her stomach. Morning sunshine glazed the window. The promise of a new day. It seemed to mock her.

Out of the corner of her eye, she kept glancing at the bloodless knuckles of Mac's hand where he gripped the wheel. "At least there's one good thing about my situation," she said.

"What?"

"I'm not going to have to spend the night biting my nails. We've already produced a new batch of antibodies using that frozen blood of Tom's. All we've got to do is draw some of my blood and test it."

Still, the closer they got to Elkridge, the more she felt like a condemned prisoner being transported the last mile to the scaffold.

Yet she had to know. The moment Mac pulled into a parking space, she hopped out of the car. "I'm going down to hematology."

"Okay. I'll meet you in the hot lab."

When she arrived fifteen minutes later with a tube of blood, she found Mac had had one of the technicians get everything ready.

"Thanks, but I can take over from here," Katie told the young man.

"Yes. I'd like to have Dr. Martin do these tests," Mac added.

If the technician thought anything about the strained atmosphere between Dr. Martin and Mr. McQuade, he didn't comment. He simply did as he was told.

At least she was going to get the news in privacy, Katie thought. Privacy, except for Mac. At the moment, she didn't really want him there, either. Was this how he'd felt yesterday morning when she'd hovered around him?

She sensed him standing close behind her while she introduced the blood into the isolation chamber. Before she could proceed any further, he took her by the shoulders and turned her toward him. Caught off guard, she froze under the impact of his smoky gray gaze.

"Katie."

The look in the depths of his eyes blurred everything else in the room. When she realized his intention, she gasped and tried to push him away. But he had several tactical advantages over her. Strength. Determination. Surprise.

"No—you—"

The words were cut off by the pressure of his mouth. His lips moved urgently, almost savagely over hers. It wasn't precisely a passionate kiss. But it was possessive and primitive and left her clinging to him, gasping for breath.

Dazed, she could only stare up at him as her heart pounded in her chest. Finally she found her voice again.

"Mac. That wasn't a very smart thing to do."

"Finish the test."

"If I have it, you—"

"Dammit, shut up and finish the test."

Time seemed to have ground to the pace of a slow-motion instant replay. Katie turned back to the isolation chamber. Still her hands were strangely steady as she took the stopper off the tube of blood. Finally the slide was ready, and she placed it on the stage of the microscope. A pulse pounded in her forehead as she closed one eye and adjusted the focus.

"Katie?"

"I—I—don't see—"

He moved her gently aside. Unsure that her knees would hold her erect, she stood slumped against the wall watching Mac bend to the eyepiece.

"Thank heaven," he gasped.

She'd hardly been able to believe her own scrutiny of the slide. Now Mac's exclamation of thanks confirmed her own observation. The terror had ended. She didn't have the antibodies. When her knees buckled, she felt Mac sweeping her up into his arms. For a moment he simply hugged her against his chest. Then he started down the hall. "What are you doing?"

"Taking you back to the motel. You're dead on your feet."

"What about the tissue samples we brought?"

"I've already given orders to have them tested. It's time for you to stop arguing. We're both going to feel a lot better once we get some sleep."

THERE WAS A TAP on the door. "One moment." Jade Nishizaka slipped the photo album back into its hiding place. No one but Akio had ever shared its secret with her.

She clasped her chilly hands together in her lap. Soon her brother would be arriving from Kyoto, and she would be glad to see him. How could she not be glad? He was the center of her life. Yet Akio was such an exacting taskmaster. And he would be angry when he learned that everything was not in perfect order.

With the discipline she had cultivated over the years, Jade schooled her features into a Kabuki mask. "Come in."

Ming entered the room. "I have the acceptance list for the Day of Beauty."

Jade's voice betrayed neither her excitement nor her tension as she held out her hand. "Good." The workshops and make-overs scheduled for this coming Monday were being held as a special program for wives of delegates to the National Economic Symposium. The number who had signed up would spell the success or failure of six years of intensive work.

But she and Akio had learned patience. Long ago there had been no choice. Their very survival had been in question. Yet they had lived and prospered and gotten the education they needed. After that had come the courting of investors and the founding of Nishizaka Pharmaceuticals. It had taken hard work and money—and years of research with the herbal products their mother had developed in her small workshop. But finally they'd been ready to create Genesis. She had made the salon a place of luxury and prestige. And she'd watched its word-of-mouth reputation grow among Washington's elite. Every rich woman who visited the nation's capital wanted to spend a day at Genesis. Soon, hundreds of them from around the country would be in one place at one time.

A thousand moths fluttered in Jade's chest as she scanned the list. As name after important name leaped out at her, she felt the tension replaced by exhilaration. Mrs. Calvin Abingdon. Mrs. Donald Treemore. Mrs. Percy Worthington. Mrs. Vincent Guccini. They were all signed up. And they would all find the secret of eternal youth—and more.

MAC WAS RIGHT, Katie decided as she toweled herself dry after a quick shower. She felt better, but she was so tired it was hard to rub two coherent thoughts together. She'd grabbed one of the bags from their shopping expedition before coming in here. But it was the wrong one.

Rummaging through the contents, she found that the only thing that might be any use to her was a package of T-shirts Mac had bought. Tearing the plastic wrapper open, she pulled one out and slipped it over her head. It was about five sizes too big, which meant it would make a pretty good nightshirt.

The intimacy of putting on Mac's clothes—even Mac's new clothes—made her glance quickly at the closed door. One moment she felt closer to him than ever before, the next he was worlds away. Maybe Mac had changed too much. He was harder, more primitive, less approachable. Maybe he didn't need anybody else, and maybe she was putting her heart in jeopardy by caring. Yet if *he* hadn't cared about her, why had he kissed her right before she'd tested her blood for the virus?

In her present state, the questions were too much to handle. With a shrug she began to clean her teeth with the blue toothbrush Mac had bought. Then, conceding she was in danger of falling asleep standing up, Katie gathered up the last shreds of her strength and opened the door. Tottering across the rug to the closest bed, she pulled back the covers and slipped underneath.

The drapes were still drawn, so that the room was in semidarkness. Mac was talking in low tones on the phone, his head bent. She sensed rather than saw that he was watching her, but he continued the conversation for several more moments before hanging up.

"I've checked in with Jo. She was worried."

"I should have talked to her." The protest was little more than a mumble from under the covers.

"Later. You're beat."

Katie felt the mattress shift as he sat down beside her. "Roll over."

She flopped to her stomach and felt him start to knead the tense muscles of her shoulders. "Nice," she murmured. Under the tender ministrations of his fingers, she drifted off to sleep.

MAC MCQUADE GLANCED at his reflection in the mirror and grimaced. He'd never before worn undershorts decorated with NFL team logos. But the choice in his size at the discount department store had been rather limited. After pulling on the shorts, he held up his left arm and examined the stump of his wrist. Twenty-four hours was an awful long time to wear a metal hand. Now that he'd taken it off to shower, he knew it would be painful to put it back on until he'd given the wrist at least a couple of hours' rest.

His gaze flicked to the bathroom door, as he imagined Katie sleeping a few yards away. Not many people had seen him without his hand. Or without a long-sleeved shirt buttoned at the cuff, for that matter. None of them had been the women he'd taken to bed. He hadn't felt confident enough to let them see him that naked—to face the indrawn breath when they got a look at his deformity up close and personal. Deep down he had the feeling that Katie was different. And maybe if she wasn't, he wanted to know about it now.

The long-sleeved pajama top he'd bought stayed in the bag. Instead he pulled on a twin to the T-shirt Katie had donned. In the brief glimpse he'd gotten of her as she'd crossed to the bed, he'd liked it better on her feminine curves.

He needed sleep. He was starting to feel like a zombie. Still he continued to hesitate before opening the door. When he finally did, he stood looking at Katie in the shaft of light from the bathroom. She was sleeping deeply, innocently, lying on her side now with her legs drawn up and her brown hair a tousled contrast to the white pillowcase. One vulnerable, gently cupped hand was extended outside the covers and lay on the pillow beside her face. Seeing her like that made him feel as if a mortar shell had just exploded inside his chest.

God, when she'd told him the face cream was contaminated and that she'd used it, he'd just about flipped out. The only thing that had kept him coherent was knowing that one of them had to stay in control. And he had—until he'd kissed her. Right before she'd bent to look at her blood under the microscope.

He didn't want to scrutinize too closely his wild swings of emotion today. Not with regard to Katie. And not with Arnie Beale, either. Yet a nagging question kept eating at him. Did the way he'd wielded the scalpel over the man mean he'd lost touch with his humanity?

When your life was on the line, were such extreme measures justified? Or had their situation been an excuse to unleash the darkest monsters of his being?

Right now his exhausted mind couldn't grapple with such subtleties. And his tired body was having trouble keeping him on his feet.

About all he could handle at the moment was a mattress and cool sheets. His eyes swung to the empty bed across the room, then back to the one where Katie slept. More than once he'd tried to send her away, and she wouldn't leave him. Now the idea of separation made his throat burn. It was more than a sexual need. It was something even more elemental—like the need to breathe. Without giving himself time to think about the difference between fantasy and reality, he crossed to the bed and slipped under the covers with Katie.

Her warmth overwhelmed him as he moved carefully up behind her, his face barely touching the tender skin at the back of her neck. She felt so soft, so feminine. She smelled of cleanly scented soap and lavender. That was the last thing he remembered before falling asleep.

KATIE WAS DREAMING about Mac. Dreaming that he was making love to her. And he was only a few feet away, in the other bed. A flush spread across her face and neck. Then, she felt the warmth of another body beside her and realized Mac wasn't as far away as she'd thought. Her eyes snapped open, and she saw his hand. He was lying on his side in back of her, his arm draped across her shoulder. She didn't question why he was there. She simply looked down at the relaxed fingers that rested against her forearm, and her heart lunged in her chest like a trapped bird throwing itself against the bars of its cage.

When she'd gone to bed, she'd been wondering how she felt about him. Now as she looked at him, all the emotions she'd choked off came swooshing back like a river at flood time. She loved this man.

If she moved just the tiniest bit, his fingers would be touching her breast. Without giving the matter further consideration, she moved.

And his hand was where she wanted to feel it. The sudden flash of sensation was so exquisite that she had to bite her lip to keep from whimpering. This was what she'd craved. This intimacy.

For a while it was enough simply to enjoy the sweet newness of the contact. The contentment didn't last for very long.

"Mac." His name was a wispy sigh on her lips.

She knew the instant he woke, the instant his fingers moved. Stroking. Pressing. Finding the hard bud of her nipple, making her breast throb. No, not just her breast. Her whole body was throbbing. And it was impossible to hold back the shaky little sound of response that had lodged in her throat.

"Button."

She rolled over to face him, her body warm and pliant only a few inches from his.

There were several pounding heartbeats when his gray eyes questioned hers. She saw longing. Desire. Hesitation.

And she knew that even though he had chosen to sleep with her, the decision about where they went from here was still hers.

She answered his question by moving the tiniest bit again, bringing her lips to his. It wasn't like the last time, or like the first time, either, when they'd both been taken by the surprise of discovering each other again.

This was deliberate. The long, deep kiss that she'd been craving. It brought her a kind of hot satisfaction. And a deep need for more, so much more. But as his lips moved more urgently over hers, the need became tinged with worry. Would he stop if he knew how much this meant to her?

She might die if he stopped. Yet she had to find a way to slow the pace to something she could handle.

"Mac." There was a catch in her voice as she spoke his name.

"Um?" He pulled her hips tightly against his and stole several small sipping kisses from her lips.

Heat zinged through her again, making it almost impossible to speak. "Mac, I haven't had very much practice at this sort of thing. I—I don't want to disappoint you."

His gaze snapped into focus, and he stared into her doubtful blue eyes. She was so desirable, so sensual, so obviously happy to have him in her bed that it had simply never crossed his mind that she might not be very experienced sexually. Had some insensitive jerk hurt her, made her cautious with men? Whatever the reason for her sudden hesitation, her whispered confession made his heart swell.

"You won't disappoint me, Button," he said gently, as his lips began to nibble on hers. "Just tell me if I'm going too fast, because I don't want to disappoint you, either."

"You won't," she repeated as she snuggled into his arms, enjoying the tantalizing responses he was bringing to life. As they kissed and touched, she found she was reacquainting herself with the man who had excited her so many years before.

He was an electrifying lover. A skillful lover. A playful lover.

She giggled as he teased her about hiding from him, his hand making little forays through the T-shirt. The laughter choked off as he pulled the thin cotton taut against her breasts and admired the way the knit fabric revealed her shape.

In the next moment, he dragged the garment up and over her head. Then in a universal gesture of male possessiveness, he reached to cup her breasts. The fingers of his right hand closed over her heated flesh. His left wrist collided with her chest under her other breast.

He froze. And she saw stark anguish flash in his eyes.

Mac started to pull away. She reached down to cover both the right hand and the left wrist with her own hands, pressing him tightly against herself.

"You shouldn't have to settle for second best," he grated.

"You're not second best. You're exactly what I want. What I need."

She brought his hand to her lips, kissing his fingers. She smiled at him as her tongue and lips and teeth began a sensual exploration. His breath stopped moving in and out of his lungs when she reached for the other arm. Her movements languid, she brought his wrist to her lips, lavishing it with the same tender attention she'd begun with his hand.

Mac could hardly believe what she was doing and hardly believe his own reaction. Since the accident, he'd treated that part of his body as nothing more than a dead end. But the caresses of her lips and tongue felt good. Very good.

The unexpected pleasure and the aroused look in her eyes broke through barriers he hadn't even known were there. He swept her into his arms, desperate to give her everything that was in his power to give, no longer hesitant about touching her in any way and every way that would please them both. Yet, the closer they drew to the ultimate joining, the more he sensed that somehow she was slipping away from him.

"Honey, what is it?"

"Mac, I have to tell you—"

She wanted to let him know about something she liked, something that would make it better for her. Some women had trouble telling a partner about things like that.

He lifted her fingers to his lips the way she'd done with his, nibbling at their tips. "Don't be shy with me, Button."

She swallowed painfully and forced the words out. "Mac, I—I haven't made love with anyone before."

There was no way to hide his stunned reaction.

She gulped. "The way I figure it, if making love really didn't mean anything, there wasn't any point in doing it. Not just to say I'd had the experience."

"And now you—"

"And now I think I'll die if we don't go ahead."

He was overwhelmed by the gift she was offering. Overwhelmed that she was offering it to *him*. Yet he tried to keep his voice light. "We wouldn't want that to happen." He pulled her close again, kissing her, stroking her, murmuring words that broke through her anxiety, making it easier for her to talk.

She smiled at him tentatively. "You don't get through medical school without learning about the mechanics of sexual intercourse. It's just that putting theory into practice is a little daunting the first time."

His eyes were teasing again. "Honey, you always were one of the best students. But don't think of this as a final exam. The important thing is to relax and enjoy it."

"I have been."

"Yeah. So have I. Very much."

"But you're probably getting a little impatient."

"Nope. Getting there is half the fun."

He knew just what to say to ease her tension. Just how to rock her on a sea of sensuality, lifting her higher and higher toward sexual fulfillment as each wave broke.

He stroked her with his hand and then his body, bringing her to climax before he'd fully entered her. Then, as she came down off that high, sun-drenched crest, he breached the last barrier. She was so limp with the joy of her fulfillment that her body easily accepted his. There was hardly any pain, only more pleasure as he began to thrust inside her, the deep powerful strokes bringing her to an even higher peak of ecstasy.

Chapter Twelve

They had slept for only a few hours, but Mac woke up disoriented. A shaft of light from the center of the drapes pierced the artificial darkness. He was in a motel room, and there was a woman's head on the pillow beside his. No, not just any woman.

Katie.

As he absorbed her warmth in the bed beside him, a great sense of serenity stole over him. It had been years since he'd felt this kind of peace. He longed to bask in the glow. Yet even as the temptation began to unfurl, he found the strength to overcome desires he had no right to claim. This was wrong. If not for him, then for sweet, innocent Katie who didn't realize what she was getting into with a misfit like him. He was easing carefully away from her when she opened her eyes.

He could tell that her awakening was different from his. There was no moment of disorientation on her part. She knew at once where she was and with whom. Her blue eyes, as they regarded him gravely, were huge and blue like the clearest mountain lakes, and he felt himself falling helplessly into them. Then she smiled, and it was like the sun coming up over the mountains.

"I used to dream about making love to you. Real life is better."

"Katie, this isn't real life."

"It could be."

Suddenly he was powerless to fight his desires. He didn't want reality. He wanted the fantasy to go on. They might have been enclosed in a time bubble where no one and nothing could reach them. With a groan that was part need, part protest, he pulled her willing body against his.

He smiled against her cheek as he sensed her confidence. This time she had a much better idea of what they were doing and where they were heading. And the rewards were even more spectacular—for both of them.

Afterward, replete, and just a little bit smug, Katie snuggled into the arms of the man she loved. "I feel cheated out of all the time we missed," she murmured.

When she felt Mac's body tense, she knew at once that it hadn't been the right thing to say. Raising up on one elbow, she looked down at him. "What's wrong?"

"Nothing."

"Don't put the barrier back up between us. Not now."

"Katie, I can't help it. I've been putting up barriers between me and the rest of the world for eight years."

"You know now you don't have to do it with me. Our being together is so—" She floundered for words and couldn't come up with anything better than "right."

"You didn't think so when we were down there at the morgue with Arnie Beale."

"That wasn't the real you."

"It's as much the real me as the man who made love to you a little while ago. Katie, you don't understand how much I've changed. I'm too messed up to give you the things you deserve."

"What exactly do you think I deserve?" She assumed he was going to spout some conventional speech about a reliable husband and a house full of kids. But she hadn't thought of herself in those terms at all. For the past eight years, her life had been her career. And when it had hit a snag, she worked herself into a fine state of trying to get it back on track. Actually it would be hard to shift gears into being a contented homemaker.

The self-knowledge made Mac's words particularly painful. "You're obviously a fine clinician and a gifted research physician. You deserve someone who can be proud of your accomplishments. Not some medical-school washout who would feel threatened every time you got a new grant or got a paper published in a medical journal."

She ran her hand down his chest. "Medizone Labs is one of the most respected research outfits in the country. You did that without the benefit of a medical degree. Not finishing school certainly wasn't your fault. Besides, it doesn't make any difference to me."

"That's fine for you. But it makes a hell of a lot of difference to me. Katie, I'm not stupid. I know that for the past eight years I've been trekking off to every godforsaken place on earth to try and outrun my anger about what happened."

"So now you want to convince me there's no future for us?" she whispered, hardly able to get the words out.

"Finding you again was a shock. I tried to tell myself I didn't want you anymore. Well, we both know that was a lie. But it doesn't mean I've figured out how to cope with my deep-rooted insecurities."

If ever a man had proved his worth, it was Mac McQuade. Yet no amount of argument was going to make him see that. If he couldn't come to the realization himself, there was nothing she could do about it. Except maybe show him how unconditional her love was for him.

He broke into her thoughts. "Right now the two of us are in a hell of a jam. And neither one of us is going to have a future until we find out exactly who wants us out of the way and why."

Mac was right. It was easier to think about the immediate danger than to do any more probing at the layers of scar tissue covering his heart.

"Then I think the next step is to test the other sample of face cream, the one you took back to your house," she said. "Only if it's dangerous to go to my place, it's just as dangerous to go to yours."

"Maybe Jo has some thoughts on that."

"Right." Katie sat up and gathered the covers around her chest. Then she phoned their friend, who'd been waiting for their call.

"I can scan the house and the area to see if anyone's watching," Jo told her. "And if Mac doesn't mind giving me the entry code to his security system, I shouldn't have any problem getting in the house."

Mac didn't mind. "The cream's on the top of the bookcase in the den," he said. "And while you're there, get my laptop computer. It might come in handy. It's on the kitchen table."

When Mac disappeared into the shower, the two women continued the phone conversation. "Jo, be extra careful when you go over there," Katie warned. "And don't touch the jar of cream. Use rubber gloves and put it into a sealed container."

"I'll treat it like a biological warhead on a Scud missile. And if I can't get there in a couple of hours, I'll call."

"We can meet in the coffee shop." As Katie spoke she looked down at the rumpled bedsheets, not quite ready to have Jo walk into the room where she and Mac had just made love.

Yet as the three of them slid into the green plastic booth two hours later, Katie knew that even though Jo hadn't said a thing, she'd detected the change in their relationship.

"Did you have any trouble at my house?" Mac asked.

Jo grinned. "There aren't too many ways to bust into an underground house short of breaking the window."

"It's reinforced glass," Mac told her.

"Thought so. Someone did make a frontal assault on the entrance, but your Randolph Security System kept them out."

"Underground house?" Katie questioned.

"It's pretty spectacular. You'll have to get him to give you a tour when we've got more time." Jo turned back to Mac. "Your face cream is in a beer cooler in the car—along with the computer. You can take it to the lab after you tell me about your adventures at the morgue. And by the way, I do have one more piece of information you may be interested in."

"Yes?" Mac asked.

"Tom Houston's body was claimed by a brother in New Hampshire."

"He didn't have any brothers."

"That's what I figured," Jo said. "Whoever is behind this whole thing isn't leaving any loose ends."

"Except that we've still got Tom's blood and the tissue sample from the morgue," Katie pointed out. "They may know about the tissue samples by now. But they can't know about the blood."

She and Mac spent the next twenty minutes telling her about their early-morning break-in—by mutual consent glossing over the part about Arnie Beale. After listening to their account, the detective pulled out a piece of paper with the name of the company that had leased the car. The Chrysanthemum Corporation. An odd name, which told them nothing.

"I'll see if I can get a lead on what else the company owns," Jo promised.

"As long as you're looking, you might want to see what you can dig up on the guy who tried to run us over." Mac pushed the hit man's wallet across the table. "But I'm pretty sure he's small potatoes."

Jo slipped the wallet into her purse.

"There's also the woman who owns Genesis," Katie added. "Arnie was supposed to leave the tissue sample there. That's where the face cream came from, too."

The breakfast broke up quickly after that, and Mac and Katie left for R & E. The tissue-sample test, although a bit more complicated than the previous procedures had been completed. There was no surprise in finding that Val tested positive for the virus. Next they introduced the second face-cream jar into the hot lab. This time, the results were the same as before. No virus in the cream.

"I was sure we'd figured it out," Katie muttered.

"Yeah." Mac's expression was thoughtful, as though he were barely listening to her. "Um, why don't you go get us both some coffee while I update my notes." He pulled a small notebook from his pocket and began to write.

Still wrapped in her disappointment, Katie went down the hall to the canteen. When she returned to the lab ten minutes later, she found that Mac had put the notebook down and was leaning over the hot lab. She could see that he was mixing something inside the hood and was having trouble trying to work one-handed.

"What are you doing?" she asked as she set the coffee cups down.

"Trying a little experiment. Come and help me get this sample where I need it, will you?"

What did he want to look at with the electron microscope? Katie wondered. Minutes later the question was answered as an image filled the screen. Katie recognized the same nasty-looking virus structure they'd looked at before. Only now there was something different. The virions appeared to be disintegrating.

They both watched the virus particles.

Katie thought about the limited number of other materials in the sterile environment. "What did you add to it? The face cream?"

"As a matter of fact, yes."

She focused on the screen again, watching the virus protein dissolve. "What in the world made you try that?"

"One of those hunches I get out of the blue sometimes."

Katie looked at him with increased respect. She'd always known Mac McQuade was one of the brightest students in their class at Georgetown. Beyond that, the work he'd been doing over the past few years had sharpened his analytical abilities. What he'd dismissed as a hunch was the kind of intuitive leap that came to truly great medical researchers.

Her hand closed over his, and her voice rose with her excitement. "Not out of the blue. We were both assuming there was some link to the face cream. When it didn't turn out to be the source of the virus, you started thinking in another direction."

His expression was doubtful. "Oh, come on. I was just angry that we'd had Jo break into my house for nothing. And I guess I was remembering you trying to show me your bruises. Only there weren't any."

Katie didn't allow his dismissive words to dampen her enthusiasm. "No, you're like Pasteur when he decided to experiment instead of throwing out a batch of half-dead anthrax virus. What he came up with was the whole theory of immunization."

He laughed. "I don't think this is exactly the same caliber discovery."

She moved in closer and wrapped her arms around his waist. "Mac, a lot of people may be in danger from this virus. And you've just found something that counteracts it."

For a moment neither one of them moved, and she knew that despite what he'd said to her a few hours ago, a special kind of closeness was growing between them. It was the kind of bond they'd had in medical school—two minds on the same wavelength sharing the excitement of new discoveries.

In the next moment, however, he put his hands on her shoulders and moved her gently away. "Don't get too worked up. All we know so far is that some component of the cream dissolves the virions after they're dead. What we need is a live human sample. And I haven't a clue about where we're going to get that."

Katie turned away, as much to hide her reaction to his dismissal as to give herself a chance to think clearly. Tom and Val were dead. Had either one of them passed the illness on to someone else? "Wait a minute. Val talked about another man she was seeing besides Tom. An instructor at the health club where she kept in shape."

"Do you remember his name?"

"Give me a minute, it'll come to me." She pressed her fist against her teeth and nibbled. "Greg something. He works at Body Electric."

"She was intimate with him, too?"

Katie nodded tightly. "I'm sorry, Mac. She wasn't the kind of woman who stuck to one relationship."

His face went hard for a moment. "Well, if he has the virus, I wonder what the chances are he'll agree to cooperate with us?"

"We're not going to know until I go down there and talk to him," Katie said.

"What do you mean, you?"

"Mac, let's face it. Even in the best of circumstances, you tend to be intimidating. Who do you think is more likely to persuade him to cooperate? Or were you planning to kidnap him?"

He considered the proposal for several moments. "Okay, I don't like it, but I'll go along with you—for now."

"Then we'd better call the club and find out what his hours are."

THE BODY ELECTRIC health club was a block and a half off fashionable Wisconsin Avenue—where the rent wasn't quite so high. The next morning, Katie pulled into the small customer parking lot and sat for a moment wondering what was going to happen when she met Greg. Dealing with Val hadn't been much fun. Was her other boyfriend going to be the same way? Worse? Better? Maybe if he was lucky, he wasn't even sick. Which would tell them something about the level of contagion of the virus. Unless Val had been lying about the relationship.

There was no use sitting here speculating, Katie told herself as she climbed out of the car and headed for the entrance. There were simply too many questions she couldn't answer until she talked with Greg. Pushing open one of the heavy frosted-glass doors with a decisive shove, she went inside. The lobby was deserted, but in a surprisingly large room to her right, she could count a dozen men and women working out on stationary bikes, stair-climbing machines, and rowers. Over the speaker system, a Madonna hit set a lively pace.

Katie was looking around for assistance when a young woman in green leotards and a Body Electric T-shirt, came out of the locker room and moved behind the front desk. Her name tag read Tina. "Platinum or regular card?"

"I'm not a member. But I have a few questions."

"If you're interested in joining, I can get Pete to show you around and explain our packages."

"What about Greg? Is he available?"

Tina grimaced. "Greg Scoggins? I don't know what's with him lately. Yeah, he's free right now, but he's supposed to be doing Nautilus training in fifteen minutes. I think he's in the weight room. Down the hall, the second door on your left.''

The weight room was empty except for a short, muscle-bound guy lying on the bench pumping a huge barbell up and down like it was a Tinkertoy.

Katie watched the play of his strong biceps as they flexed and contracted. If you judged a person's health by their physique, he was in great physical shape. But Val had been, too.

''Pardon me. Are you Greg?'' she asked.

''Yeah. What can I do for you?'' After setting down the barbell, he tipped up a plastic bottle of water for a drink, realized it was empty and threw it down disgustedly.

''I understand you might have been dating my sister, Val Caldwell.''

Greg's blond eyebrows knitted together. ''I wouldn't call it dating. She worked out at the club, and we got it together in bed a few times, that's all. Nothing heavy. That babe sure had an itch, and I was glad to scratch it.'' Almost as an afterthought, he added, ''Sorry to hear about her accident.''

Katie tried to keep the look of repugnance off her face. He was putting his relationship with Val in the crudest of terms. But then her sister hadn't had much control over her tongue, either.

Out of the corner of her vision, Katie saw two men enter the room and start their own workout.

''Is there somewhere private we could talk for a few minutes?''

Greg scratched under his left armpit. ''Don't think so. My next appointment's going to be here soon. And I'm booked till closing. Besides, there's really not much I can tell you. Why are you hounding me?'' Without waiting for an answer, he walked past her and dug a bottle of chewable vitamins out of his gym bag. Shaking a half dozen into his hand, he began chomping on them loudly.

"Who the hell took my water?" he mumbled under his breath. When he spotted the discarded container under the bench press, he picked it up, tried to drink from it again, and seemed shocked to find it still empty.

Katie watched him, trying to maintain her professional detachment. From her brief observation of his unguarded language and his disorganized behavior, she'd bet that Gary had the virus. Was she going to be able to reason with him?

Katie glanced over her shoulder and then lowered her voice. "Greg, my sister may have had something contagious."

His blond head whipped around, and a frightened look flashed in his light eyes. "Wha'da'ya' mean? AIDS?"

"No, not AIDS. It's a long story. But I've got to talk to you today. You might be at risk."

He seemed to waver indecisively for a few moments. "Okay. There's a sub shop across Wisconsin. Come on."

As they passed the front desk, Tina called out to him about his next appointment, but he ignored her. Pushing Katie toward the door, he followed her outside without even bothering to change into street clothes.

When the frigid air hit his heated body, he shivered. "Cold."

"It's a long way to the sub shop. Why don't we go sit in my car? It'll be more private."

"Yeah. I'm not hungry anyway."

They were halfway across the parking lot when two long shadows fell across their path. Katie glanced up to find the way blocked by a couple of large, Asian men. Sumo wrestlers in three-piece suits. It wasn't just their size but also the dangerous looks on their faces that sent a stab of fear to the pit of her stomach.

She might have turned and run, but one of the goons clamped a hammer-hard hand on her shoulder.

"Greg, do something!"

"Take your mitts off the lady!" Crouching down, the exercise trainer jabbed at one of the assailants. He got in a couple of quick blows, but he left his back unprotected. A chop to his neck crumpled him like a piece of dry toast.

The thug turned his attention back to Katie, muffling the scream that would have torn from her lips. Frantically she tried to twist from his grasp. But she might as well have been a dove fluttering in an eagle's talons.

The other man opened the door of a yellow van advertising a cleaning service. Then he tossed a still-unconscious Greg onto a pile of laundry bags inside.

As her captor pushed Katie toward the gaping door, his grip loosened for a moment. Katie went limp and tried to slide under his body. He only laughed, scooping her up and dumping her on the laundry bags beside the unconscious Greg. A gun was out of its holster and pointed toward her as his companion started the engine.

The man with the gun jumped in behind her and slammed the door. As they swayed out of the parking lot, he slapped strips of adhesive over her mouth and around her wrists, pulling her arms painfully behind her back while he trussed her like a lamb on the way to market.

Chapter Thirteen

A half block down the street, Mac watched in grim horror as the kidnap vehicle sped away.

"Oh, God! No!" His stainless steel hand clamped the steering wheel so tightly that the hard plastic started to give. With an exclamation that was half curse, half prayer, he switched on the engine and pulled out after the van. He'd thought Katie would be safe enough if he staked out the gym. But he hadn't been prepared for something like this.

It had all happened so damn fast. In a matter of seconds the two big men had whisked Katie and the jock out of sight.

He'd had to stop himself from leaping out of the car and dashing across the street—because a grandstand play could have gotten Katie shot.

Stomach churning up corrosive acid, Mac followed several car lengths behind the van. If only he had a weapon. Or some reinforcements. His eyes flicked to the portable cellular phone on the passenger seat. He needed help. But whom could he call? Certainly not the police. For all he knew, they might be behind the abduction.

What about Jo O'Malley? No, she'd told him she had to take care of some urgent business of her own north of Baltimore. Was there a chance she'd changed her plans? When he reached her on her car phone and told her what had happened, she instantly dropped the other project. But that didn't do him any immediate good.

"Mac. It'll take me an hour to get there."

"I can't wait that long."

"Call me as soon as you know where they're taking her."

"If I can."

ONLY A THIN RIBBON of light sneaking in at the top of a window illuminated the back of the van. Fighting not to gag on the damp, musky smell coming from the laundry bags, Katie struggled to a sitting position and looked around. Both thugs were up front now, and neither one of them was paying any attention to her and Greg. They must be certain there was nothing to worry about.

Mac, she thought. *Did you see what happened? Are you out there following us? Or did they know you were there and get you while I was inside?* The terror of that speculation brought a silent scream bubbling up in her throat.

For long moments it was all she could do to keep the fear from swallowing her whole. Then, she pulled together the tattered shreds of her equanimity. With all her strength, she tried to break the tape that bound her wrists. Still the bonds held as effectively as if they were metal cuffs.

No good. Was there some sharp projection she could use to cut herself loose? In the semidarkness she could see almost nothing. Moving awkwardly, she felt along the side walls of the van and encountered only smooth vinyl. Maybe there were bolts where seats had been removed from the floor. She'd have to dig down with her feet through the bags of laundry to find them.

Through his gag, Greg moaned feebly. The physician in her wanted to find out if he'd been seriously injured. But the realist knew that if she didn't get away, they might both be facing extremely shortened life spans. Besides, with her hands and mouth taped, there really wasn't much she could do for Greg, anyway.

As she continued to dig for a cutting tool, Katie tried to assess the situation. From the stop-and-go traffic, she imagined that they were still on Wisconsin Ave. Where were they headed? And what was waiting for them when they got there?

By the time her mobile prison had come to a halt, Katie's arms and shoulders ached from her struggles and the strained position. One of her captors flung open the door of the van, pulled her out and set her roughly on her feet. It was the one who'd laughed when she tried to get away. He laughed now as her knees gave way, and she slumped against the side of the van.

Greg was still unconscious. The other thug hoisted him over his shoulder as if he were almost weightless.

They were at the loading dock of a warehouse. Before Katie could register any more details, the tape on her ankles was cut. Then she was stumbling inside and down a dimly lighted hallway.

"Why are you doing this?" she tried to mumble through the tape.

The only response she got was a hard twist to her bound wrists that shot a bolt of pain up through her shoulders and brought tears to her eyes.

At the end of a hall, Katie was separated from Greg and ushered through an unmarked door. Inside she was astonished to see a fully equipped doctor's examining room.

With frightening efficiency, her captor cut the tape from her wrists, stripped her down to her bra and panties, and strapped her onto the table.

The room was cold; but that wasn't the only reason goose bumps bloomed on her skin. She had to clamp her teeth together to keep them from chattering. What was her guard

thinking now? She turned her head away from his probing
dark eyes, praying he wouldn't touch her.

He stood with his hands clasped behind his back until a
man in surgical dress—mask, gown and gloves—entered and
issued an order in a foreign language, maybe Japanese. After a quick, subservient bow, the thug filed out, leaving Katie alone with the newcomer. Most of his features were
hidden beneath the paper mask. But she could see his dark
eyes in back of thick lenses. Their sharp interest as he studied her tightened the goose bumps on her arms. Dr. Jekyll.

With sudden terrible insight, Katie knew how Arnie Beale
must have felt strapped down on the table in the autopsy
room. She squirmed against the bonds that held her to the
table but it was impossible to break away.

If her mouth had been free, she might have started
pleading with the doctor. In growing horror, her gaze followed him around the room as he made methodical prepa-
rations for some procedure. Oh Lord. Was he planning to
operate on her? Or something worse—like infect her with
the virus? Katie felt a wave of nausea edging up her throat.

Somehow she had to keep her fear from overwhelming
her. With deep, steadying breaths through her nose she
managed to hold the terror in check.

Dr. Jekyll turned back to her and pressed two fingers
against the side of her throat.

"Congratulations, you look very calm under the circumstances, Dr. Martin. However your pulse is one-eleven," he
said in heavily accented English.

She swallowed.

Reaching to the table behind him, he held up an empty
syringe in his hand. "I will be taking a blood sample and
doing an examination. With your cooperation, the pain will
be minimal. Without, I make no guarantees."

Katie closed her eyes and felt a swab of alcohol and the
jab of a needle in her arm. No, she'd better watch. Strug

gling to keep the breath moving in and out of her lungs, she forced her lids open and watched him fill three vials with her blood.

When he was finished, the doctor opened a panel in the wall, set the blood inside and closed the door.

"We have a very quick test for HDV15. The results will be available in a few moments."

There were all sorts of inferences Katie could make from those simple sentences. He was very familiar with the virus. It even had a name, which ended in a rather high number. Had he discovered that many natural variations? Or had there been that many laboratory trials?

The speculations made her skin break out in a cold sweat against the slick plastic of the table. The sensation grew more pronounced as the doctor's skilled fingers began to poke and probe her body.

MAC STUDIED the windowless facade of the Rockville warehouse, his eyes narrowed to slits. The goons had taken Katie and the unconscious Greg in through a metal door beside the loading dock. Every cell in his body urged him to leap out of the car and charge that door. Except that the odds were even worse now. The place could be full of bruisers, for all he knew. Or there might be an alarm system guarding the door. Getting himself killed or captured wasn't going to save Katie.

Stealth, speed and surprise were his only weapons. Time and miscalculation were his enemies. If he didn't act quickly, if he didn't make the right split-second decision, they might—

Shuddering, he cut off the thought. Instead he pulled the car back onto the road, drove down to the next parking lot and took sixty precious seconds to tell Jo his location. Then he jogged back to the warehouse.

Just as he rounded the corner, one of the thugs who'd captured Katie and the jock came out of the building, got back in the van and drove off. Well, that had to improve the odds, but it didn't alter his plan of attack.

Mac's mind and body were reacting with jungle instincts now. He had switched into a sort of super aware state in which physical details seemed to leap out at him and contingency plans were processed at lightning speed.

No external surveillance system, or they would have picked him up already. He circled the warehouse and decided that a series of rungs fixed to the side of the building and leading to the roof offered the only other feasible way of getting in. Since the accident, climbing had become awkward because he couldn't pull himself up with the artificial hand. The encumbrance hardly slowed him now.

Once he gained the flat gravel roof, the hand became an asset instead of a liability. With the twitch of an internal circuit, he produced a cutting tool. It sliced through one of the large aluminum exhaust ducts like a sharp knife through gelatin.

Moments later he had lowered himself inside to the edge of a dusty second-floor catwalk. Crouching low and moving quietly through the shadows, he studied the layout below. Most of the large building was either empty or being used for storage. In the center was a section where suspended ceilings blocked his view. Since he couldn't spot Katie, he assumed she was in there.

Near him were several roughly partitioned rooms. Some were piled with shipping crates. Thankfully most were empty—of both people and equipment.

He froze as his eyes swept over a canteen with a sink, microwave and tables. One of the goons who'd scooped up Katie was slipping two slices of frozen pizza into the microwave oven.

One-on-one made better odds than Mac had anticipated. Slipping under the balcony rail, he leapt. He would have caught the man squarely in the middle of the back, except that just at the wrong moment, his target turned and saw a body hurtling toward him from above.

KATIE TRIED to close off her mind, tried to endure the examination with cool detachment as if the body tied down on the table belonged to someone else. The ploy was only partially successful.

After Dr. Jekyll was finally finished, he busied himself with some of the equipment in the room. When a buzzer sounded, Katie's body jerked. But the doctor calmly turned and opened the pass-through in the wall again.

She watched him study a computer readout.

"Congratulations again, Dr. Martin. You are in excellent health." Stripping off the mask, cap and gloves, he tossed them into a trash container in the corner.

They were face-to-face now. Hers must be pale and bloodless. His was subtly lined—his nose flat, his lips thin, his eyes darkly intelligent. Under other circumstances she might have called him a good-looking man. Now his most prominent feature was the ice behind his dark eyes. She wanted to turn away; instead she used the opportunity to observe him, her mind memorizing details.

For one thing, he wasn't as calm as he pretended to be. A muscle under his right eye twitched, and she suspected that below the surface of his cool oriental manner, he was holding violent emotions in check. Then there was his age. At first she might have said he was in his late forties. A second glance made her suspect he was older.

"There are some questions I must ask you," he said, his accent becoming more pronounced. With a smooth, sharp motion, he ripped the tape from her mouth.

Katie gasped in pain.

"I've found it's best to get the worst over with first. Wouldn't you agree?"

Katie nodded tightly.

"So let us proceed to the meat of our discussion. You and your sister, the spy."

"What?"

"Val Caldwell. Sent to spy on us. Sent by whom, Dr. Martin? Who is your group working for?"

"Nobody. I—that's crazy."

"Please do not strain my patience. You and Mr. Mc-Quade have been conducting research on HDV15 at Medizone. You've stolen tissue samples from the D.C. morgue. And now you have the good fortune to turn up at the health club when we went to pick up Mr. Scoggins. What else do you know about our plans?"

Katie felt her heart thumping wildly inside her chest. "Nothing."

"Who else knows about the virus?"

She had to protect Jo. Yet telling him nobody else knew would be putting herself and Mac in even more jeopardy. "We've talked to the D.C. police and the Centers for Disease Control in Atlanta."

"Lying to me is taking a great risk," he said sternly. "You and I both know the D.C. police are no problem. And I know you have not made contact with CDC. Besides, you had nothing to send them. We removed all the evidence from Medizone, although I conclude you must be working with the tissue samples from the morgue in another lab. Where?"

The extent of his knowledge and the menace in his voice made her blood turn to ice, yet she looked at him defiantly.

"We don't have another lab."

He reached out and stroked her cheek in a parody of an affectionate caress, then brought his hand down in a stinging slap that made her eyes water.

"You're either very foolish or very brave to defy me, Dr. Martin. But I must know about this spy ring of yours. You weren't carrying any identification when you came to talk to Mr. Scoggins. Wouldn't you call that suspicious? Are you the brains behind the operations? Is it Mr. McQuade? Or was Mr. Houston in charge?"

"There is no spy ring." She prayed her voice didn't betray her fear. She prayed she had more time than she thought.

"Where is your accomplice, Mr. McQuade?"

Katie tried to hide the relief that flooded through her. He'd just told her that they didn't have Mac. Unless he was trying to trick her.

"I don't know."

He touched her cheek again, and she cringed. This time, he didn't slap her. But the implied threat hung between them in the chilly air.

"Your answers are remarkably monotonous, Dr. Martin. But you're not going to destroy plans that have taken years to come to fruition. I have a way to make you talk. You've seen what HDV15 does to the human brain. I can arrange to have you experience the disorientation and the mental deterioration firsthand. Believe me, once you have the virus, it will only be a matter of time before you start to babble out answers to any questions I put to you. Suppose I give you a little bit of time to think about it?"

THE BIG MAN'S REFLEXES were excellent. The pistol was out of his pocket before Mac hit him. As he lifted his arm to aim and fire, Mac acted with a well-honed sense of self-preservation. His alloyed hand came down with the force of a hammer on the thug's skull, sending him to the floor like a block of concrete sinking in a lake. Kneeling, Mac made a quick examination. The guy wouldn't be getting up soon. Mac picked up the gun and waited tensely to find out if anyone had heard the brief scuffle. Apparently no one else was aware of an intruder in the building.

Cautiously Mac pressed his ear against the door and listened. One down. How many more were there? All he could hear was the throbbing of equipment somewhere. Opening the door, he stepped into the corridor and began making his way toward the area that had been hidden from the balcony.

A guard sat at a battered metal desk where two corridors crossed. Luckily he had his back to Mac, who was able to take care of him with a sharp karate chop to the neck. After binding his hands and feet and gagging him with tape from his own desk drawer, he dragged him into an empty room and closed the door again. Two down. He was leaving a trail of unconscious bodies around the warehouse. Sooner or later they were going to come back to life and haunt him.

"WELL, DR. MARTIN, your time is up, I'm afraid. What is your decision? Would you like to experience the virus that drove your sister and Mr. Houston mad?"

"I'll—I'll trade you information."

His eyes flicked to the straps that held her arms and legs. "You're in no position to bargain."

Katie fought the swell of fear that threatened to choke off her breath. "At least tell me what's going on. What does the face cream have to do with this?"

"Ah yes, the face cream." He smiled with satisfaction. "One of my more profitable discoveries. It's a big seller at Genesis because it restores youth and beauty by cleansing the cells of destructive elements. Moreover, in the case of someone with the virus, it slows the course of the infection."

"I don't understand. Val was using it. And she was very sick."

"I assume she had to ration her stolen supply sparingly. She didn't have enough to be totally effective."

"Why are you doing all this?"

"To right an old wrong," he snapped, his eyes boring into her. "But we're wasting time, Dr. Martin. It's my turn to ask the questions. How long have you known your sister was infected? Where can we find Mr. McQuade?" He raised the hand with the hypodermic and held it in front of Katie's face.

"Right here, pal." Mac slammed the door open and strode into the room. It took less than a second for him to comprehend the scene and point the gun at the doctor's midsection. "Drop the syringe and back away from her—or you're dead."

Dr. Jekyll's eyes flicked from Mac's grim face to the gun. The hypodermic slipped through his fingers and clattered to the floor.

Katie stared at Mac, trying to absorb the sudden shift in reality. "Katie." His smoky eyes locked with hers, and she saw relief, outrage, anger. Then his gaze swept down her body, taking in her state of undress and the straps around her arms and legs.

"What did that bastard do to you?" He snapped his head toward the doctor cowering in the corner.

She tried to reassure him, but she could feel tears welling up in her eyes. She struggled to hold them back. With her hands bound, there was no chance to wipe them away.

"Hang on. We're getting you out of here."

He was stepping toward her, the gun still pointed at Dr. Jekyll, when she heard the sliding panel to her right open again.

"Mac, watch out. There's someone on the other side of the wall." The only gesture she could make was to swing her head frantically toward the opening to alert him to the danger. A second later, it was all too obvious.

There was an ominous hissing sound from behind the sliding door, as if a cage full of snakes had just awakened. But it wasn't an animal threat. In the next second, a white cloud of choking vapor spurted into the room.

As the mist touched her face, Katie's eyes began to sting, and she started to cough. Mac and the doctor were coughing, too.

Poison gas? Would they kill one of their own people to prevent a captive from escaping?

Katie tried to hold her breath. But it was too late. She'd taken in some already.

The noxious mist filled the little room, obscuring the shapes of people and objects. Katie sensed Mac bending over her, fumbling frantically with the strap that held her right wrist. A blade sliced through the restraint, nicking her flesh, and she gasped, taking in more of the contaminated air.

The indrawn breath set off a coughing fit.

Above her, Mac had also started choking. That was when she realized she was only hearing the two of them in the little room now. "The doctor," she gasped. "Gone."

Mac had been between Dr. Jekyll and the door. Had her captor somehow slipped past? Or was there a bigger panel in the wall—one that could serve as an emergency exit?

Katie could tell that Mac was trying to work more quickly—without nicking her again. As he reached for the hand that was still bound, he inserted his finger under the strap before he cut.

Both arms were free. Katie tried to bring her hands together so she could rub some circulation into her numb wrists, but her muscles didn't respond to her mental commands.

Her vision was beginning to blur. Above her, Mac's face wavered—a friendly spirit come to watch over her in the poison mist. Like the last grains of sand sliding through the funnel of an hourglass, she could feel her grip on consciousness sliding away. Closing her eyes, she sank back heavily against the padded surface of the examining table.

"Don't conk out on me, Button." Mac's voice was urgent as he moved to the end of the table and began to work on her feet. Dimly she sensed that she was free. Yet there was no way she could lift her leaden limbs now.

Mac hauled her up and tried to set her on her feet. When they hit the ground, her knees gave way.

"Sleep," she murmured.

"Not yet." Coughing as if his lungs would burst, Mac hoisted her over his shoulder and staggered like a drunken sailor into the hall.

"Breathe," he gasped, between his own shaky gulps of air. Swaying, he helped her stand against the wall.

Katie obeyed. Still she felt as if her head were stuffed with mattress ticking. Why didn't Mac just let her sink to the floor so she could sleep? Why didn't he give her a blanket so she wouldn't be so cold?

His hands gripped her bare shoulder, shaking her. One was flesh, the other cold metal. "Katie, I came in from the roof. You've got to tell me how to get out of here. Quick!"

"Umm..."

A stinging slap to her cheek brought her eyes popping open, and she cringed away. "No, please. Don't do it again."

His features were pinched as they swam into focus above hers. "Come on, Katie. I know you breathed in more of that stuff than I did. But you've got to tell me how to get you out of here," Mac repeated urgently.

The shock treatment worked. Mac's face solidified above hers. Her brain was functioning again, at least on a basic level. Straining to clear the fog from her head, she tried to reverse the route she'd taken earlier. "Right, I think."

They both began to move down the hall. To her surprise, she found that her legs were working fairly well. So was her mind. There was something important they were both forgetting.

"Wait. What about Greg?" she gasped as they approached the juncture in the hall where the two captives had been separated.

"Damn! I wasn't thinking about him. Where in the hell did they put him?"

She pointed. "In there. At least they took him through that door when they separated us."

The door led to a room that could have been transported straight from Georgetown Medical Center—except that there were no windows.

Greg, still wearing his shorts and T-shirt, was just climbing out of a bed with metal rails along the sides. Canvas restraints hung around his wrists like oversize bracelets. He backed away when he saw Mac.

"Hey, man, I was just mindin' my own business talking to that broad about her sister. First you conk me on the bean. Then you stick me with needles. Why are you doin' me like this?"

Mac jerked his head toward Katie. "I'm with the good guys. I've already sprung the 'broad.' You want to come with us?"

"You betcha."

A pair of folded pajamas lay across the chair. Mac grabbed the striped top and thrust it toward Katie. As they fled down the hall, she struggled to fit her arms into the sleeves. Mac slowed his pace to hers.

"Are you all right?"

"I will be as soon as we get out of here."

He put her in front of him, and she knew he was intent on shielding her from whatever danger might be creeping up behind them. Greg brought up the rear. But for some reason he wasn't keeping pace with them.

"Hurry up." Mac turned to urge the exercise instructor on.

"Got a cramp, man." Greg leaned down to massage his thigh.

Their luck ran out as they reached the exit. Mac was still trying to urge Greg on when the door opened and the other sumo wrestler stepped back into the building. For a split second he goggled at the two escaping prisoners and an armed escort. Then, with a whir of motion, he pulled a gun from a holster under his arm and aimed it at Katie's midsection.

"Drop your weapon and hold it right there or your girlfriend gets it."

Chapter Fourteen

With a vivid curse, Mac let the pistol slip from his fingers.

"All right. Now move back down the hall," the big man ordered, flicking the gun.

Greg balled his fist and made a growling sound. Katie put a restraining hand on his arm. "We can't do anything now."

"No talking!" the thug bellowed. "We're gonna find out why you're not back where you belong."

Katie had begun to turn around, when a flicker of movement in back of their captor made her heart jump in her chest. Another figure had crept up stealthily behind him. It was Cameron Randolph, Jo's husband.

"Oh, Lord, another one," Greg moaned and pointed.

The man with the gun half turned. There was a dull whoosh, and he crumpled to the ground like a marionette whose strings had suddenly been cut.

Cam stood over him holding a peculiar-looking handgun.

"Thank God! But, Cam, what are you doing here?" Katie exclaimed.

"I met Jo at Security Mall. We got here about ten minutes ago and were evaluating the situation." He gestured toward the man on the floor. "When we saw him come in, I figured I'd better follow."

"Thank God you did," Katie said.

Mac stooped to reclaim his borrowed weapon. "Let's get out of here. No telling how many hornets are left in the nest."

Katie took Greg by the arm. The health instructor wrenched out of her grasp and stampeded forward. Dropping to his knees, he started pounding the unconscious thug with balled fists. "You bastard. You're not so tough without your gun."

Cam and Mac tried to pull him up. Katie had more success with words. "If we don't get out of here, the others may come back and strap you in bed again."

Greg looked at her like a little boy who'd been caught punching out a buddy on the playground. "Strap me in bed again?"

"Come on. It won't happen if we get the hell out of here." Mac grabbed the health instructor's arm and jerked him to his feet.

As they left the building, Cam pulled a small box from his pocket and set it on the floor at the edge of the door.

The motley group that stumbled into the parking lot was met by a tense-looking Jo O'Malley who popped out from behind one of the cars, gun drawn.

"I told you to stay in the car," Cam reminded her.

"You're over my time limit." She turned to take in Katie's scant attire and her deathly white face. "Honey, are you all right?"

"Yes."

"We'll fill you in later. I want to get out of here before somebody else bursts through the door," Mac grated.

"The portable EMP unit I brought along will stop them for a while," Cam told him, referring to one of the devices he'd invented.

When Mac raised an eyebrow, he continued, "It generates electrical waves that disrupt brain activity. Anybody who gets near it is going to get dizzy and pass out."

"Glad you're on our side," Mac murmured.

Even with that extra measure of safety, the group hurried across the blacktop and around the corner where Jo and Cam had parked. As Cam opened the door, Mac gestured toward Gary. "This is Val's former boyfriend. Greg Scoggins."

"Pleased ta meetja," the jock mumbled, extending a large hand, which was ignored by both Cam and Jo.

"Can you take him with you?" Mac continued. "He needs to go to a medical facility that you can trust," he added in a lowered voice.

Still, Greg picked up the key words. "No! No more doctors." The exercise instructor's eyes bulged, and he cringed away from the open car door.

He had just turned to run when Cam raised his pistol and fired. Like the thug before him, Greg slumped to the ground.

"What is that, a tranquilizer?" Mac asked.

"Same idea. But it's not invasive. It uses electronics." As he spoke, he was already folding the unconscious man into the back of his car.

Katie looked around for Mac's car. "Do we need a ride, too?"

"We're in the next parking lot." Mac pointed down the street.

"What happened in there?" Jo asked, her voice strained as she twisted around in her seat to look at her friend.

Katie knew she had to say something to reassure her. "They have a fully equipped examining room inside," she told her. "A man dressed as a doctor took a blood sample from me and did a physical. He was questioning me when

Mac burst in." She got the explanation out all right, but the little speech ended with a shudder.

Mac's arm tightened on her shoulder. "Then someone flooded the exam room with gas," he took up the story. "The doctor got away."

"Let's get out of here," Katie added in a weak voice.

Jo nodded in agreement. "I think I know where we can stash the patient."

"Thanks. We'll get back in touch with you when Katie's rested." Mac looked at Jo. "Wherever you're taking Greg, make sure the staff avoids any communicable contact."

"Got it."

Jo looked as if she wanted to say something more. Instead she squeezed Katie's shoulder before her friend exited the car. "We'll talk later," she said.

When they were alone, Mac pulled Katie into his arms for a quick thankful hug. "Are you really okay?" he asked urgently.

"Yes." She clung to him tightly. "Mac, he was so creepy. He kept insisting Val was some kind of spy, and that you and I were in on it."

"What?"

"I know it's crazy."

Mac started the car, accelerated rapidly, and zoomed down the road in the opposite direction from the warehouse. Once they were out of the industrial park, he slowed to the speed limit, and Katie knew he was trying not to call attention to the car. He didn't speak until they put several miles between themselves and the danger.

"I didn't like slapping you."

"Oh, Mac, I know. But you didn't have any choice. I was really spacey from that gas." Knowing he needed reassuring, she squeezed his arm hard for a moment, and he seemed to accept the gesture. Yet now that the ordeal was over, she couldn't keep up any sort of front for long. As Mac drove

toward the motel, she pressed her shoulders into the seat so
she'd feel the connection with something solid. Burying her
hands in the oversize pajama sleeves, she closed her eyes and
prayed that Mac wouldn't ask her any more questions for a
while. She'd always had a pretty good idea of who she was
and what she believed in. Dr. Jekyll had called all that into
doubt. Maybe now, if she didn't have to talk about what had
happened to her, she could hold herself together.

Mac seemed to understand her need for privacy, because
he drove in silence. When they pulled up in front of their
room, she looked down at the pajama top. "I'm glad I don't
have to walk through a lobby."

"Let me unlock the door before you get out."

When Katie stepped into the room, she headed straight
for the dresser where she pulled out some underwear and a
comfortable cotton shift. "I need to wash that place off."

"Do you want me to bring you something to eat?"

"Not now." Before he could say anything else, she
stepped into the bathroom and pulled the door shut behind
her.

Mac sat in one of the wooden armchairs by the window,
listening to the running water, fighting the impulse to follow Katie into the bathroom, pull her out of the shower and
hang on to her—dripping wet and naked. He wanted to be
close to her. Physically, if that was the only thing she could
give him right now. Or maybe she couldn't even give him
that. God, he never should have let her out of his sight. If
he'd stayed by her side, none of this would have happened.

And now she was hurting. All the way back in the car,
she'd been hiding behind her closed eyelids. And her dis-
appearing act into the shower had just been an extension of
her withdrawal.

Metal fingers gouged through the wood of the chair arm.
He couldn't let her clam up like this. Not when she needed
him. Even if she wasn't willing to admit it.

He tried to get control of his thoughts, but the horror show in the examination room blazed onto the screen of his mind. Katie. Nearly naked and looking terrified. Strapped down on a table with a fiendish doctor hovering over her. Dr. Jekyll, she'd called him. He'd had her in his clutches for almost an hour. What the hell had he been doing all that time? The question sent his imagination into lunar orbit.

Yet, he didn't have the right to make her tell him. Not when he'd walked out on her eight years ago without an explanation. Not when he still couldn't say the things he knew she wanted to hear.

It was then that the irony of the situation hit him. After all these years of shutting people out, the shoe was on the other foot, and he didn't know whether he could cope with the pinching sensation.

When he finally heard Katie's hand touch the doorknob, his whole body jerked. Unclenching his hand from the splintered chair, he struggled to make his expression casual as she opened the door. Despite the hot shower, her face was still pale, and she looked as if she'd shatter if she moved too fast.

"Feeling better?"

"I guess." She walked across to the table under the window and stood fingering the room service menu.

"Hungry now?"

"I—no."

"Katie, for God's sake, stop it!"

"Stop what?"

"You've got to talk to someone about what happened. It might as well be me."

When she didn't reply, he forced himself to continue. "I've got a pretty vivid imagination, you know. You were tied up—in your underwear. And all he did was give you a physical examination?"

"He hit me once when he thought I was lying. Mostly it was just a very impersonal going over," she clipped out. "At least he wasn't interested in my body."

Mac let out the breath he'd been holding.

"The physical part wasn't the worst," she said in a low voice.

Had he detected a tiny chink in the armor Katie had donned? Was it safe to try and pry it wider?

Safe or not, it couldn't possibly be worse than the defeated look on her face now. "Whatever happened, don't shut me out. Let me help you deal with it." Levering himself out of the chair, he crossed to where she stood and folded her into his arms. For just a moment she stiffened. Then, with a tiny sound that was half sigh, half sob, she turned and slumped against him.

"I want to help you. Please. Don't be afraid to need someone."

She pressed her head against his chest, and he could feel the beat of his heart thumping against her cheek. After a while, he lifted her up in his arms and sat down again, pulling her with him into his lap and cradling her protectively. But he didn't push her to talk.

Long moments later she began on her own. "Mac, I was so scared of him."

"Anybody would have been."

"He was a—contradiction. Unpredictable. All cool and collected on the outside. But underneath, he was like a volcano ready to erupt if I didn't give him what he wanted. That was terrifying."

"What did he want?"

"Information," she said, the word muffled by his shirt.

He felt her suck in a deep breath and let it out in a rush "Mac, he was going to inject me with the virus if I didn' talk. He was standing over me with the hypodermic wher you came in." Her voice broke, and she started to shiver violently.

"That bastard. I should have shot him when I had the chance." The words were fierce, but he held her tenderly, rocking her in his arms, kissing her hair and her neck, giving her all the comfort he could.

After a few minutes, she stopped crying, but she kept her face hidden against his chest. "The whole time I was in the shower wondering how I was going to face you, I kept thinking about *No Exit*—you know, that movie where the man and two women are locked in a hotel room in hell."

"Yeah. By Sartre. We saw it at an arts festival on campus."

"Remember the scene where you find out the guy went to hell for betraying his friends, because he was afraid of being tortured?"

"Katie, stop it! You haven't done anything to be ashamed of."

"I was going to try to lie to Dr. Jekyll, to stall for time. But eventually I would have told him where we were hiding out."

"So? I wasn't there."

"I know what the virus did to Val and Tom. I didn't want that injection."

"Katie, don't beat yourself like this. You were in an impossible situation. This isn't the Geneva convention where you're only supposed to give your name, rank and serial number. Think about those captured pilots on TV during the Gulf War. They were spouting false confessions to save themselves. That's what you have to do when the other guy isn't playing by the rules. You would have been crazy not to give him what he wanted if that was your only alternative."

"*You* wouldn't have."

He lifted his head and stared down at her. "Who do you think I am, James Bond? The right threat can make anybody talk."

"I know you, Mac. You would have called his bluff. And if he'd injected you with the virus, you would have kept your mouth shut and hoped you could get away so you could come up with a cure."

"Oh, come on. I honestly don't know what I would have done. Anyway the important thing is that we got out of there before anything serious happened."

She nodded against his shirt. This time, he felt an elusive difference in the way her cheek moved against him and the way her body shifted in his arms. When he reached to tip her face toward his, he found she was looking at him expectantly.

"Mac, I need you. Make me feel whole again."

"Ah, Katie."

Her hands went to the back of his head, pulling his face down to hers. Then she was taking his mouth with the same hunger and demand he felt.

Between hard, urgent kisses, words tumbled from their lips.

"Mac, it was horrible."

"I know, honey. I know."

"I didn't want to talk about it. But you were right. I needed to."

"I couldn't let you do that to yourself. It's my fault he got you in the first place. I never should have let you go into the health club alone."

"No. I wanted to do it. You don't have anything to be sorry for." She stopped his protest with a fervent kiss.

He stood, crossed the few feet to the bed with her in his arms, and followed her down to the yielding surface of the mattress. Even before they were prone, they were locked in stormy passion, kissing wildly, fumbling with each other's clothing, trying to get more of each other, all of each other—everything that a man and a woman could give. And there was no way to know which of them needed the other more.

IT WAS LATER in the afternoon before either one of them wanted to stir.

"Think you could eat now?" Mac asked.

"I have the feeling you're hungry."

"Will you be okay if I go get us something?"

"I'm fine."

While Mac was gone, Katie got dressed and made the bed. Feeling restless, she unfolded the complimentary *Washington Post* the motel had left at the front door. At least she could make sure their visit to the morgue hadn't been reported. There was nothing in the Metro section about stolen brain tissue or a courier found strapped to one of the autopsy tables. However she wasn't able to put the section aside without reading the lead story. It was about George Wright, president of Wright Chemical Corporation, who had murdered both himself and his wife, Helen Austin-Wright, in their Georgetown home. Friends had been shocked to hear about the tragedy, although a number of Wright's colleagues said that he'd been worried about a buyout of the company's stock.

So much violence in the world, Katie thought with a shudder. The name Helen Austin-Wright plucked at some string of memory, but she wasn't able to place the woman.

When Mac came in, she piled up the paper and set it on the floor.

"Anything interesting?"

"Nothing about our unauthorized visit to the morgue."

"I didn't think there would be. They'd want to keep it quiet. Whoever *they* are."

Katie murmured her agreement as she watched Mac set their milk shakes, burgers and french fries on the table. A little while ago, they'd both been swept up in a firestorm of desire. Yet what exactly did she say to him now? she wondered. Thank you for being there when I needed you? Does your making love to me with all that passion change anything you said yesterday? Specifically the part about our not having a future together? She wasn't about to ask that kind of question.

"I made yours a gourmet burger—with lettuce and tomato," Mac said with a grin.

"Don't worry about me, I can live for extended stretches on carryout if I have to."

"I remember, back in the bad old days." Mac ended the sentence abruptly and began unwrapping his cheeseburger.

Katie cast around for a less personal topic. "I was thinking back over the scene with Dr. Jekyll," she murmured.

"Umm?"

As Mac's dark eyes focused on her face, she wished she had kept her mouth full of hamburger. "I'm not going off on another guilt trip."

"Good."

"I was trying to make sense of some things he told me."

"I'm surprised he told you anything."

"I offered to trade him information."

"Uh-huh. So even while he had you at a horrible disadvantage, you were plucky enough to manipulate him."

"I was just—"

"Stop denying your effectiveness and eat your lunch," he said, taking a healthy bite of his own sandwich.

The order coaxed a tentative smile from her lips. But after she'd taken a couple of bites, her expression sobered again. "Maybe he was bluffing, but he sounded as if he has an informant at the CDC."

"What?"

"I wanted him to think we'd been talking with them. But he told me very emphatically that the CDC hadn't gotten anything from us. Which must mean our sample hadn't arrived yet. And when it does, somebody will probably scoop it up."

"Damn! Every time we make a move, we're blocked."

"Do you know anyone down there personally?"

Mac quickly came back with a name. "Perry Greenfield."

"Is he someone you can trust?"

"He used to be at Medizone."

"Maybe if we contact him and explain some of what's going on, he can help."

Mac pulled a notebook out of his pocket. "I think we'd better start making a list."

While he finished scribbling several notes, Katie finished her burger.

"Okay. What else do you have?" he asked.

"Dr. Jekyll told me some interesting things about the face cream. It restores cells—and in the case of the virus, it slows the course of the disease."

"That explains what we saw in the lab yesterday, but why didn't it work for your sister?"

"He said she'd stolen her supply, and she didn't have enough to do the trick."

"I wonder what the critical dosage is. Maybe we have enough left to start treating Greg."

"But we're going to run out. Then what?" Katie folded down the end of her plastic straw. "Maybe I could pretend I'm a customer and go buy some from Genesis."

"Forget it! If those goons who scooped you up at the health club knew what you looked like, so will the staff at the beauty shop. I'm sure as hell not going to risk your getting into their clutches again."

For several minutes Katie picked at her french fries, and Mac worked on his second burger. When he was finished, he wadded up the wrapper. "Maybe we can't do anything for Greg, anyway. Once a brain cell is dead, you can't bring it back to life. It may be that you can only prevent deterioration—not reverse it."

"I hope for Greg's sake you're wrong."

Mac nodded. They were both silent for several minutes.

To keep from thinking about Greg, Katie began going over the facts they'd assembled. She put down her milk shake. "Remember how we thought the face cream might have been accidentally contaminated before it was shipped to the U.S.?"

"Uh-huh."

"The way Dr. Jekyll was talking makes me think disseminating the virus is a deliberate plot. But who's the target?"

"Well, he admitted there's a connection to the face cream. And that leads back to Genesis."

"Okay. Then let's get at it from a different angle. Who uses the face cream?"

"Women who go to Genesis. Women who can afford to pay high prices for an exclusive beauty product that will make them look young," Mac answered. "And they don't just run in to the salon for a quick haircut at lunch time, do they?"

"No. Val told me they're likely to spend the day, getting the works."

"So they're having all sorts of treatments. What if while they're there getting beautified and pampered, they also get infected with the virus?" Mac asked. "You wouldn't have to use a hypodermic. Any instrument that broke the skin would do it. It could even look like an accident."

"But why? Why give a bunch of women a deadly disease and then keep them from getting sick?"

He shrugged. "I don't have a clue."

"Dr. Jekyll told me he was avenging an old wrong."

"On a bunch of society women who don't have anything better to do than spend their days getting pampered? Maybe they didn't invite him to their debutante balls."

"Debutante balls! It's got to be more significant than that. He's bought off the D.C. police and someone at the CDC to make sure the plot isn't uncovered. And he's so sure that what he's doing is important that he thinks someone has loosed a team of spies on him." Katie was trying to fit all the known facts into some kind of theory when the phone rang. Mac picked up the receiver.

"Hello?" he asked cautiously. A moment later he was smiling. "It's Jo, she wants to know if we're ready to receive company—and some information."

"Sure. How long will it take her to get here?"

"A couple of seconds. She's in the parking lot."

Katie got up and opened the door just as Jo raised her hand to knock. The detective stepped inside and gave her friend a brief but comprehensive inspection.

"Do I pass muster?" Katie asked, a bit more sharply than she'd intended.

"You're looking a heck of a lot more chipper than the last time I saw you. How are you feeling?"

"Much better."

Jo set down the briefcase she'd been carrying. "Honey, I have a pretty good idea of what you went through. So if you need someone else to—"

"How could you know what it was like?" Katie demanded.

"Because something pretty similar happened to me. Before I met you, a nut kidnapped me and held me captive for a couple of days. I spent most of that time trying to figure out how to keep him from killing me."

Katie gasped. "Oh, Jo, I didn't know."

"I don't talk about it much. I guess I thought I'd put it behind me. But when Mac told me those goons had you, I started flashing back to it."

"I'm sorry."

"Not your fault."

"A couple of days," Katie murmured. "It must have been horrible. How—how did you get through it?"

"At first I felt so alone and scared, I didn't think I was going to make it. Then I started pretending Cam was there with me, giving me the strength to match wits with the guy."

Katie reached for her hand and squeezed it. "That's how I felt. Isolated. Like I wasn't strong enough to stand up to him when he started asking me questions."

Mac who had quietly been clearing away the remains of their lunch, stopped moving. For a moment there was an awkward silence. Then Katie reached out, grabbed his hand, and stood holding on to him and Jo.

"Thank you both," she said, resting her head against Mac's shoulder for a moment. Then she cleared her throat. "We've got a lot of work to do."

Mac pulled up another chair, and they all sat down.

"How's Greg?" Katie asked.

"Worse."

Mac nodded tightly.

"He's at a very discreet private sanitarium—Tucker Manor, in Clarksville."

"I've heard of the place," Katie said. "You did make sure they know he has a contagious, fatal disease that's causing his dementia?"

"I was very clear about his being infected with a virus," Jo assured her. "And I took a blood sample to R & E. What's going to happen to him?"

"We don't know. We're hoping treatment will make a difference—and that we can start working on a cure for the infection."

"Dr. Jekyll must already have a cure," Katie muttered. "Otherwise it would be too dangerous to have the stuff around."

"Maybe somebody has to go back to that warehouse," Mac suggested.

"They've probably cleared out by now," Jo said. "Still, we might as well drop an anonymous tip to the Montgomery County Police that something illegal's going on there."

Mac nodded toward the briefcase. "What have you got for us?"

"A folder on Jade Nishizaka, the owner of Genesis."

"You found out who it was!" Katie exclaimed.

"Yeah, but I don't have much on her. It looks as if she went to a lot of trouble to cover her tracks." Jo stopped and looked uncomfortable. "I don't like dropping this whole thing in your lap. But I promised Laura Roswell that when Mickey Donaldson got out of jail, I'd be available to protect his wife. He made some nasty threats against her and the baby when she instituted divorce proceedings. Now he's back and acting psycho again, and she doesn't have the money to pay someone else for protection. Are you guys going to feel like I'm abandoning you if I leave the stuff and cut out?"

"Of course not," Katie assured her. "You can't just bow out of something like that."

"I can handle things," Mac assured her.

"You're not going to do anything risky without consulting me," Jo clarified.

"If there's an emergency, we'll call you," Katie assured her.

After the detective had left, Katie picked up the folder.

"What does it say about the Nishizaka woman?" Mac asked.

"Not a lot. She's been in D.C. for about three years. Before that she was the president of a Japanese pharmaceutical company."

"From pharmaceuticals to running an exclusive beauty salon. Isn't that a little unusual?" Mac asked.

"It's not illegal. And her record in the States is absolutely clean. She hasn't even gotten a traffic ticket." Katie scanned the few paragraphs. "Her driver's license listed her date of birth as June 15, 1932. From what Val told me, I expected her to be younger."

"She must be well-preserved. Maybe she uses her own face cream," Mac tossed in.

"Of course! Why not?" Katie went back to the meager information. "She was born in some place called Onodo. But that's about all there is. Her marital status is unknown. So is her citizenship and her education. She's really covered her tracks, which you might want to do if you were up to something illegal. Or masterminding some sort of revenge scheme."

Chapter Fifteen

"It still doesn't make a lot of sense," Mac muttered. "We're only talking about getting revenge against a bunch of women who happen to patronize a certain exclusive beauty salon."

"No, Mac," Katie contradicted as a sudden insight struck her. "It's not just a bunch of women."

"What do you mean?"

"You remember when you thought you might have the virus? You were trying to protect me. And when I thought I had it, I wanted to make sure I didn't give it to you."

They both went very still for a moment as they looked into each other's eyes. When Mac didn't speak, Katie continued. "Think about the situation with the Genesis patrons. You give them a deadly disease and prevent them from developing symptoms. But they're all carriers."

Mac was nodding as he followed Katie's logic. "The virus is spread through sexual contact. You wouldn't just be giving it to the women, you'd be passing it on to their husbands, too. But the husbands aren't using the face cream. So they're the ones who get sick. Like Tom and Greg."

"And the husbands can afford to send their wives to a very expensive salon," Katie murmured.

"We don't have any names," Mac pointed out. "But, my God, we've got to assume we're talking about individuals at the very highest levels of government and industry. If men like that started going berserk the way Tom did, it could do all kinds of damage."

Katie felt the top of her scalp prickle. "I think I've just had one of your intuitive leaps." Leaning over, she fished up the Metro section of the *Washington Post* and spread it out across the table. "Maybe we're talking about something like this," she whispered as she pointed to the story about Helen Austin-Wright and her husband.

Mac scanned the text. "Was she a patron of Genesis?"

"When I read the story, her name sounded familiar. I think Val bragged about doing her hair. But I'm not absolutely sure."

"I believe we need a list of Genesis customers," Mac said.

"Is that our top priority? Or is it making sure the CDC gets the sample?"

"Both."

Mac took his laptop computer out of the bottom dresser drawer where he'd stashed it. Over one of the government networks, he sent an urgent message to Perry Greenfield at the CDC, telling him there might be a foreign agent intercepting information at the facility. Next he alerted him to a package arriving from R & E labs, summarized what they knew about the virus, and asked if any other cases had been reported. He also asked if the agency could order autopsy results from George Wright and Helen Wright.

"Well, that's all we can do for the moment on that end." Katie picked up the folder on Jade Nishizaka again and began to scan the information. "Wait a minute, there's something I didn't notice before. Something strange. Val told me Genesis had plans to expand nationwide. Yet according to this, they're not even renewing their lease on the D.C. salon. In fact, it's up next month."

"Maybe they're moving to a new location."

"Maybe . . ." Katie murmured doubtfully.

"Or maybe they're getting ready to skip town—"

"Because they'll be all done with their revenge business," Mac finished.

Katie nodded.

"We've got to find out what they're up to," Mac muttered. "Fast."

"Wait a minute," Katie objected. "Don't you think it's time to call in the authorities? I know the D.C. police are out. What about the FBI?"

"And tell them what?" Mac asked. "We've been running around for days. All we have at this point is a mysterious virus, some allegations we can't prove, and a mass of speculation. I'll bet that if the FBI broke into the warehouse, they'd find every trace of that hospital setup had vanished. Besides there's no proof that the virus is connected with Genesis. We've got to take them something concrete."

Katie sighed, bowing to the inevitable. "You're right. I guess that means getting in there tonight when the place is closed."

"After what's just happened to you—"

"I need to prove to myself that I haven't turned into a quivering mass of gelatin," Katie finished the sentence, her fists anchored on her hips.

"You don't have to prove anything. You're a research physician, not a spy."

"That's a good line, coming from the man who's devoted the past eight years to proving himself."

He scowled. "That's different."

"Not really. And if you can't see why not, there's no use discussing it."

Instead of answering, Mac began to put the computer away.

He hadn't gotten any better at dealing with a direct confrontation between them, Katie decided. Moreover, she was too weary to go another ten rounds with him at the moment. "I need some sleep," she told him. "Set the alarm for nine."

Turning her back on Mac, she pulled off her shoes and dress and slipped under the covers. She was going to roll on her side away from him, but she changed her mind and lay on her back watching him stand in the middle of the room looking from her to the other bed.

She'd reached the point where there was absolutely nothing left to lose with this man. But he was hers for now—if she didn't use his aloof tactics when the going got rough. "If you're thinking of sleeping by yourself, it's too late for that," she murmured. "At least if we can't have a civil conversation, you can hug me. A hug would be good fortification for the evening's activities."

She heard him mutter something she couldn't quite catch. For several moments he continued to hesitate. Then he began to unbutton his shirt.

"Probably you want to rest your wrist before we go out," she said.

He didn't comment. Instead, after he'd stripped down to his underwear, he unfastened the high-tech hand and set it on the dresser. Their eyes held for several heartbeats. Then he sighed and slipped into the bed. At first he lay stiffly beside her. But when she snuggled up to his lean body, he wrapped his arms around her. Pressing her face against his chest, she closed her eyes and tried to absorb the essence of Mac McQuade. After this episode in their lives was all over, it might be all that was left to keep her warm.

EVENING FOUND THEM back in D.C., both dressed in new jeans and casual dark shirts, heading for Genesis. It was in a seven-story structure in a fashionable uptown stretch of Connecticut Avenue. A number of the older buildings along the broad avenue had been torn down in the sixties and seventies to make way for boxy yellow brick apartments. But Genesis was housed in a vintage art-deco structure that had been carefully restored to its former glory. Mac drove around the block, sizing up the possibilities for illegal entry. "The roof worked last time I staged a break-in," he mused. "Why don't we try it again?" Katie squeezed Mac's hand. The last time he'd staged a break-in, he'd been rescuing her. He squeezed back.

"How do we get up there?" Katie asked.

"If we're lucky, from the roof next door."

Katie looked up at the adjoining new appartment. It was taller than its neighbor—eight stories high, to be exact. Clambering across a roof that far above the ground wasn't exactly on her list of ten favorite things to do, but she didn't protest. At least, she consoled herself, since the building housed a Middle Eastern restaurant, they ought to be able to get into the lobby as if they were part of the dinner crowd.

In fact, no one even glanced at them, knapsacks slung casually over their shoulders as they made their way to the elevator. They took the car to the top floor and climbed a flight of stairs to the roof. Mac taped the latch on the door so it wouldn't lock and trap them, in case they had to come back that way.

"Picked up that trick from the Watergate burglars," he quipped.

Katie gave him a weak smile.

Eight stories above Connecticut Avenue, there were no guardrails, and a strong wind was moaning across the darkness. Katie grabbed for Mac's hand as they stepped from the shelter of the stairwell. They couldn't risk flashlights because someone in a nearby building might spot them, so they took a few moments to make sure of their orientation.

Katie craned her neck at the stars. Above the glare of the city, they were spread across the sky like sequins winking on black velvet. But their beauty was far less important than the fact that they gave enough light for two fledgling cat burglars to find their footing.

Crouching low, they made their careful way across the exposed gravel surface. After lowering himself to the next roof, Mac helped Katie down. Neither spoke, but when they were both safely across the barrier, he hugged her tightly, and she returned the strong embrace.

"Okay?"

"I've done worse."

Now they were on the wrong side of a locked door, and Mac had to open it before they could gain entrance to the stairs. Katie didn't ask where he'd acquired either the expertise or the set of master keys. Instead she huddled out of the wind in the shelter of the brick wall while he worked.

Finally the door was opened, and they were able to descend the stairs to the second floor, where Genesis was located. This time, Katie stood guard while Mac studied the lock.

It seemed to be taking forever. Then she heard a string of muttered curses.

"What's wrong?"

"I guess it was stupid to think it was going to be this easy. They have an alarm system. Twenty or thirty seconds after I touch the lock, either there's going to be a bell ringing in the hall or a buzzer going off down at police headquarters."

Katie thought about the high and windy roofs they'd crossed—for nothing. "Cam would probably know what to do about it," she suggested, her voice tentative. She really didn't want to get him involved in a breaking-and-entering charge if something went wrong.

Mac shook his head, agreeing with the tone of her voice not her words.

"Maybe there's a back entrance, but it's probably wired, too," Katie muttered. As she spoke, her eyes scanned the hall and began to take in the details. The building was about the same age as 43 Light Street, only a lot more money had been put into sprucing up the interior. Her eyes fixed on the panels above her head. "Mac, the ceiling's been lowered."

"And?"

"The building's a lot like the one where I have my office. I'll bet the drop ceiling is covering the old transoms above the doors. If they're still there, maybe we can get in that way."

"It's sure worth a try."

Katie tried not to think about how this was going to look if someone happened to come through the hall. Instead she donned the gloves she'd brought along and let Mac boost her up so she could push aside the buff-colored ceiling panel in front of the door. By standing on his shoulders, she was able to pull herself up.

"Well?"

"It's here!" She heard Mac grunting as she moved around on his shoulders trying to pry the transom open. "It won't budge," she reported after several fruitless minutes.

"Do you think you can give me a quick boost up?" Mac asked.

"I can try."

They reversed their positions, and she made her body into a step stool. Mac had to put his full weight on her shoulders for only a moment. Then he used the edge of the ceiling for support as he pulled himself up and disappeared.

It was worse waiting down here, Katie thought, as she listened to the blood pounding in her ears. When she heard a grinding sound, she tensed. It was followed by a muffled exclamation of triumph from above.

Mac came slithering back through the hole and reached down his gloved hand.

The man was strong. With a steady pulling motion, he brought Katie up and off the floor. As she joined him above the ceiling, she saw that the transom panel was lying beside the door. Mac wiggled backward through the opening he'd made. Before she joined him, Katie replaced the ceiling panel.

A few moments later, they were both breathing hard and standing inside the reception area of the Genesis salon.

Katie's face split into a broad grin. Mac grinned back, and they shook hands.

"Maybe we can get a job with Barnum and Bailey," she quipped.

"The one-armed bandit—"

"—and the brunette pushover."

"I believe you were pulled. And I'm not making a career of this unless it pays better than medical research."

"Speaking of research, let's get our work done and get the heck out of here." Katie opened her knapsack and took out a flashlight.

Mac followed suit.

They'd both been too busy for more than a quick glance at their surroundings. Now they took the time to absorb the plush atmosphere. Most of the lights were out. A few dimmed bulbs provided enough illumination to set off the Italian tile floor, blooming hibiscus and white wicker furniture.

"You could go right from here to Club Med," Mac muttered.

"You're going to have to take a rain check for a shampoo and scalp massage."

They both moved to the front desk. A gold engraved invitation to a "Spectacular Day of Beauty with Genesis" lay on top of the schedule book. Katie moved it aside so they could take a quick look at the customers who'd come in over the past few weeks, in case they couldn't find more detailed information.

Mac pulled out the camera they'd brought along and photographed several dozen pages. Looking over his shoulder, Katie pointed to Helen Austin-Wright's home number. Mac nodded. By itself it wasn't proof of anything. Nevertheless it was a good bet her patronage of Genesis wasn't a coincidence, either.

Katie began to search the contents of one of the hair-dressing stations. Unless the virus was in a bottle labeled Setting Lotion or Extra Hold Mousse, it wasn't in evidence. Which meant it must be stored somewhere else, because using a container that anyone could pick up and use by mistake seemed much too dangerous.

Mac moved past her toward a closed door. After easing it open, he gave a low whistle. Katie came over and stopped in her tracks. The rest of the salon was elegant, but this room was in another class altogether.

They stepped onto a priceless Aubusson carpet and crossed to a richly polished Louis XIV desk. The traditional furnishings were set off with exquisite oriental accents like a two-foot-tall terra-cotta figure of a Japanese warlord mounted on a stallion. In the corner was an antique Japanese screen decorated with chrysanthemums.

"Want to bet this is Jade Nishizaka's private office?" Mac asked.

"Unless someone else holds the real power at Genesis."

A book inside the top desk drawer had what they'd been searching for—a list of customers, apparently in order of when they'd had their first appointment. It was annotated with each woman's phone number, address and personal information like hair color and makeup selections. Also included was a wealth of personal data such as number of children, entertainment preferences, favorite foods and social affiliations. There was an additional listing for the woman's husband. If he was in the private sector, his company's Dun & Bradstreet rating was included. If he was with the government, there was an evaluation of his political and policy-making influence.

"Pretty detailed for beauty parlor chitchat," Mac observed.

"I agree."

"Why do you think there's a star next to some of the names?" Mac asked.

"I don't know. But Helen Austin-Wright was one of them."

"We'll figure it out later. Right now I want to make a record of this stuff." Katie continued to skim the information as Mac began to photograph the entries. They were both so intent on the book that neither one of them heard the front door open and quietly close. The first inkling of danger was the dark form that suddenly filled the doorway.

"All right, raise your hands above your heads and back away from the desk," a steely voice ordered.

The command was reinforced by a large automatic pistol.

With a sick feeling in the pit of her stomach, Katie lifted her head. She was no more astonished than the man who held the gun. It was D.C. Police Detective Cornell Perkins.

He let out a surprised breath. "I'll be hog-tied! Dr. Martin, what the hell are *you* doin' here?"

"Are you going to arrest us, Officer Perkins?"

"I don't know. What are you up to?"

"Getting the goods on whoever has hatched a plot to give a virus called HDV15 to half the influential men in Washington," Mac answered.

Perkins whistled through large white teeth. "Say what? I just got back into the game." His eyes flicked to the metal hand. "Better start by telling me who you are and what's HDV15 virus."

Mac recounted the last few days' activities and findings, ending with their frightful theory of the deadly virus.

The detective took several moments to digest the information. "Sounds like you had a busy week. You're talking conspiracy?"

"We hadn't put it in quite those terms," Katie told him. "All we know is that there's some kind of revenge scheme."

Mac looked at the weapon in the detective's large hand. "I function better when someone isn't holding a gun on me."

Perkins studied the unlikely burglars. "This may be the stupidest thing I've ever done." With a sigh, he put the gun on the desk between them.

"So now we're supposed to trust you." The aggressive tone of Mac's voice hadn't changed. "How do we know you're not just interested in having us disappear?" he challenged.

"I was taken off this case to keep me from digging up the facts. Now I'm back—and workin' on my own time."

Katie touched Mac's arm. "He helped me that night at Val's apartment. I think we can trust him." She nodded to Perkins. "How much do you know?"

"I don't know squat. Not the real stuff, anyway. So far I've cottoned on to the autopsy switch and the small-time hood who ended up in a drawer at the morgue without any record of how he was brought in."

"Oh God." Katie shuddered. "That must be Arnie Beale."

"You folks know something about that?"

"The first time we saw him, he tried to run us over at the Columbia Mall. The last we saw him, he was very much alive and strapped to an autopsy table," Mac said. "Which is just more proof that somebody in your department is working like mad to cover this whole thing up."

"How did you end up here?" Katie asked.

"A tip from someone who'd like to blow the cover off this whole thing. He even gave me the access code for the Genesis alarm system. There's a cover-up all right, but somebody's running scared."

Katie felt the hair on the back of her neck bristle. "That could mean this is a trap—for you. And we've walked into it."

Mac's protective gaze swung to Katie. "Then we've got to get out of here. Now."

"Not yet," she objected. "We don't have enough information." She looked at Perkins. "Add a mole at the Atlanta Centers for Disease Control to your list of conspirators. And since you're here, could you make sure there's only one door to this place and then stand guard while we keep searching?"

"The Centers for Disease Control. The D.C. police. A beauty salon. Doc, I'd feel a heck of a lot more comfortable if I had the whole picture."

"*We* don't have the whole picture. That's why we're here. We'll tell you everything we know as soon as we finish going over this place. But I'll feel safer if you're watching the door."

"I'm a trained police officer and you're rookie crooks. Who do you think has a better chance of turnin' this place upside down?"

"Ordinarily, you. Except that what we're looking for is the transmission method for a deadly, mind-destroying virus. If you stumble on it and don't know what you're doing, the consequences could be fatal," Mac told him.

"I get your drift," Perkins muttered. "Okay, I'll play watchdog for you."

Mac picked up the campaign chest sitting on the stand beside Jade's desk. "Before you go on guard duty, could you try fooling with the lock on this thing? You're probably better at it than I am."

"In for a penny..."

It took the detective only a moment to open the box.

"A picture album," Katie murmured as she took out an old-fashioned leather-bound book and turned to the first page. Inside the front cover was a tattered map of Japan. The place names were in Japanese. Two cities were circled.

Black-and-white photographs yellowed around the edges followed the map. The first few shots were of a smiling Japanese family, the young mother in traditional kimono, holding a baby, the father in a business suit. They were standing in front of a modest Japanese-style cottage. The captions were no more readable than the words on the map.

On the next few pages the photographs chronicled the family's growth. Sometimes a whole raft of other people were also in the pictures. Uncles? Aunts? Cousins?

The small family appeared again. Now there were two children, a young girl and another baby. Several pictures later it became clear that the second child was a boy.

Katie asked. "Do you think this is Jade Nishizaka's family? I remember she came from some city I never heard of. Onodo. If this is the place, it looks like a small town."

The next pictures must have been from a few years later. The family seemed to have moved to the city, to a larger house with a beautifully landscaped traditional garden. The children were older, and the man had exchanged his suit for a military uniform. With the mother, father and children were an older woman and man, both in traditional dress.

"I think I can finally date these," Mac said. "It looks like the father joined the Imperial Japanese Navy."

"In World War II?" Katie asked.

"Uh-huh. I guess he moved his family to town for the duration."

"I'll bet they were living with the grandparents," Katie suggested.

Katie studied the background and the faces, but her gaze kept coming back to the boy. Something about him seemed familiar.

Expecting to see similar snapshots, Katie turned the page. As the new pictures came into view, everyone in the room gasped. Suddenly they were looking at a ruined city, the buildings flattened almost beyond recognition, the landscape charred. Then there were photos obviously taken in a hospital—of disfigured women and children.

There was more horror. Pages and pages of ghastly photos of victims of some sort of terrible disaster. No one wanted to examine them too closely.

Perkins, who had been leaning over Katie's shoulder, put several feet between himself and the book. "Lordy! It looks like the place was hit by an atomic bomb or something."

Katie felt the words like rocks crashing into a concrete wall. "I think that's exactly what happened," she breathed. Quickly she flipped back to the map in the front. "Two cities circled. Probably Hiroshima and Nagasaki. Jade must have lived in one of them."

Mac nodded. "We were all told that dropping the two atomic bombs saved a lot of American lives because we didn't have to invade Japan."

"From the allies' point of view, the devastation was a necessary evil. But if you'd lived through it, you'd probably have a considerably different opinion," Katie whispered.

"Yeah. Your home gone. People around you killed or dying slowly of burns—or radiation sickness. It could warp your whole personality," Perkins agreed.

Katie felt a wave of cold flow across her body. "To right an old wrong," she repeated Dr. Jekyll's phrase. "Do you think this is what he was talking about?"

Mac put a steadying hand on her shoulder. "It's a logical theory," he agreed. "Revenge on a grand scale. And think

of the irony. You take away the customer's inner beauty—
and leave a hollow shell.''

"What do you mean a grand scale?" Perkins objected.
"This place may be posh, but it's just one salon."

"With a very selective clientele," Mac countered. "Except that you're right. It's a slow process. You could only do
a few women in one day."

Katie went very still, her face a study in concentration.
Then she pushed back the desk chair and lit out of the room.
A moment later she was back with the gold engraved card
that had been in the reception area. "What about this?" she
asked, as she set the cream-colored rectangle carefully on the
desk. "It's an invitation for the wives of delegates to the
National Economics Conference at the Wardman Park
Hotel on Monday. How many women whose husbands are
high up in the country's major corporations do you think
they'll have access to then?"

"I don't know. Maybe there's a list of invitees," Mac
suggested.

They found what they were looking for in one of the side
drawers of the desk. Not only was there a list of women who
had been invited, there was also a notation of who had accepted. It read like a Who's Who of Mrs. Corporate America.

Perkins whistled through his teeth.

"Two or three months from now, you'll get an effect like
a bomb exploding in the brains of high-powered executives
all over the country."

"Mac, I told you, we've got to let the FBI in on this,"
Katie said.

"We've still only got a half-baked theory. We need proof
that they're going to infect these women with the virus." He
glanced at Perkins for confirmation, and the detective nodded in agreement.

Katie shivered. "I wish we could get out of here."

"You could leave."

"I'll stay until we're finished."

Perkins took up his position at the door. At least it was reassuring having an armed police officer on guard duty. At Mac's request, Perkins also took the scheduling book and began searching for the appointments of women whose names had an asterisk on the master client list. "See if you can find out which treatments they received," Mac requested.

He and Katie began going over the salon. One of the first things they discovered was the environmental room, a chamber about the size of a large sauna where all sorts of natural environments could be simulated. At the moment, it was dark and silent as a tomb, and it hardly seemed a suitable depository for anything that could be damaged by heat, cold or moisture.

A more promising storage facility was near the back of the salon. On the top shelf of a locked metal cabinet they found the supply of face cream.

"Well, back to square one," Mac muttered. "We've still got to find the viral induction agent."

"Let's try the refrigerator." Katie pointed to a large, restaurant-size unit.

Inside were several large boxes labeled Cosmetic Sensitivity Allergy Test Kits.

"Is testing for allergies usual for a beauty salon?" Mac asked.

"I don't think so. Not in the ones I've been to."

He opened a box and took out a kit. It was sealed inside an outer plastic bag and an inner foil pouch, each labeled Handle With Extreme Care. Results Will Be Invalid If Tester Touches Any Surface Besides Customer's Skin.

Using his metal hand, he opened both wrappers. Inside was a small metal device similar to the those used for TB tests—although the grasping handle on the back was longer. The business end was peppered with dozens of quarter-inch metal projections—sharp enough to pierce the skin.

"I think we've found the viral induction agent," Katie said.

"I think you're right," Mac agreed. "But we'll have to do a test." He slipped one of the packets into the protective case inside his knapsack.

Katie looked at the shipping labels on the boxes. "There are at least three hundred of these things here. I'll bet they're for the conference."

"Yes, they're probably going down to the Wardman Park tomorrow."

They both came out of the back room to show Perkins another one of the test kits.

"Do you know if the women whose names are starred got an allergy test?" Katie asked.

The officer ran his finger down the list. "Every one of them," he confirmed. "And another thing, all of them were scheduled for a session in the environmental room—whatever that is."

"We saw it back there," Mac gestured toward the interior of the salon. "It's a place where you simulate various natural conditions," Mac told him. "A rain forest at sunrise. A tropical island in the evening. Stuff like that. It's supposed to be relaxing."

"I hope so." Perkins snorted. "They charge $125 for a half-hour session."

"I think we'd better give it a second look," Mac said.

"I suppose you're going to leave me here at the door while you get the grand tour," Perkins groused.

"Afraid so." He and Katie headed back toward the chamber. Mac studied the sophisticated control panel for several minutes before touching it. He turned on only the lights—to bright.

As he opened the door to step inside, Katie put a restraining hand on his shoulder. ''I don't like you going in
there. What if it's dangerous?''

''If it was dangerous, the customers would complain. But
I'll leave the door open.''

Still not entirely reassured, Katie leaned into the room,
watching as Mac began to inspect the floor, walls and contour couch. Her full attention was on him, so that she didn't
see the shadow loom up behind her. Suddenly the lights in
the ceiling blinked off.

She screamed as powerful hands gave her a mighty shove.
Then she tumbled into the chamber with Mac, and the heavy
door slammed and locked behind them.

Chapter Sixteen

"Katie!" In the dark, Mac scrambled toward her. They collided, winced, caught their balance as they grasped each other's shoulders. Mac pulled Katie to him, holding her with a sure, firm clasp. Around her the room seemed to spin, and he was her only anchor to reality.

"Are you all right? What the hell just happened?"

Reaching behind her, she fumbled for the knob and found that it wouldn't turn. "Somebody killed the lights, pushed me in here and slammed the door. It's locked." She tried to keep her voice steady; it was wobbling by the time it reached the end of the sentence.

The room came to life. The twitter of a forest full of birds materialized around them in the dark, and a faint pink glow rose above their heads, as if it were the beginning of a new day. At the same time, the air was suddenly filled with the scent of a pine forest. Even the shapes of the trees were vaguely visible. "Somebody's putting on a show for us," Mac growled.

In itself, the spectacle wasn't frightening. Under other circumstances, Katie would have enjoyed the magic of the illusion. Yet somehow the scent of the trees and the soft pink glow held an unknown threat.

"I wish I knew what was going to happen next," she whispered.

"Yeah. Somebody's playing with the controls." Holding
Katie against his side, Mac moved to the door and banged
with the stainless steel hand. "Perkins?" he called. "What
the hell is going on? If this is your idea of a joke, we're not
amused."

There was no response.

"I'm sorry, Mac. We never should have trusted him."

"It's not your fault."

They clung to each other, trying to cope with the terrible
isolation of the chamber. Inside, there was no indication
that the outside world even existed. Katie shivered, suddenly unable to shake the apprehension that all the oxygen
was being pumped out of the little room. Heart pounding,
she began to suck air into her lungs.

When she started to feel light-headed, she realized she was
hyperventilating. Cupping her hands around her nose, she
dragged some of her own carbon dioxide into her system. It
helped.

"You okay?" Mac asked. She could tell he was trying to
stay calm, but there was a strained edge to his words.

"I'm not going to give them the satisfaction of falling
apart."

"Good."

That was easier said than done. It was hard not to imagine the walls of the little room pressing in around them.
Closing her eyes, Katie tried to focus on the logic of their
problem. After a few moments, she felt a bit calmer.

"Maybe it's not Perkins out there," she finally murmured. "Maybe they got him first."

"Unless he was a ringer all along, and he was just waiting to find out what we knew," Mac countered.

Katie nodded, but she was listening to the noises in the air
as much as to Mac. The twitter of birds was suddenly replaced by the buzz of insects. It was so real, she could
imagine their wings beating. As she listened, they turned

into a swarm of hornets, zeroing in on her. She ducked. They were all around her head now. Unable to contain her panic, she screamed, swatting wildly with her arms.

"Easy. Easy," Mac soothed. "They're not there. It's all special effects."

She gulped. "I know—it's just—not knowing what's going to happen next."

As if to confirm her words, the hornets vanished and the sound of waves took their place. At first they were a gentle rolling sound far in the background. Then it was as if she and Mac were rushing toward a rocky shoreline. At the same time, the lights went out again. Katie cringed away from the assault of the unseen, giant breakers. Somewhere deep in her mind, she knew it was all an illusion, yet she clung to Mac, unable to dispel the fear that she was about to be swept away by the crashing surf.

Katie shivered as she felt the wet spray break against her face, felt the waves shake the ground on which she stood. The spray became a choking mist, like the gas that had overwhelmed them in the examination room. Only that had been like breathing essence of rose petals compared to this. She was gagging, gasping as every breath became an agony of stinging pain. It was over. Finished. "Mac—I—love—you—" she managed to get out. Then, as the burning in her lungs became too much to bear, she sank into oblivion.

KATIE CAME BACK to consciousness slowly. Her head felt as if it were a giant, throbbing hollow log on which a native drummer was beating. Her lungs stung, and her body might have been battered by hurricane-force winds. Perhaps it had. They were just as likely as anything else in here.

Her eyes snapped open. "Mac?"

In the dark, he was beside her instantly. "Right here."

"Are you okay?"

"Yes. But don't talk, and try not to move around. I don't think there's much air getting in here."

She fought off a shudder of panic and tried to make herself comfortable against the rubberized floor. Mac was working at something.

"What are you doing?"

"Trying to short out the control mechanism."

She didn't ask any more questions. Instead she reached out and found his thigh in the darkness. He squeezed her hand. Then he went back to working. Her mind drifted on a sea of thickening air. This was so silly. They were trapped like two bears in their cave because somebody had rolled a giant rock in front of the door.

Katie knew the symptoms of oxygen deprivation. And these were it, she thought with a little giggle. Maybe she could write a paper about it for *The New England Journal of Medicine.* No, they'd be stuffy about her not having taken notes.

She went to pull Mac over so he'd curl up with her. No he was busy doing something. She couldn't remember what. It was getting harder and harder to make her mind work.

Then she heard a popping noise. A moment later, dim light and cold air flooded into the chamber. Grabbing her under the shoulders, Mac dragged her to the door and pulled her out. For several minutes they both lay gasping on the floor.

Finally Mac sat up and rubbed his hand against his forehead. "That was too damn close."

"I know. How did you get us out of there?"

"I found the service panel and I used my personal mechanical toolbox." He held up the prosthetic hand. "They should have taken it off while we were out cold."

"I'm glad they didn't realize their mistake."

Katie watched Mac push himself up. She wanted to tell him to take it easy, but she knew that they didn't have the luxury of resting for too long.

Mac staggered into the storage room. He was back with a triumphant look on his face. "It's still here."

"The virus?"

"Yeah. We've got to kill it before they cart it down to the Wardman Park."

"You have something in mind?"

"You're damn right I do." He took her hand and pulled her up, watching to see how steady she was on her feet. "Think you can help me move the boxes?"

Her body protested with every step she took, but she didn't turn him down.

Mac opened the box and removed one of the packets. "They took my knapsack. I want another sample for the lab," he explained, as he rummaged on the storage shelves for a carrying case and put the deadly cargo inside.

As they began to transfer the virus, Mac told Katie what he'd thought of while he was trying to get them out of the environmental chamber.

"I like the way your mind works," she approved.

"Let's hope we have enough time to pull it off."

"What if they come back?"

"With all those lives at stake, we've got to take the chance," Mac insisted.

Half an hour later, they finished with the special treatment for the virus and began putting the boxes back.

"You think they'll realize what we've done?" Katie asked.

"I hope not. Everything looks just the way we found it. Now let's split."

"What about the door alarm?" Katie asked as they made their way back to the front of the salon.

"You don't feel like climbing back through the transom?" Mac asked as he stuffed the carrying case with the virus into his pocket.

"I'm not feeling quite as spunky as when we came in."

"I can check the cutoff box. Wait right here."

He went back toward the interior of the salon, and Katie turned to watch his broad shoulders disappear. The click of the door lock behind her made her turn. To her horror she found she was facing Dr. Jekyll. An attractive Asian woman stood slightly behind him. But she couldn't compete for attention with the gun the doctor leveled at Katie's chest.

"Raise your hands and back up, Dr. Martin," he ordered.

Wordlessly Katie obeyed.

The three of them stood in the reception area staring at each other. Katie's eyes went from the man to the woman beside him. She couldn't be anyone else but Jade Nishizaka—and there was a definite family resemblance between her and the doctor. In fact, they were grown-up versions of the children she'd seen in the photographs. Jade and her younger brother.

"How did you get out of the environmental room?" he hissed.

"I—Mac did it. I don't know how."

"Akio, it might have been better to have killed them when we had the chance," the salon owner murmured. There was both deference and apology in her voice.

"Are you questioning my decisions?"

This was a woman with complete power in her own realm. Yet she shook her head and cast her eyes down.

"We must know the extent of the plot against us. This time there will be no interruption to the questioning session." Akio's manner changed as he gestured with the gun. "Back up, Dr. Martin."

Katie obeyed and found her shoulders flattened against the wall. The solid vertical surface gave her a false sense of security.

"Where is Mr. McQuade this time?" Akio demanded. "He wouldn't have left you here."

Katie's mind scrambled for a plausible explanation. "He went to get help from a detective friend of ours. I was guarding the virus induction kits."

"Perhaps." He turned to his sister. "Go make sure they're still there."

Katie held her breath as the woman scurried away. What if Mac were in the storage room? What if she discovered him there? However, Jade returned a few moments later—alone.

"Everything's fine." She held up one of the virus packets. "This time I don't want you to wait. Just give it to her."

Katie's gaze flicked from brother to sister. She had to buy some time—for herself and Mac. "I know why you want to infect the women at the conference," she told the pair.

"You couldn't possibly know," Jade snapped.

"Was your mother killed by the bomb the Americans dropped on Hiroshima?" Katie asked.

The beautiful features contorted with pain. "My mother. My grandmother. My grandfather. My aunts and uncles. My cousins. Some of them died in the blast. Some of them, like my poor mother, lingered on—burned, suffering from radiation sickness. She wasn't one of the *Hibakusha*—the survivors. The worst would have happened to me and Akio, too, but we were in the country for the day, visiting friends."

"It had to be horrible for you, losing everyone like that. My father died when I was little. I know it must have been so much worse for you," Katie murmured, hoping she could communicate with the other woman.

Jade ignored the expression of sympathy. "Your father! You only lost your father. *My* father was killed at sea when his ship was torpedoed by the Americans. When he died

Akio and I were alone. But Akio was strong. And he lent me his strength. He helped me understand what we had to do. Do you know how I scraped together money so I could start producing my mother's cosmetics again? I made myself available to the American soldiers. They were willing to pay for a young, beautiful Japanese girl. Even now when I remember the shame of that, it makes me sick."

"You did what you had to," Katie whispered.

"Yes I did what I had to—to survive and grow strong." She glanced worshipfully at her brother. "I revived my mother's cosmetic business and started our pharmaceutical firm. I paid for Akio's education. And now he is one of the world's great researchers. His discoveries have made it possible for us to avenge our ancestors. If his work had taken a different direction, he would have gotten the Nobel Prize."

"What was your field?" Katie addressed herself to the brother.

However, the sister answered. "The field of revenge. But we are selective in our punishment. The women we give the virus to tomorrow are all married to men whose companies participated in the war effort. Fitting justice, wouldn't you say?"

Katie swallowed. "But they're innocent. They haven't done anything."

Jade fixed her with a fierce look. "My mother was innocent. My grandmother. It didn't save their lives. And you are not innocent. You and your sister must have been conspiring for months to stop us. Tell me, did she break into my campaign chest? Did she look at the pictures? Was that why she wanted to stop us? You must have been the brains of the operation, since she was stupid enough to infect herself."

"Val didn't know anything about it. I didn't know anything about it until after she died."

"You can do better than that," Akio snapped. "And you will." He looked at his sister. "I am tired of this farce. Infect her with the virus, then we will proceed."

Jade opened the protective wrapper on the kit. Carefully she removed the inductor and held it by the handle on the back.

Katie felt every cell in her body tense. "Please, not that," she whimpered. "Not the virus."

"It's what you deserve."

"Please. Anything else. Please."

There was a look of satisfaction on Akio's face.

It barely registered with Katie. The blood pounded in her ears. Yet she didn't move a muscle. They were counting on her to be paralyzed with fear. It wasn't hard to be convincing. Her eyes were fixed on Jade as the salon owner moved forward. Maybe if she were lucky she could get herself out of this and then find out what had happened to Mac.

Jade had stepped between her and Akio, between her and the gun. Steeling herself, Katie waited until the tiny needles pressed against her flesh. Then she grabbed the woman's wrist and yanked her forward. A moment later she was standing with Jade in front of her like a shield. And ownership of the inductor had changed. Katie was holding the metal needle lightly against Jade's neck.

"Drop the gun or I'll give the virus to your sister," Katie said in a dead-level voice.

Akio looked at the two women in horror.

For a moment there was silence in the room. Then Jade began to say something in Japanese, something that changed her brother's expression to one of uncertainty. He looked pleadingly at his sister, shaking his head no. *"Iie."*

Her insistence was just as emphatic. *"Hai."*

Just then from the back of the salon came a high-pitched screech that made the hairs on the back of Katie's neck stand on end. It was followed by a crash of thunder so loud

that the whole building seemed to shake. Another volley
followed and then another, the noise crashing around them
like the waves in the environmental room.

The truth registered in a millisecond. Mac must have seen
Jade and Akio come in. Now he was doing the only thing he
could to pull the gunman's attention away from her. He was
working the controls of the environmental room, amplify-
ing the effects to inhuman proportions.

Katie pushed Jade forward. As she stumbled against her
brother, Katie dashed through the doorway to her right and
slammed it behind her.

Two shots tore through the wood. She barely registered
the sound above the roaring of the thunder. But she saw the
splintered wood and ducked behind one of the nail-polish
carts. Did she hear a shout from the outer office? She
couldn't tell. Then more shots rang out.

Moments later a uniformed police officer barreled
through the doorway, his gun drawn. He didn't see Katie.
Instead he barged right past her, heading for the back of the
salon. Oh God, he was working for Perkins and he was going to shoot Mac. Without any regard for her own safety,
she picked up a cut-glass vase, dumped the flowers on the
floor and dashed after the policeman.

Suddenly the cacophony of the sound system died, casting the area in an eerie silence. Still clutching the vase, Katie moved to the entrance of the door, her eyes searching for
Mac.

She found the police officer first. He had leveled the gun
at Mac who held up his high-tech hand as if it were a
weapon. "McQuade, take it easy. I'm one of the good
guys."

"Then why are you pointing a gun on me?"

"So you don't kill me first and ask questions later."

One of the questions was answered by a loud sob from the
front of the salon. "Akio, Akio, don't die," Jade wailed.

"Perkins got him," the young officer explained. "He's not gonna die if the ambulance gets here ASAP."

"Perkins! Isn't he working for Genesis?"

"Naw. In the past four hours he's shaken up the whole D.C. police department. He's gonna get a medal for sticking his neck out to blow this conspiracy. The guy who set him up has told us everything he knows—including about the mole at the CDC." The officer grinned. "Now, if I put my gun back in the holster, will you promise not to jump me?"

"Okay," Mac agreed. "But you walk in front of us, just in case."

"Sure thing."

In the reception area, Jade was crouched over her brother, still wailing.

"Let me see what I can do for him," Katie offered.

Jade's eyes snapped toward the physician. "Stay away from him. You have the virus."

"Katie, no!" Mac took her shoulders and turned her toward him, searching her face.

She shook her head. "Mac, she's wrong. I don't have it. She was going to give it to me. But she got the inducer from the dead batch we put back in the refrigerator—after we cooked it to 212 degrees in the environmental chamber."

The breath whooshed out of Mac's lungs as he folded her close. She buried her face against his shirtfront, wanting to stay that way for a long time—just the two of them, holding each other. However they weren't alone.

There was a muffled curse from the floor. As Katie raised her head, she saw that Jade had fixed them with a look of pure hatred. But she didn't have much time to spare for Katie and Mac because two paramedics with a stretcher were just coming through the door. They took the wounded Nishizaka down to the ambulance. A weeping Jade was handcuffed and led to a squad car.

When the brother and sister had departed, Perkins turned to Katie and Mac. "I guess you thought I was lying to you the first time we met up here."

Mac nodded.

"Well, I was the one being messed with. The guy who gave me the combination to the security system set me up. Trouble is, you got caught in the trap."

"How did you get away?" Katie asked.

"Jade had two men planted in the D.C. police department. Lucky for me, one of them had second thoughts. He turned me loose and told me what was supposed to come down. That was enough to get me in to see the chief. I would have been back sooner except that I knew they weren't planning to kill you until after they'd questioned you."

"Thanks," Katie told him.

"The Nishizakas aren't a very nice pair," Perkins observed.

"You can feel sorry for the terrible things that happened to them when they were kids. You can even understand why it warped them," Katie said.

"Warped, yeah," Mac agreed. "Nobody in their right mind hatches a plot like that."

"It was Akio's idea," Katie told him. "He was the one with vision, if you want to call it that. Jade had to go along with him because that was the traditional way in Japan. The men made all the decisions."

"Now we've still got to find out exactly how many people have the virus—and what we can do for them," Mac said. "But I have a hunch there's an antidote. Otherwise a meticulous researcher like Dr. Nishizaka wouldn't feel safe working with the stuff. Not when a lab accident would spell disaster."

"I hope you're right. If some of the effects are created before brain cells die, maybe close to normal function can even be restored. Maybe we can still save Greg. But we're going to have to find someone who reads Japanese to look through Akio's materials.''

"When we find out where he moved them."

Perkins interrupted the exchange. ''There are plenty of other people who can take care of that now. Probably you folks want to go home and get some rest, and we can continue the discussion tomorrow down at police headquarters.''

Katie was suddenly feeling distinctly disoriented. It had seemed like she'd been carrying a boulder around on her shoulders for weeks. Now somebody had just lifted it off. No, that wasn't quite right. She and Mac had reduced it to rubble. Now a cleanup crew was going to take care of the pieces.

She looked uncertainly at Mac and saw that he had the same bemused expression she assumed was on her own face. "Come on. Let's take the man up on the offer before he changes his mind," she urged.

Perkins laughed.

Mac nodded.

A few minutes later they were climbing into their rental car. It was early morning again. Another night on the graveyard shift, Katie thought. As she watched Mac start the engine, she felt her chest tighten painfully. It was all over except for the shouting. Only there really wasn't going to be any shouting. It would be a nice, civilized ending to a very strange interlude in both their lives. Now Mac was going to take her back to the motel to pick up her stuff, and then he'd drive her home.

But she wasn't going to let it happen that way, with no muss and no fuss. She wasn't going to slip quietly back into Mac McQuade's past. She loved him. And if explaining to a very stubborn man why they'd be crazy to simply walk away from each other was going to cause a shouting match, so be it. Only the car was no place to do it. She wanted Mac

McQuade's full attention, and she didn't want him running off the road into a tree when she got it.

Silence seemed to suit Mac just fine as they headed north out of the city. Wishing it was a shorter trip, Katie leaned back and pretended to sleep. When she opened her eyes again, she was surprised to see that they were not heading for the motel. Instead they were on a two-lane road in the Maryland countryside. The scenery changed from woods to newly plowed fields, and then to expensive new houses dotting former farmland. It looked like the area south and west of Columbia.

Mac turned in at a gravel drive between two aging sections of fence. The narrow road wound upward through a stand of oaks and maples. As they cleared the trees, Katie saw the summit of a hill. The sun glinted off Mac's sports car parked at a bend in the road. But there was no other indication that they'd reached any sort of destination except an open field. Maybe he knew they were in for a shouting match, and he was going to make sure that she had all the open space she needed to exercise her lungs.

When he pulled up beside his car and cut the engine, she looked at him inquiringly.

"My house."

"Where?"

"Under the hill."

"Right. I forgot you were the dragon under the hill," Katie murmured.

"What?"

"Nothing."

"I thought this would be a better place to talk than the motel room. Maybe it's not such a good idea."

"No, no. This is fine." Katie followed Mac about fifty feet up the road and around a bend to the front of the house, which featured a broad expanse of glass looking out over a meandering river in the valley below.

"Brighton Dam Reservoir," Mac answered her unspoken question.

"Nice view."

"I like it." Mac turned abruptly to unlock the door.

Katie wasn't sure what she'd expected. Once Mac had closed the door, she noted that the floor-to-ceiling window and a skylight kept the room from being dark. Yet there was a feeling of safety from the protection of the earth around them.

Safety from outside interferences. Now that they weren't going to be interrupted, neither one of them seemed to want to start a serious discussion.

Katie focused on the room's decor. The furniture was pine—more serviceable than showy. It contributed to the solid, homey look of the interior.

"Do you want anything?"

"Not now. I—I should call Jo and let her know we're all right."

"Yes. There's a phone in the kitchen."

Katie assured Jo they were safe and gave her a few details about the Nishizakas. Yet as she hung up, she found herself taking a deep breath before she went to find Mac.

He was standing stiffly by the window, looking down at the lake, and she imagined that he often studied the view while he was thinking. "Everything I said the other day about us was true," he said without turning.

Katie felt her heart plummet to her toes. "And?" she managed.

"But I feel like something inside me is going to shrivel up and die if I have to give you up again."

She didn't want him to see the sudden blooming of hope on her face. It would be too terrible if he were only trying to find a way to tell her that he still couldn't place her in his future. Instead she came up behind him, slipped her arms around his waist and pressed her cheek into his shoulder.

"You don't have to give me up. In fact, it's going to be a hell of a lot harder to get rid of me this time."

He laughed. "I kind of sensed that. But this is more than just the happy ending tacked on to the dangerous adventure we've just been through. It's dealing with all the day-to-day things I haven't been able to face since the accident."

"I think part of the problem is that you've been imagining my life has been something like 'Dr. Martin Makes It Big.' It hasn't been quite that way. In fact, there's something that happened to me a couple of years ago that was pretty hard to take."

He turned so that he was facing her, draping his arms loosely over her shoulders.

She tipped her face up toward his. "I don't talk about this much. Maybe I should have told you before, but I didn't quite know how to start. Do you remember the big scandal at the Sterling Clinic? Front page in the *Sun Papers* for a couple of weeks?"

"The Sterling Clinic. You mean that place in Mount Washington that had to close because of what a few of the doctors were doing? *You* worked there?"

"Yes. Abby Franklin, a friend of mine, uncovered the plot. Of course, I wasn't involved with what was going on. But like everybody else on the staff, I got covered with the debris when the dirt hit the fan. For six months I couldn't get another job. Even Medizone rejected me for a research position that was advertised. The director of personnel said I was overqualified." She shrugged. "Maybe that really was the reason. Who knows?"

"I'm sorry it happened, but I never saw your résumé."

"Even if you had, you wouldn't have called me in for an interview."

"Not because of a medical scandal that had nothing to do with you personally."

"Well, it was only one of a slew of rejections. Having a medical degree isn't the guarantee of success that you've built it into."

He stroked his hand up her back. "I guess you had a pretty hard time. I'm sorry."

"For a while I was depressed. Abby—she's a psychologist—helped me put things in perspective. She suggested I try getting myself a foundation grant. I wrote a proposal and it was accepted. She even offered me the use of her office while she was out of the country. And I've been pleased with what I've been doing. Now I realize that I'm really happier in research than in clinical practice. I thought everything was going fine, until I bumped into you in that closet and found out what's been missing from my life."

"Ah, Katie. What the hell are we going to do?" He didn't give her a chance to answer the question. His hand tangled in her hair and brought her eager mouth to his. Her tiny, indrawn murmur of approval was swallowed up as his mouth covered hers and he kissed her with all the hunger that she knew he'd been trying to hold in check. His hunger matched hers. So did the tension in his body. When he finally lifted his head, they were both trembling.

"Are you going to show me your bedroom?" she asked in a breathy voice.

"I want to." He shook his head slowly. "When I'm with you, when I hold you in my arms and kiss you, all I want is to make love to you."

"Mac, that's the way I feel, too. That's the way it's supposed to be between a man and a woman who've discovered that they love each other," she said softly.

He gazed down into her glistening eyes and swallowed. "Yeah. I heard you say it. You told me you loved me just before we went under. I could have said it, too. Knowing I love you is the hardest part. I've been alone a long time. I haven't been able to go back and see my family. Hell, I don't know the first thing about being a decent husband. I don't know if I—"

She pressed gentle fingers over his lips. "Hush up and listen to me. Eight years ago, something terrible happened to you. You lost your hand. You lost your career. You lost your sense of self-worth. You felt abandoned by your family. And you told yourself you didn't want the pity of the woman who was closest to you."

"That's quite an analysis."

"Let me finish. That was then. This is now. You're different. But that doesn't mean weaker. It means stronger. You've proved you can manage very well without a left hand. In fact, you can do some pretty extraordinary things with the replacement you're wearing. You've shown the world you could succeed at a tough, demanding career. You've found out that the last thing the woman you sent away wants to give you is pity." The words had been bold. Now, almost afraid to hear Mac's response, Katie removed her fingers from his lips.

"How long have you been working up to tell me all that?"

"It came to me in bits and pieces—things I knew I had to say to you if the two of us were going to make it. I decided it was easier to get it out in one fell swoop."

"Well, there was more you could have touched on. Like my anger and resentment. You know, the kind of anger that came out when I had poor Arnie Beale strapped to that autopsy table."

"Poor Arnie Beale was a hired killer. He tried to run us over, remember? You had plenty of reason to be angry with him. Not only that, you were under a lot of stress. We both were. People act out hostilities when they're stressed. But if you want to take your emotional temperature, I think the way you made love to me is a better indicator."

He closed his eyes for a moment and she knew he was remembering that first time—just the way she was.

"Or the way you saved my life," she whispered. "Or the way you kissed me when you didn't know whether I had the virus."

They were both silent for several heartbeats. Finally she began to speak again in a low voice. "If the MD after my name still makes a difference and you're worried about competing with me professionally, you could give me a job as medical director of Medizone. Then we won't be competing. We'll both be on the same team. And if I write any papers for medical journals, it will be with you as the coauthor. In addition, I have one other stipulation. Either you find someone else to send on those jungle trips, or you take me along."

A slow grin spread across Mac's face. "You really did think this whole thing out, didn't you?"

"I had to. I knew I had to have a viable proposal ready."

"Are you sure you're not bucking for the job of administrator instead of the medical director?"

"I can help you out, if you're in a bind. But I'm afraid I like research better."

"You're so sure of yourself. What if you're wrong about this jerk named Mac McQuade who left you flat eight years ago?"

She laughed. "Let's put that in the past tense with a lot of other old stuff. Mac, I love you. Nothing has ever seemed more right than the two of us together."

"Oh God, Katie. I don't think I can keep fighting any longer. Not when the idea of giving you up is making every nerve in my body raw."

"Thank the Lord."

"Katie, I love you so much." He traced her lips gently with his finger. "It feels so good to say that."

"It feels good to hear it."

He pulled her tighter against the length of his body. "I guess Tom was right all along."

"Tom?"

"I didn't tell you about going through his files after he died. The reason he got together with Val in the first place was because he wanted to contact you."

"What did he want from me?"

"Tom was the only person I could really open up to. A couple of times I talked to him about you. I guess he figured out I needed you."

"How did you feel when you found that out?" she murmured.

"I was upset. Now I'm grateful."

"Oh, Mac. I wish I'd met him—when he was all right."

"I wish you had, too."

They stood holding each other for several moments. "So many terrible things have happened," Katie whispered.

"Then let's make sure something very good comes out of it."

She tipped her head up and gave him a radiant smile. "That proposition, McQuade, deserves some in-depth research."

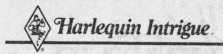 *Harlequin Intrigue*

43 Light St.

It looks like a charming old building near the Baltimore waterfront, but inside 43 Light Street lurks danger ... and romance.

Labeled a "true master of intrigue" by *Rave Reviews*, bestselling author Rebecca York continues her exciting series with TRIAL BY FIRE, coming to you in August.

Sabrina Barkley, owner of an herbal shop at 43 Light Street, finds that the past has a bizarre way of affecting the present when she's called in by ADA Dan Cassidy to consult on a murder case—only to be herself accused of murder *and* witchcraft. Sabrina's only defense is four hundred years old and an ocean away....

Watch for TRIAL BY FIRE in August, and all the upcoming 43 Light Street titles for top-notch suspense and romance.

my VALENTINE 1992

Celebrate the most romantic day of the year with
MY VALENTINE 1992—a sexy new collection of four
romantic stories written by our famous Temptation
authors:

GINA WILKINS
KRISTINE ROLOFSON
JOANN ROSS
VICKI LEWIS THOMPSON

My Valentine 1992—an exquisite escape into a romantic
and sensuous world.

 Harlequin Books

VAL-92-R

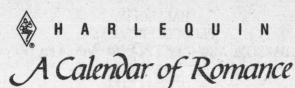

HARLEQUIN

A Calendar of Romance

Be a part of American Romance's year-long celebration of love and the holidays of 1992. Celebrate those special times each month with your favorite authors.

Next month, live out a St. Patrick's Day fantasy in

			MARCH			
S	M	T	W	T	F	S
1	2	3	4	5	6	7
8	9	10	11	12	13	14
15	16	17				21
22	23					
29						

#429 FLANNERY'S RAINBOW by Julie Kistler

Read all the books in *A Calendar of Romance,* coming to you one per month, all year, only in American Romance.

HARLEQUIN
PROUDLY PRESENTS
A DAZZLING NEW CONCEPT IN ROMANCE FICTION

One small town—twelve terrific love stories

Welcome to Tyler, Wisconsin—a town full of people
you'll enjoy getting to know, memorable friends and
unforgettable lovers, and a long-buried secret that
lurks beneath its serene surface....

JOIN US FOR A YEAR IN THE LIFE OF TYLER

Each book set in Tyler is a self-contained love story;
together, the twelve novels stitch the fabric of a
community.

LOSE YOUR HEART TO TYLER!

The excitement begins in March 1992, with
WHIRLWIND, by Nancy Martin. When lively, brash
Liza Baron arrives home unexpectedly, she moves
into the old family lodge, where the silent and
mysterious Cliff Forrester has been living in seclusion
for years....

WATCH FOR ALL TWELVE BOOKS
OF THE TYLER SERIES
Available wherever Harlequin books are sold